Eye for an Eye

Featuring Arlon Grey

Book 3

Josef Peeters

Copyright © 2020 Josef Peeters

All rights reserved. This book or any portion thereof
may not be reproduced or used in any manner whatsoever
without the express written permission of the publisher
except for the use of brief quotations in a book review.

This is a **work of fiction**. Names, characters, businesses, places,
events and incidents are either the products of the author's
imagination or used in a fictitious manner. Any resemblance to
actual persons, living or dead, or actual events, is purely
coincidental.

Edited by: Rosemary Hillyard

Editing Services, rmhillyard@aol.com

Cover design by Rocking Book Covers,
https://www.rockingbookcovers.com

ISBN: 9780645028805

Other books by the author

Fiction:

Dumped (action/adventure)

Daintree Denizens (thriller)

Mt. Moulamein (sci-fi)

Transience (magic realism)

Black Heart (psych. thriller)

Endure (dystopian) Out soon

Horror Series:

Eat What You Kill (Book 1)

B.A.M. (Book 2)

The Guardians (Book 4) Out soon

Non-Fiction:

Wood Whisperer Volume 1

Wood Whisperer Volume 2

Wood Whisperer Volume 3

Giving Up (Short, autobiographical)

Visit Josef's web page for all purchase links and book descriptions;

http://lakesidecaravanpark.wixsite.com/josef

DEDICATION

This mild horror series was inspired by a trip to visit my brother and sister-in-law in their newly acquired township of Allies Creek, where my fertile imagination was allowed to blossom freely.

ACKNOWLEDGMENTS

Without the indispensible contribution of my highly-skilled editor, Rosemary Hillyard, I would not be able to produce these volumes.
I would also like to recognise the creative genius of my cover designer, Adrijus Guscia, of Rocking Book Covers, for the sensational artworks he supplied for this series.

PROLOGUE

Deep in the temperate rainforests of Victoria's rugged hinterland, where crisp, white snowdrifts decorated the tips of the numerous mountains surrounding the area, in a ravine known to only a handful of locals, sat an elderly lady beside a babbling brook.

With mere starlight penetrating the chilly darkness, Hilda Haggerty hummed softly as she held out her hand with a morsel to tempt the local fauna out of hiding. For nigh on eighty years, Hilda had maintained the annual ritual, travelling the length of her cleared property within the hidden ravine, to sit upon the stump at midnight on the eve of the winter solstice and await her guest.

From her fifth birthday, introduced to her inaugural pilgrimage to the stump by her blessed father, Hilda had followed the routine set out by Jason Haggerty eighty times since. It was to mark her passage on earth, the day she entered the world. It was also the day she lost her mother. Twenty years later, on the very same date, she lost her beloved father in a logging accident.

Death and birth, joy and heartache: two faces of the same coin flipped into the air on any given day to randomly reveal which face will decree another chapter in a person's life. Though the date held sad memories for Hilda for the loving father she lost and the mother she never knew, it also foretold a special event that she shared with no other living soul after her father, one that brought immense joy to the old woman.

Her exhalations formed small clouds of vapour in the still night air. The temperature was below freezing, as expected for that time of year in the Victorian forest of towering mountain ash, some trees taller than seventy metres. A thick fog had yet to emerge above the frigid soil, where it stayed until well past midday during the depths of winter. Snows would descend on the slopes of her mountain, only a few hundred metres higher than her clearing in the deep ravine, immersed in shadow for much of the winter cycle.

By re-enacting the annual ritual, Hilda held to the promise she made to her father eighty years ago on the first night he carried her down the slope from their cottage to the stump by the creek. There, he placed the young, tired girl on the stump, wrapped in many blankets to protect her from the biting cold and rising damp. Without a word spoken, Jason made sure his daughter remained absolutely still and silent.

There they waited for the miracle that occurred each year at the same time, when humankind would commune with nature: when the Haggerty family of two honoured a debt and paid homage to the creatures of the forest that blessed them with their trust. Her father explained to the young Hilda that no other human contact of the kind had ever been recorded in Australia's history. He invoked a pact of complete secrecy about their assignation upon the impressionable young girl, a pact that Hilda swore to uphold until her dying day.

She was the last Haggerty. The secret would perish upon her deathbed unless something miraculous occurred in the time she had remaining to her. Hilda doubted her old body was capable of reproducing and so held little hope of passing her secret on to her offspring, just as the recipient of the midnight tryst had done with hers. She couldn't determine exactly how many generations she had celebrated the ritual with over so many years. Her old eyes had developed cataracts some time ago, ensuring that she could no longer distinguish individual markings as she once had done.

Like the fogs that rolled in over the clearing each night, so had the mists invaded her eyesight so long ago, leaving her nothing but blurry white and indistinct shapes to witness on the eve of the anniversary. Hilda now saw only ghosts haunting her vision. Spectral apparitions swam before her, whether day or night, wafting in and out of view, retreating to the periphery whenever she attempted to focus on an image.

Her other senses had taken up the mantle of responsibility to guide Hilda through her daily chores, senses that she had sharpened to perfection over time. Senses that transcended the norm, were heightened and honed to a razor edge by necessity. She had acute hearing, exceptional olfactory perception and an intuitive perspicacity that came from living alone for a lifetime. The gradual loss of her vision had not impaired the redoubtable Hilda Haggerty. It had enhanced her in many ways, beyond the belief of most, unacccptable to others and downright spooky to the rest.

Alone in the dark, unafraid and highly attuned to her surroundings, Hilda waited patiently on her stump beside the permanent creek, listening to the gentle splash as the crystal-clear waters washed against the many stones and boulders in its downward path. Much had occurred in the clearing of late and Hilda held fears that her guest might not appear, might no longer be able to appear. She felt intensely sad about that possibility. It would not be worthwhile continuing if she could no longer experience the event that had been such a large part of her existence.

All that she did, everything she accomplished each year, was designed to follow through on the promise made to her father. It was to continue the ritual he began in his youth, before she was born, before he met her mother. Her entire philosophy of life revolved around the anniversary of her birth, to continue the crucial act of reunification.

Succumbing to lethargy and her ageing anatomy, Hilda's eyes blinked in an attempt to remain awake. Gradually, her eyelids descended, as gravity and age took their toll. Unable to remain awake for the first time since being introduced to the sacred tryst, Hilda nodded off, releasing the morsel she held in her hand to tempt the creature from its forest refuge. The titbit rolled from her wrinkled and liver-spotted hand onto the frosty grass at her feet. From there it continued for a metre down the slope before coming to rest against the base of another small tree stump.

Staring up blankly from its final resting place, the gelatinous globe remained there until it was finally found and consumed by the secretive recipient hours later.

CHAPTER ONE

"Where are we going?" whispered Harry, as they crept through the understory of vibrant and plentiful tree ferns, each vying for their share of the limited sunshine leaking through the leafy canopy far above.

Underfoot, the rotting leaf matter squelched with retained moisture as Harry and Noel made their way slowly across the slippery slopes. The ethereal aspect of the Black Spur Forest had encouraged the soft tone adopted by the young men since they left their 4WD ute at the end of the ancient forestry road to continue on foot.

"I already told you where we're going: to make some money," answered Noel.

"You trying to tell me that you buried some of your loot out here or something?"

"What loot?"

"When you knocked over old man Jonkers' shop."

Noel stopped to look at Harry, taking in the round, freckled face, the impossibly buck teeth, and the stupid grin he always wore.

"Harry, don't be a fuckwit. I got a few bucks from his till, some smokes and a few bottles of rum. That's all. 'Sides, that was a year ago, mate. Why the fuck would I want to bury anything, anyway? Especially way out here in the middle of nothing?"

"You're the one leading me into this 'nothing'. Can't see no way of making money out of it, otherwise."

"How long we been together?" asked Noel, peering down at his friend from a superior height.

"We growed up together, Noely, since we was little tackers."

"And have I ever let you down, mate?"

"Fucking heaps of times," admitted Harry with a grin.

"Ungrateful cunt," Noel admonished with a good-natured

shove. "C'mon. Not much longer. Hear that?"

"Kookaburra, so what?"

"Na, mate. See? Changed already. Sounds like a butcher bird, don't it?"

"Sounds like a bloody rooster now."

"Lyrebird, Harry, me old mate. They mimic all the other birds and then some. They've been known to mimic jackhammers while they were doing construction work at the Healesville Sanctuary. You don't think they'd be worth a bloody bob or two, eh?"

"Now I know you're bonkers, Noely. How the fuck are we gonna catch us a lyrebird and who the fuck are we going to sell it to?"

"Nah, not the lyrebird, mate. Black gold, that's what. Know what you can get for a black cockatoo from the right buyer?"

"Nuh."

"Well, not that much in Australia. Overseas, yeah, hundreds, maybe thousands. But the real money is in eggs or chicks, mate. I got a bloke what'll pay me coupla hundred per viable egg and five for a chick. Mainly the two types hereabouts; the red-tailed black cockatoo and the yellow-tailed black cockatoo. They build their nests high up in these trees."

Harry cast his eyes upward. "How the fuck you think we're getting up there to find nests?"

"Don't have to if you know the right place to look."

"And you know this place, do you?"

"Me mum does."

"So how do you know where to go?"

"Followed her a year ago, then came back a coupla times. She was down here earlier today. Believe it or not, this is a path we're following."

"How does your mum know about it and what's she doing coming in here alone?"

"Jeez, Harry! You ask a lot of useless questions, you know that? Been doing it ever since pre-school."

"Only way I get to learn anything, Noely."

"Well, it's bloody annoying. Now, let's get going. Be dark soon and that's what we want."

"That what the torches are for?"

"What do you think? Just don't bloody turn yours on unless I tell you."

"Why not?"

"Fair dinkum, Harry, if you weren't me mate, I'd have knocked your block off ages ago. Now shut up. We have to be bloody quiet from here on. Don't you dare ask," warned Noel, with a glare that brooked no challenge.

The chilled air of early evening, as the sun disappeared over the western peaks, crept into the pair as they made their way through the gathering gloom. Noel had not been completely honest with his friend. In truth, he had been down the meandering deer track through the forest only once after secretly following his mum. He had obsessed over the mystery for years, as his mum brought home the prize-winning poultry year after year.

Betty Payne, Noel's mother, entered her bantam roosters in the Melbourne show each year, never failing to place in the top three, always receiving accolades and ribbons for her prized cocks. When questioned about her breeding methods and selections by anyone, she always became vague and unresponsive. She never revealed her secrets to another soul, including her son.

By the time Noel reached his late teens, he had become so entrenched in the mystery of the phantom roosters, showing up in their backyard pen each year, that he began to follow his mum around everywhere she went. After trailing her for close to a year, he finally found an alteration to her routine that he couldn't explain immediately. In his beat-up jalopy, held together with chewing gum and tie-wire, he managed to shadow her VW Kombi van as she made her way from their Yarra Junction home towards Healesville.

Noel became confused when his mother turned off the main highway after Healesville to follow a narrow road, and then veered off onto an old forestry track barely discernible through the thick foliage of tree and ground ferns disguising its entrance. She travelled a further kilometre or two before pulling to a stop at the end of the track. She wasted no time before leaving the car and heading straight through the dense growth to make her way along an even narrower track.

Noel knew he couldn't simply leave his vehicle parked next to hers. He had to find a siding that would accommodate his car, ensuring it would be well-hidden, before trekking through the forest to follow his mother on foot. He knew he had to hurry or he would assuredly lose her in the bewildering undergrowth of the rainforest. After ten minutes of frantic searching along a track that was nothing more than an impression of someone's passing, he saw the back of her bright blue cardigan. Fortunately, she appeared to be in no hurry to reach her destination, stopping occasionally to dig up a plant or two, highly illegal in a state forest, which she placed into a little pail she carried.

Orchids and bromeliads, together with seeds of exotic palms and ferns, made their way to the Payne household every year. Noel was happy to discover an answer to that vexing conundrum that had occupied his mind for many years as well. It was interesting for him to make the connection that the seed hadn't fallen far from the tree as far as he was concerned. Noel Payne had probably inherited his penchant for obtaining goods in less than legal methods from his lovely mother. He smiled when he realised how close they were in personality.

Noel understood immediately why his mother was bound to secrecy about her actions. His father, Gordon Payne, was a very pious man who ruled his castle with an iron hand, never wavering from absolute adherence to the law of the church and the land. If he knew his wife was breaking the law to procure the myriad of plants around their family home he would have gone ballistic. His sermonising and pompous preaching could bore the most ardent criminal into going straight. Or so he thought.

Not so, according to what Noel witnessed that day, creeping through the ethereal quiet of the forest to follow his mother, who gained great esteem in the eyes of her only child. Noel was not a violent boy as he grew, but he was lazy and a thief. If there was a quick way to make money that involved anything of an illegal nature, Noel was all for it, if only to spite the old man. He'd had enough of the Bible and all the hocus-pocus to last him a lifetime.

Noel had challenged his father as he grew older, often rebuking the man for his arcane beliefs and superstitions. Noel could no more stomach all the guff about religion than he could defer to the notion of elves and fairies in the garden. It made so little sense to him, as he slowly grew out of the indoctrination he'd received from birth, that he rebelled in the only way he could. By going against everything the old man held sacred and dear, Noel was exacting a form of silent and secret revenge. That his mother was doing the same pleased him more than he could state.

The descent, from the crest of the ridge where they had left the car to the bottom of the deep ravine, took more time than Noel thought possible. Despite the pervading gloom in the understory of the forest, where only dappled light passed through the dense canopy above, making it many degrees cooler, Noel was sweating profusely as he struggled to keep up with the figure in front of him. She disappeared occasionally as she walked behind the massive trunks of the towering mountain ash. Judging by the old growth about him, Noel decided that fire and the lumberman's axe had yet to make their mark in this particular section of the forest.

Deeper and deeper she went into the eerie forest, along a track that he could never have discovered on his own. Bird calls and minor movements of scurrying insects and, possibly, lizards were all that could be heard within the cocoon they travelled. The muted sounds seemed to be diminished by the awe which the creatures held for the magnificence and grandeur of their surroundings. The deeply scented odours emanating from all about him projected the riches of rotting matter, adding its nourishment to the soil. The verdant forest gained its longevity and endurance from the abundant rainfall and millions of leaves, adding to the heady mix below.

Noel assured himself that the only possible explanation for his mother's odd behaviour was that she was meeting someone, clandestincly, to procure her next winning fowl. He had no idea how she would have come across such a beneficial source in the middle of a forest. If not that, could she be trapping somc wildfowl that had managed to breed on their own after escaping captivity? If so, how was she accomplishing that task? So many questions, so few answers. He had no choice other than to follow if he hoped to gain an understanding.

Although the sound was muffled by the surrounding vegetation, Noel heard the orchestration of a lyrebird as it went through its repertoire of stolen sounds. Amongst the plethora of noises emanating from the clever creature came a weird yipping that Noel had never heard before. It did not sound like any bird he had ever come across. He listened closely for a repeat of the sound to determine its origin, but the bird finished its recitation, leaving the forest silent once more.

A gentle susurration crept through the quiet as he came close to a small stream at the bottom of a deep ravine. Ahead, Noel saw his mother enter a clearing, where only the massive stumps of the forest giants remained to tell of their existence in a time gone past. Tell-tale signs of the axeman's craft told of the era in which the trees were felled, long before modern chainsaws and the like changed the industry.

High on the cleared slope stood a small derelict cottage surrounded by structures. Greenhouses, Noel assumed, though not panelled in glass, as far as he could tell. Some had a solid roof and mesh sides, while others were fully enclosed with translucent fibreglass sheeting. One largish shed at the rear of the property made its purpose known to Noel when he heard the distinctive clucking of hens and the raucous cries of the tiny bantam roosters he knew so well.

Upon closer inspection, Noel began to notice the many bird-feeders and nesting boxes adorning the trees around the perimeter of the clearing. The sounds and calls of numerous birds could be heard as they flitted about from one to the other. Male king parrots, sporting their bold orange breasts and bright green wings, magnificent crimson rosellas and so many other varieties of bird life boggled the mind. Most obvious of all were the normally shy black cockatoos, making their distinctive calls as they flew to their nesting boxes.

Noel observed as his mother made her way up the steep, grassed slope toward the cottage. After knocking on the door several times, she was eventually allowed to enter by an unseen occupant. Several moments later he saw her emerge at the rear of the house, making her way along a dirt path to the large shed housing the poultry. The selection process did not take long. His mother quickly exited the shed, carrying a covered cage containing what Noel expected to be that year's newest addition to their bantam menagerie at home.

Noel had known all along that his mother had not been breeding the prize-winning birds herself, though he was mystified about the need for such secrecy. He'd never heard of the rules governing the entrants of fowl to the Easter Show, and supposed there might be some clause about the birds being bred by the owners. He didn't know and didn't need to speculate. He had the answer he required for the time being.

His thoughts meandered in a different direction as he watched his mum exit the clearing and return to the path she had taken to enter the property. Noel did not follow her. He was hatching some ideas about how he might profit from his discovery. He decided that surveillance of the property would determine if his scheme held merit. Over the following months, he attempted several journeys to the isolated property, managing to get lost when the track became almost impossible to identify. Recognising his inability to find his way back to the cottage in the forest, Noel waited until the following year to trail his mother's return. When Noel followed her earlier that day, he made sure he could relocate the track and the cottage by leaving markers.

Harry began to lag as the steep terrain took its toll on his flagging energy. Being overweight and particularly lazy did not help the youth when it came to any form of exercise. He struggled behind Noel along a path he was unable to identify. He had only his best friend's word that the path existed and that thcy would find some means of making money at the end of it, as unlikely as that seemed.

The air became quite cool in the late afternoon and the waning light made it even more difficult to navigate the track. Noel was moving far too quickly for him, and he became fearful of being in the forest at night.

The Black Spur Forest had been the subject of many stories during his childhood: stories that involved missing persons and strange goings-on in the dead of night. Harry did not necessarily believe the stories, but he feared being there at night, nonetheless. He couldn't conceive a single reason for their expedition, couldn't imagine any way of making money by trekking through the cold, damp gloom. Were it not for his mate, Noely, he would never have been persuaded to go along with such a harebrained scheme.

The night descended quickly for the pair, stumbling along the path that threatened to see them slipping down the steep slope with every step. Harry was uncomfortable and winded, tired of the pointless trek and waning in his trust for his friend. He wanted to scream in protest, wanted to slam his mate up against the bole of a tree and deliver a message about how he felt.

Unfortunately, Noely was bigger, stronger, tougher and far more charismatic than Harry could ever hope to be. If it hadn't been for Noely, his life would have been shit. Considered nothing more than a troublesome, fat nerd during his school years, Harry owed his peace of mind to the good nature of his mate, who rescued him. He never understood the reason. Noely was considered one of the cool guys in school, yet from the time they attended pre-school together, Noel Payne had remained a loyal friend to Harry. In truth, Harry loved his 'mate' more than he would ever know. Never fully admitting it to his friend or himself, Harry nonetheless recognised the passionate yearning he felt at times. He almost ached to be apart from Noely as they grew up together, sharing so very much of each other's lives. Sleepovers rated among the best of those occasions, when they shared a bed.

It became increasingly difficult to hide his feelings as they grew older, often skinny-dipping together in the local creeks or showering at school after sports. However, what he suspected of himself could never be admitted, not to himself and, most of all, not to his friend.

Harry almost ran straight into Noel when the young man stopped suddenly.

"We're here," Noel whispered.

"Where?" asked Harry desperately.

"Hear that creek? That's at the boundary to the property at the bottom of this ravine," explained Noel quietly.

"I don't understand, Noely. What's this all about? It's cold and I'm a bit scared," admitted Harry.

"Of what? Nothing to be scared of, Harry."

"You've heard the stories."

"Jeez, Harry. They're stories. Kid's stories, forest legends."

"Forest legends?"

"As opposed to urban legends?"

"Huh?"

"Never mind. Around the perimeter of the clearing ahead are a bunch of breeding boxes for birds. I seen them. If we can snaffle a few eggs and chicks, we can make some good bucks. Nothing to it. They aren't even high up. Whoever lives there must have been feeding them and encouraging them for years. Got a couple of cloth bags here with some cotton wool in them. That should protect the eggs and the chicks from the cold until we get them back home."

"What's that?" asked Harry, hearing a strange noise, almost like a puppy yipping.

"Lyrebird, mate. Heard them make that sound and a heap of

others last time."

"Okay, I suppose. Only..."

"Harry, we're broke, no food at home and no money for petrol, rent or anything else. Unless you can come up with a better scheme for making some quick dough, shut the fuck up. Nothing to be worried about and bloody nothing to be scared about. Now let's..."

As Noel turned to continue the small distance down the path to the creek, a sudden movement through the foliage in front of him stopped him in his tracks. Harry paused behind his mate, wondering what had occurred. A slight bubbling sound from Noel had Harry fumbling for his flashlight. When he eventually located the switch on the torch, Harry saw his friend standing motionless before him. It was only when he stepped to the left to peer into his friend's face that he became truly alarmed.

Noel was blowing bubbles. In the yellow light provided by the torch beam, it was not immediately clear that the bubbles were red. Looking down from his friend's shocked and unblinking stare, Harry discovered a horizontal board at the level of Noel's chest. Upon further inspection, it became clear that the board had several wooden spikes protruding from it. The realisation that a number of those spikes had entered his friend's chest, puncturing his lungs and possibly his heart, did not register immediately.

"Noely? What is it, why is that board there? What happened?" asked Harry in slow recognition.

His body held in place by the strong sapling bearing the horizontal board, Noel's eyes began to glaze over with the sure signs of approaching death, blood no longer being supplied throughout the body by a damaged heart, lungs no longer supplying oxygen required for life to continue. Harry's eyes grew wide with horror and fear, incomprehension befuddling his mind. It didn't make sense to him. It couldn't be true that his best friend, his only friend in the entire universe, was dying and there was nothing Harry could do to prevent it.

Frozen with indecision, Harry felt the first of many tears

welling up at the corners of his eyes, as well as a warm flush infusing his groin and trouser leg. Panic swelled within the mind of the bewildered young man, rendering him incapable of clear thought. Indecision gripped him, forcing him to remain rooted to the spot, face to face with his mate.

When his mind could no longer cope with the gruesome and heartbreaking sight, he turned and fled.

CHAPTER TWO

"What about this one? It sounds like it might be less about bizarre and mysterious and more about good old-fashioned detecting; a missing person enquiry," suggested Clarice Grey to her recently acquired husband, Arlon Grey, the detective element of the Bizarre and Mysterious Detective Agency.

While it seemed that their agency should have prospered since its inception, having been well paid by their last client, the opposite was closer to the truth. The bills were barely being paid and, while they did not want for necessities, they still struggled to find a steady list of paying clients to keep their business afloat: clients of the variety Arlon preferred, the non-bizarre and mysterious kind.

His conservatism threatened the solvency of their agency. Clarice had long been an advocate of the other side of life, the outer edge of 'normal'. She trawled through the websites associated with the supernatural and the paranormal. Anything of a nature that didn't fall within a conservative category intrigued the wife of Arlon Grey.

Clarice glanced over at Arlon, who sat behind a newspaper at the breakfast table ostensibly ignoring her, though she knew he'd heard every word. She smiled. It was the happiest she had ever been. She'd even managed to lose a couple of kilos since their wedding.

Never truly obese, Clarice had, nonetheless, been concerned enough about her figure to adopt an exercise routine with her new husband, though far less strenuous than his. She would never have the stamina to keep up with the gruelling routines he followed. Arlon Grey was a true martial arts master with black belts in many disciplines. His ritualistic routines took Clarice's breath away at times. Not only was he magnificent to watch on a purely selfish and erotic level, but he was also a superb technician of the lethal arts.

His brilliant blue eyes would be deeply set in concentration as he went about the stylised moves, with none of the accompanying sounds normally associated with the dojo. Only the sibilant sounds of controlled breathing were heard while Arlon trained. The rigorous and exact movements were exhilarating to observe, a veritable dance of combat. Clarice often fantasised about watching him train while he was naked. She quickly dismissed that distraction from her thoughts as Arlon folded his newspaper to attend to her question.

"Tell me about it," he requested, in his soft voice redolent of the Australian vernacular.

"Seems a bit tame compared to...you know?" she said with a shrug.

"Tame is preferable, surely?"

"A bit less dramatic than our last case, for sure. I mean, how many times can a man save the world, maybe even the universe?"

"Stop exaggerating, Clarice," he admonished.

"Oh, exaggerating, am I? Who was telling me about how serious it all was at the time? Who was it that nearly died? How did that amazing silver streak appear in that beautiful black hair of yours, pray tell?"

"I tried dying it out," he admitted weakly.

"That's hardly the point. Arlon. You shouldn't try to deflect the grave danger we all faced on that island. The world may never know what happened, but we certainly do. Don't we, pumpkin?"

"Sure do," agreed Tara Blaze-Grey, adopted daughter of Arlon and Clarice Grey, with a mouthful of Froot Loops. Tara had been a victim of the tragedy from their last assignment. Months after the incident and the consequent wedding, her new parents had officially adopted her. She had never known such love and devotion. It fulfilled her every desire and she could want no more than to spend the rest of her life as their daughter. She spared little thought on her biological parents, who had perished so recently. They had never truly loved their only child. She was tolerated at best by the rich couple.

She had offered her new parents every cent of her substantial inheritance. They politely refused. They arranged for a trust account that would mature when Tara reached the age of eighteen, when she could do as she pleased with the full amount.

Until then, she would earn interest on the amount, which would see her attain a bright future if the money were soundly managed and wisely invested. A portion of the interest paid for her private school tuition. Arlon ensured that money management and economics played a large part in her education. When the girl came of age he wanted to feel confident that she could handle the responsibility of being wealthy.

"Go on, tell me about the case," insisted Arlon.

"Email from a Betty Payne, who lives in Yarra Junction, Victoria. She says her son, Noel Payne, has been missing for over a year. His best friend, Harry Sommers, was found after the disappearance of her son and had to be institutionalised. Betty is at her wits' end with the dead investigation. The police have nothing and the friend is non compos mentis. Betty believes the friend holds the answers. They had been inseparable since early childhood. They lived together in a rundown little cabin in the back yard of another friend's parents: little more than a tool shed, by the sound of it.

"Her marriage has ended as a result of the disappearance, and her workplace let her go a little while back. She refuses to give up on her son and won't move on. She's offered a ten-thousand-dollar reward for any information leading to her son. She's willing to pay us a handsome retainer as well as the reward if we succeed."

"If she's out of a job and has no husband providing for her, how can she afford our retainer, let alone the reward?" asked Arlon quietly.

It was impossible most times to tell if Arlon was interested or not. His condition precluded the appearance of tell-tale emotional signs. Clarice often had to guess at what he might be thinking. The man had undergone profound changes to his physiognomy and mental acuity during their last assignment, namely; a brilliant silver/white streak through his obsidian hair after a debilitating irradiation, and the presence of emotions, but he had since lost any evidence of the latter.

Clarice was in two minds over the temporary alteration to Arlon's condition while it was in effect. Having never before experienced emotions, he became almost overwhelmed during the short term of the infliction. Arlon suffered greatly on a physical level from the ordeal, taking many months to fully recuperate without any discernible after-effects. However, on the emotional level, he underwent profound changes that sought to undo him.

Clarice was happy to witness the end of the disturbing behaviour that had her husband weeping and in turmoil for no apparent reason. It gradually decreased and for that Clarice was glad. When his normal personality returned; unfeeling, uncaring and unconcerned, she was less than thrilled, but content that he was no longer suffering. Alexithymia was on the autism spectrum, and Arlon Grey was a poster boy during his youth as a person in the highest percentile of the condition.

Somehow, during the last assignment, subjected to the intense radiation of a completely unknown nature, Arlon Grey began to experience emotions for the first time in his life, emotions that crippled him. Just as a full meal given to a starving person could overwhelm their digestive system, so too, did Arlon become debilitated by the sudden influx of feelings. As a consequence, he spent a long time alone in a locked room, attempting to come to terms with the affliction.

When he recovered, the only visible evidence of his ordeal was the silver streak in his hair, adding even more flair and dash to the impressive man, in Clarice's opinion. One other side-effect of the experience was a reluctance on Arlon's part to participate in any further assignments of a non-conservative nature.

Fortunately, as far as Clarice was concerned, it was the only type of enquiry they seemed to attract thereafter. This was not so unusual when her particular interests were taken into account, or the type of advertising she employed in a variety of obscure websites and magazines. Clarice hoped that she could dissuade Arlon from returning to conveyancing investigations for solicitors, or sneaking around trying to find evidence of a spouse's infidelity. Unfortunately, Arlon no longer wanted any part of the mysterious and bizarre, so their agency had gained no new clients in months.

"Chooks," claimed Clarice with a bright smile.

"Eh?"

"She can sell prize-winning poultry, or has done, to pay our fee and the reward."

"You can't be serious? A ten-thousand-dollar chook?" asked Arlon.

"Roosters, actually. Bantams. Not one, though. I did some research and there doesn't appear to be any single bird worth anything like that much. There seems to be a real point of pride amongst the show crowd to produce the best in show each year, and people are willing to pay top dollar for extraordinary birds. Betty Payne has produced the best in show many years running, always placing in the top three, and no one can understand how she does it."

"What do you mean?"

"Well, it seems that these folks talk about how they come up with their pedigrees, the breeding processes and the sort of cross-cultivation it takes to arrive at new colours, shapes and so on. They are quick to boast about their methods. Not so the private Mrs Betty Payne. Everyone is dying to find out her secrets. Some say she doesn't do the actual breeding herself, which is deemed somewhat unethical, though not strictly against the rules, as far as I can tell."

"Well, she wouldn't, would she?"

"Wouldn't what?"

"Do the actual breeding herself. One would think that was entirely impossible."

"Was that a joke, Mr Grey?"

"Not a very successful one, judging by your reaction or lack thereof."

Tara giggled.

"Hadn't you better get yourself ready for school, young lady?"

"Yes, Mummy."

Clarice frowned as Tara wiped her mouth with the sleeve of her pyjama top, then smiled as the young girl skipped off down the hall of their Indooroopilly home to her bedroom.

"I never get tired of hearing that," Clarice mused.

"Hmm?" asked Arlon.

"Hearing her call me 'mummy'. It's just...well, bloody terrific."

"Hmm."

"You aren't listening to me, are you?" asked Clarice, as she set about clearing the breakfast dishes, sopping up the spilled milk from Tara's messy consumption of her favourite cereal. Try as she might, Clarice was unable to dissuade Tara from insisting on the overly sweet cereal every morning.

"I thought we agreed that you didn't want me venturing too far away from you two. Victoria qualifies as quite a distance, doesn't it?"

"Arlon, we have a small niche market when it comes to our speciality. I knew that going in, and it still doesn't deter me from pursuing that direction. There are tons of other agencies handling the mundane stuff, the terrible divorce investigations, the due-diligence work and the rest. I figured early on that your personality just didn't gel with that line of business. I still believe that, which means we have to take what's on offer sometimes and go where the business takes us," explained Clarice, going to sit on his knee, placing her arms around his neck.

"Us?"

"School holidays coming up shortly. I thought we could take the caravan down and spend some time at Lake Eildon. Combine the job with a bit of a family holiday. You could trip off during the day, even if you have to stay away for a couple of days elsewhere, while Tara and I soak up some sun, swim, fish, have some fun."

"Oh, I see. You've already made up my mind and organised everything, have you?"

"Not...everything," Clarice admitted, beaming innocently at Arlon as she sat on his lap.

"When are we leaving?"

"This Friday."

"Does Mrs Betty Payne know?"

"She will when you email her this morning."

"That was her deposit into our business account yesterday, was it?"

"Oh, you already know about that?"

"With business being so tight I keep a daily check on our balances, yes," explained Arlon, with a certain look that Clarice had come to recognise.

"You're not angry?"

"I don't get angry, Mrs Grey."

"Not ever, Mr Grey?" Clarice said, in her best imitation of a swooning woman.

"Stop that."

"Stop what, Mr Grey?"

"You know damn well what."

"You mean this?" she said, rubbing her fleshy bottom into his groin.

"You are a wanton woman, Clarice Grey!"

"Bloody oath I am. I'm wantin' you right now," she said, leaning in to kiss him aggressively.

"Listen," said Arlon, when he finally managed to extract himself. "Don't you think it's inadvisable to take Tara along on a work assignment?"

"Why?"

"Our track record has been perfect for attracting dangerous jobs of late. I never want Tara to be subjected to danger again. It wouldn't be fair."

"I agree."

"Well, then?"

"Tara and I won't be anywhere near your work area and it's an investigation for a missing person. How dangerous can that be?"

"He could be a hitman, for all I know. A member of a bikie gang, a crime syndicate, any number of things, making it a dangerous proposition to be poking around in."

"Or it could be a young man sowing his oats somewhere his loving mum can't find him. He might have gone to the snow."

"The snow?"

"Yes, Arlon. The snow. Falls Creek is near there, or Mt Bulla a bit further away, according to my researches."

"Why would he go there?"

"Jeez, for fun, Arlon. You know, skiing, snowboarding, and having fun?"

"In the snow?"

"Well, where else can someone go skiing?"

"On a lake, on a grassy hill...in the sun."

"Just because you don't know how to have fun doesn't mean the rest of us are boring."

"Can't see the point of freezing your balls off in the snow."

"There are ways to keep warm, Arlon; thermal underwear and proper garments to keep out the wind, moisture and cold. Rugging up, dummy. It's all about layers in the southern states, especially Melbourne. They have four seasons a day there. There is nothing quite like waking up to a clear day on the top of a mountain that is sparkling white in the sunshine. Riding the chairlift up to the runs is just as much fun as the ski back down, and mulled wine at the bar, in front of a roaring fire, is the perfect end to a day in the snow. If I were young and living close by, you wouldn't see me for dust, getting up to the snow every chance I got. My bet is that's where he is. Maybe he got a seasonal job up there as a bartender or something."

"You're not taking into account one vital piece of information, Mrs Detective."

"What's that?"

"He's been missing for over a year. Snow doesn't fall all year round."

"Oh, yeah, I forgot about that."

"So how about you leave the detecting to me? I'm not too bad at it, in case you didn't know."

"So, we're taking the case?"

"If we've already been paid a deposit, I don't see how we can back out now, do you?"

CHAPTER THREE

Yarra Junction is a small rural township nestled outside Melbourne in the famed Yarra Valley. The Yarra River, originating in the mountains close by, flows through it and the many other townships and suburbs along its banks before arriving in Melbourne, where it quickly broadens into a major and iconic waterway. Mt Donna Buang towers over the valley, at a height of twelve hundred and fifty metres, just north of the township. It provides the area's closest access to snow in the coldest months.

The sleepy little burg sees a major influx of traffic on weekends and holidays as Melburnians make their way from the city to the country or the mountains. The aqueduct trail is a very popular walking and cycling track halfway up the mountain. Warburton, only a few kilometres to the north, commands a loyal following for day-trippers, stopping for coffee or lunch before making their way up the winding mountain road to other scenic parts of the mountainscape.

Betty Payne owned a small rural holding outside Yarra Junction on the road to Noojee. The neat cottage nestled among vibrant and verdant temperate flora; towering mountain ash and other native hardwood trees bordered the rear of her property. Between the cottage and the rear fence stood a large, fenced shed housing what Arlon presumed to be her prize bantams. Most of the birds were rooting around outside the shed, scratching the bare earth in search of seeds, worms or insects inhabiting the soil.

Betty went to great lengths to explain all the minute differences in shape and colour to Arlon, who was hard-pressed to distinguish the variances. While Arlon shivered with the damp cold of the morning, Betty was dressed in only a light, patterned shift with an accompanying green cardigan that had seen better days. A diminutive woman, as thin as a rake, Betty could have been mistaken for being in her sixties. Although her face was drawn, with dark circles under the eyes, Arlon could see evidence of former beauty. Had she the motivation to care for herself, she could have appeared quite pretty. The sadness in her was evident the moment he met her.

"Can we go back inside?" asked Arlon abruptly.

"Aren't you interested in the birds?" Betty asked in reply.

"No," he replied in his deadpan manner.

"Well!" harrumphed Betty.

"No need to take offence. I'm too bloody cold to be interested in anything at the moment."

"Are you normally this blunt, Mr Grey?"

"Yes."

"I see. Maybe I should find myself another detective to assist me."

"You wouldn't have contacted *me* if that were an option, I'm guessing."

"That's quite rude."

"No, it isn't. Just a fact. I'm pretty sure I'm your last resort. Let me guess. Everyone else told you to leave it to the cops or suggested you wait for your son to return after he's expended whatever energy that made him go astray?"

Betty Payne stared at the handsome man with a tear quivering at the corner of her eye. It was exactly what she had been told. Everyone she approached either wanted to rip her off after promising her the world or refused to take the job, citing the very words the detective had used.

"You're upset."

"Of course I'm upset. I've lost my only son and no one seems to want to do anything about it. The cops are useless and the private detectives are either scam-artists or uninterested. Yes, you are possibly my last resort, and I fear I may have wasted my time in contacting you through your lovely wife."

"Did my 'lovely wife' not explain my condition to you?"

"What condition?"

"Obviously not. I'm on the autism spectrum, Mrs Payne. It doesn't show in any way other than a complete lack of emotions. You expected someone to be sympathetic to you, perhaps empathetic? I'm not that person. You want that, hire a shrink. I'm a detective, a relatively good one if I'm given the opportunity. If you want me to do what I'm good at then you need to dismiss the hurt you're feeling. If you can't do that, I'll be off."

"Are you being honest with me?"

"A dishonest person would answer that in the affirmative as well as an honest person."

"I suppose."

"Can you suppose inside rather than out here?"

"Oh, you are not a likeable person."

"Correct. Now, either we go inside to talk or I leave through the front gate, get in my car and that will be the last you ever hear from me."

"What about my deposit?"

"It will be returned to you in full. I have no intention of adding to your scam-artist list."

"Are you?"

"Am I what?"

"Any good."

"I had a near-perfect solve rate when I was in the force. My personality made it impossible for me to continue with that profession, though."

"You really are autistic?"

"On the spectrum, yes. Inside or out?"

"You'd best come along, then," Betty said, as she sighed and led the way to the back of the cottage.

She removed her gumboots immediately upon entering, and slipped into a pair of sheepskin slippers. Betty frowned as she watched Arlon enter with mud on his highly-polished shoes. She led him through the slate-floored hallway to the kitchen, where a combustion stove was warming the house comfortably. Without asking, Betty went about preparing some espresso by placing the aluminium percolator on the stove after filling it with an aromatic blend that filled the small area with its delicate nuances.

"It's a local blend made up the road."

"Good to know."

"Go on, sit down."

"If you don't mind, I'll just stand by the stove for a bit."

"It isn't that cold."

"You're acclimatised. I'm a Queenslander, born and bred. This is freezing for me. I can feel it way down in the marrow of my bones. I don't think I'll ever be warm again. If I felt hatred, I would hate it here."

"Well, that's something, I suppose," said Betty after a moment of reflection.

"What is?"

"That you can't hate. You can't do anything normal without emotions, can you? That's very, very sad."

"My wife said the very same thing before she married me."

"Why did she?"

"Marry me?"

"Yes, I don't understand that. If you can't hate, you can't love. What's the point in getting married if you don't love someone?"

"While I am not offended, that is still a very personal and rude question."

"Oh, you can be as rude as you like, but others have to refrain?"

"*I* was born that way. What's your excuse?"

Betty was taken aback by the forthright answer. She would never intentionally be rude and yet this man had somehow triggered that. While her spirit had been flagging of late and her despondency made her less than ideal company, she did not wish to be rude.

"You're right. It was none of my business and quite rude of me. I apologise. Why don't you sit at the end of the table where it's nice and warm? My husband used to sit there."

"You want me to stay?"

Sighing, "You're right about that, as well. I've tried almost everyone else. If you are good, then...then you may be my only hope for answers. Understand this, Mr Grey. I don't expect you to find my son alive. I feel he isn't."

"What makes you say that?" asked Arlon, as he made his way to the proffered chair.

After taking the chair cater-corner to Arlon, Betty answered: "His best friend, Harry Sommers. What happened scared the living daylights out of him, and those two were joined at the hip for some obscure reason that I could never figure out. Harry saw something happen to my Noel, I know it. Must have been bad for him to go like that, real bad."

"You believe he was with your son?"

"They lived together, schemed together, and went everywhere together. He was with Noel that day, no doubt about it."

"Schemed?"

"I don't make any bones about it. My son was a thief and a scoundrel, Mr Grey, pure and simple. I loved him, anyway. He was my only boy and, as long as he wasn't violent toward others, he continued to earn my love."

"One might say that stealing from others was far from being passive, Mrs Payne."

The percolator started to burble, so Betty moved to the stove to retrieve the pot.

"I hear about armed robberies where innocent people get shot. I see the drug dealers and biker gangs involved in horrific and violent crimes on the news all the time. Noely wasn't a crackhead or on that ice, or anything like that. He didn't kill or injure anyone, Mr Grey, didn't hospitalise them like some you read about. That's what I meant. I didn't say he committed victimless crimes. A crime is a crime. He was what he was."

"Can you tell me anything from your perspective that might not be on the police reports?"

"Hard to say what I might add that might be of any use."

"Can you pinpoint the day he went missing? The report was pretty vague about that."

"N-no, not, not really."

Noticing the hesitation in her voice, Arlon placed a mental marker on the question and her evasive answer for the time being.

"It was around the same time of year as this, though, wasn't it? About a year ago?"

"Near enough."

"Do you know his regular movements around this time of year? Any patterns of behaviour? Do you have a birthday around this time? Are there any events you deal with in which he would play a part? Are you close?"

"We were very close when he was still living at home. It was usually around this time of year that I would reveal my next contender for the Royal Melbourne Show in September. Noel was always very excited by that when he was younger. Even when he was older he would come around to watch me unveil my latest."

"Did that happen last year?"

"No," she said, with a break in her voice.

"So, was it usually a specific day on which you revealed your contender?"

"Yes. It was the same day every year. Noel never missed one. That was why I knew something was wrong. Whatever else he did during the year, he would always take the time to come home for that. It was our special time together. He was very proud of his mum when she won at the show."

"I don't get something. You're a breeder. You have a system of sorts for pairing up hens with cocks to produce a particular strain, be that a different colour, plumage, size, etcetera. Have I got that right?"

"Sorry, I don't give out my secrets."

"I wasn't asking you to. I was asking in general terms only. You just wanted to bore me to death with this subject matter in the back yard. Now you're reticent? Anyway, my problem is that while you were all living together it would have been impossible for him, or your husband, or even close neighbours, not to notice your latest batch of prize chicks and watch them grow? I mean they're in plain view in your back yard. So how could you surprise them?"

"I...umm."

"Mrs Payne, I don't want this to come out wrong, but I don't give a shit how you come up with your chooks. It doesn't interest me in any way, and I certainly have no intention of ever revealing your secrets. I'm interested in finding your son for you, that's it. I'm trying to establish his possible movements around the time of his disappearance. We've just possibly established the day on which he disappeared. That's more than the police have. The fact that you revealed your show entry on the same day each year, which could be the day he vanished, is a big help. It narrows my focus sharply in that direction. The less you tell me about...everything, the less likely I am to succeed. I need it all, from the dirt to the glory, if there is any."

"Oh, you make it sound like I have a deep, dark secret."

"No, you're the one making it sound that way. I deal in information. It's an essential tool for me. The more I have to work with the quicker it is for me to complete the task. What about *your* movements, then?" asked Arlon, realising she would not be forthcoming with anything else.

"Nothing particularly different from any other day," she said guardedly.

"Very well. I won't have coffee, thank you. I'll have a refund cheque to you in the mail before the end of the week. I'll see myself out."

Arlon rose quickly, while Betty Payne stood rooted to the spot with shock.

"What? Why?" she asked, seeing that Arlon was about to exit the kitchen.

"Because you're lying to me and that will only hinder the investigation. I refuse to work *against* someone. You want your son found or answers given, but you're unwilling to tell the truth or cooperate."

"I resent that. I didn't..."

"Now you're lying again. You just finished telling me how extraordinary that day was to you and your family. Then you tell me that you did nothing special on the day in question. Bullshit! You probably have some cockamamie idea that anything you tell me about your stupid chook business will be leaked to your competitors. Nothing could be further from the truth. Let me be clear...I don't care how you do it or why. I don't care where you house your precious birds. My only reason for asking is that you just said that your son would always come home when the day came to reveal your next show cock. If that was the day he disappeared, I need to know everything about that day, including your movements. You're unwilling to do that. I get it. You don't trust me and you probably don't like me. I'm not easy to like, I know. So, no hard feelings and I'll be on my way."

"Please, I, I have no one...left," she begged.

Arlon watched as the proud woman almost crumpled in on herself with despair. She sat heavily on the wooden chair, with her elbows on the table, clutching her face and sobbing pitifully. Arlon was unmoved, as always. He understood the reasons for the display. He had even had a brief experience of similar emotions not so long ago, but he could find no sympathy for the woman. He simply didn't have any.

Arlon did have moral obligations that gnawed at him during moments of another person's distress. It was ingrained in him by whatever forces that governed his personality, urging him to help others less fortunate than himself. Or, at least, in greater need than he. He weighed up the pros and cons for continuing with the case. Any leads the police had were over a year old. The trail, if ever there was one, had turned cold long before it began. He had only two potential witnesses, neither of whom were cooperative: one by choice, the other by circumstance.

He knew he would eventually winkle out the truth from the woman before him. It would possibly take a great deal of time to garner that trust from her; time he didn't believe she could afford. Arlon estimated that Betty Payne had mostly sold off whatever she retained of value to reach her present circumstances. He had seen the shed containing her chooks at the rear of the property, which seemed depleted even to Arlon's inexperienced fowl-breeder eyes. What remained did not impress him at all.

When he peered about the sparse kitchen, with its threadbare curtains and dusty, empty hutch shelves, he could see that the woman was on her last legs financially. The deposit she had placed in Arlon's business account was probably scraped together from the dregs of her remaining funds. Arlon opened a few cupboards in the kitchen while Betty sobbed. The pantry was bare and so were the cupboards. He found only one packet of soup and one can of baked beans. He noticed that her coffee tin was now also empty, as she had used the last to make him a cup.

He poured some of the rich brew from the percolator into an enamelled cup set beside the stove. He poured the other half of the contents into a china cup, which he placed before the bereft woman. He sat at the head of the table, closest to the warm stove, noting the absence of wood with which to keep the fire going. Arlon then became aware that only candles and the open stove provided light within the kitchen. He hadn't realised how dark the cottage was upon entering. It could mean only that Betty no longer had the funds to pay her electricity bill.

It was abundantly clear that Betty had basically given up on life after the disappearance of her son. Her husband had given up on her as a result of the neglect he suffered. Arlon sipped the aromatic brew with reverence, always appreciating a good coffee. He would have to get the name of the local who roasted his own blends to make such a fine brew.

Only the crackling of the dwindling fire could be heard when Betty finally fell silent. Arlon greatly valued the quiet of the country setting...until the roosters started up in the back yard again. They had been blessedly quiet for a time. He would never understand how anyone could put up with the racket of crowing roosters at all hours.

"I suggest you drink your coffee before it cools. Wouldn't pay to waste such a delectable brew."

Betty looked up with red eyes telling the tale of grief and pain. Nodding her head slightly to acknowledge his wise words, she picked up the cup to sip the coffee.

"If I am to conduct my investigation in this area, I'll have to have a base. With your permission, I will use your house for that base. I assume you have a second bedroom I can use?"

Betty nodded her head uncertainly.

"I understand your mistrust of a complete stranger, especially a man, in your home. You don't have the funds to put me up at a hotel and it seems the only alternative. I demand certain standards of my living arrangements, such as sufficient warmth. You will contact your wood supplier immediately and order enough to last a week, which I will pay for out of the money you gave me.

"Your deposit will give you a week of my time, no more. If I fail to find your son in that time, you will have to accept that and move on with your life. Not everyone gets answers for runaways or missing persons. That is just a simple fact of life, Mrs Payne. It won't do anyone any good for you to keep pining over your young man to the detriment of yourself and your lifestyle.

"When you're ready, I want the truth from you about your movements on the day in question. Until then I will exhaust what other avenues of enquiry are open to me. I'll need you to arrange permission from the Sommers boy's parents for me to visit him. I'm going to leave you now to head back to Lake Eildon, where I have left my wife and child. I'll return tomorrow morning, early, with sufficient supplies to cater to my dietary requirements for the duration of my stay. I assume you're capable of cooking a satisfactory meal?"

"What, what are your special dietary requirements?"

"I didn't say they were special requirements, only that I was to be fed. I find I need a certain amount of food each day to keep going. Quite a nuisance, really, but there it is."

Betty Payne was not sure how to take the strange man's comments. She knew she was being given a certain amount of charity, which did not sit well with her. Because he displayed no humour in his voice or facial features, she couldn't be sure if he was being insincere or making a joke at her expense. Then she told herself that couldn't be true, because he had admitted that he was incapable of being deliberately offensive. The offer rankled with her, nonetheless. Betty was a proud and stubborn woman.

"No, I can't accept that. I have some super put away, which I can access in an emergency. If you will kindly pay for whatever you require at the moment, I will pay it back, and the rest of your fee, for however long it takes."

"I will still only give you a week of my time, regardless of what you pay. If I haven't managed to find your son in that time it's highly unlikely that I will, therefore it would be a waste of your money to keep me here longer. As I said, I need a base from which to work. I can't keep heading back to Lake Eildon every night. It's a three-hour drive on some very icy roads at this time of year: dangerous in great visibility, treacherous in the thick fogs and any snowfall I may encounter. I don't even have snow chains."

"Can hire them easy enough," remarked Betty unenthusiastically.

"Look at me, Mrs Payne. I'm barely functioning in the cold of this room, let alone mucking about with unfamiliar things like snow chains out there. If you don't want me staying here, I have no alternative. I can't afford to stay at a hotel or motel for a week. Your deposit wouldn't cover my accommodation and my time. It isn't charity, if that's what you're thinking. It's practicality."

The silence stretched out between them as Betty weighed her pride against her need to discover the truth about her son. The fire in the stove began to dim as the wood burned down to glowing red coals. Only the roosters could be heard. Arlon once more debated the pros and cons.

"You're married, you say?"

"You're testing my patience, Mrs Payne. Even if I had normal feelings of lust I'd be hard-pressed to find anything attractive about you in your present state. Have you bothered to look in a mirror lately? I don't know how old you are, but you look like you could pass for my grandmother. I get it. You're upset about your boy and you've practically given up on life. Big deal! Plenty have it worse than you and I'm sick of your mistrust and self-pity. No wonder your husband left you, if this is the way you've been behaving since it happened."

"That was uncalled for," said Betty, rising from her chair.

"No, it wasn't. Whatever you may have been before this happened, you aren't the same now. Someone changes that much it's almost impossible for anyone to get through to them. I don't know what sort of a man your husband was, but he obviously didn't like what you'd become and left because of it. If your husband no longer found you attractive enough to stay, why would you suspect others to have designs on you? Particularly a man who admitted that he has no emotions? Sit down!" ordered Arlon, with a slight rise in volume.

"That...that was a terrible thing to say," said Betty, collapsing into the chair.

"I'm not here to be your friend. I don't care about you, or your son, for that matter. I was paid to do a job. I'm here to gather information and nothing more. You're unable to pay for my normal expenses, such as accommodation, while I'm investigating remotely. If this happened in Brisbane you wouldn't have to be providing accommodation. It didn't, therefore I do. I don't want to upset my family's holiday by insisting we bring my caravan over here, where there would be little for them to do. So, you have a clear and simple choice. Either you trust me enough to agree to my practical solution or you ask me to go."

"You're not a nice man."

"You aren't the first person to tell me that and you most likely won't be the last. Doesn't bother me in the least. I need your help to solve this mystery, Mrs Payne, and it won't help if you continue with this antagonistic attitude and self-pity. I need the strong, dependable woman you once were to come back to the land of the living. I need you to start caring about life again, about yourself and especially about the son you profess to love so dearly. If you want answers, if you want to prove your worth to the boy you brought into this world, then start building a bridge and get over whatever it is that's holding you back. If you were hoping for someone to mollycoddle you through this you definitely chose the wrong man."

CHAPTER FOUR

When Betty Payne finally left her house at noon in her Volkswagen Kombi, Arlon, staying well back, followed her. It had taken most of the morning for her to realise that she had to follow through with a line of thought.

When Arlon told her he would leave to join his family in Lake Eildon, he lied. It was never easy for Arlon to lie convincingly. He worked at it for one simple reason; that it was sometimes necessary in his line of work.

Betty Payne was hiding information from him. Whether that had an implication in the disappearance of her son or not, he couldn't yet determine. What he intuited was that she would lead him to some answers, one way or another. Something had shown in her eyes when they figured that Noel Payne probably disappeared on the day she normally revealed her next entry for the Royal Melbourne Show.

Somehow, that particular piece of information had not been revealed during her dealings with the local detectives. Arlon saw how the police were most likely treating the case as just another unsatisfied youth, running away to find himself, or whatever youths did these days. He was probably holed up in a crack den, the modern equivalent of the opium den, where kids became hooked on the latest trending drug. Ice seemed to be the drug of preference, as far as Arlon could tell.

The report he read didn't reveal much and smacked of boredom on the part of the reporting detectives in charge. He didn't bother chasing up the detectives to question them. Arlon knew he wouldn't get any more than what he read. They didn't care for chasing up runaways of that age. Had Noel Payne been a child it might have been very different, but no one on the force thought very much of youths in their mid-twenties going off the radar.

Arlon hung back as far as he could in his Toyota Prado as he followed Betty's van, heading in the general direction of Healesville, according to the maps in his head. It didn't appear to him that she had any idea she was being followed. She didn't use a circuitous route or double back anywhere in an attempt to discover a tail. She knew exactly where she was headed and made no efforts to conceal her movements. Arlon had already phoned Clarice to inform her of his intentions. At some point he would have to stop somewhere and purchase some basic groceries to keep in with the lie he told Betty.

While Betty had insisted that she would be able to compensate him for any expenses once she accessed her superannuation funds, Arlon was equally insistent that he would purchase the necessities and pay for the firewood in the interim. Betty didn't trust him on any level before he departed, but accepted his services and decisions with reservations. Arlon wasn't sure if he should have pushed for the case, but, without anything in the pipeline, he didn't see any other choices for himself, either. They were stuck with each other.

When Arlon left the cottage he drove his Prado to the cul-de-sac at the bottom of the drive, where he waited. Something about Betty's story rang false. Her secrecy about her breeding methods had Arlon's antennae quivering as well. It seemed to him that, if someone was boastful about their prize fowls and wanted to chew his ear off about them, it stood to reason that she would want to include some titbits about the breeding processes. It was certainly possible to talk in generalities without giving away the farm. That she clammed up tight made Arlon curious: curious enough not to simply walk away from the case or drive to Lake Eildon immediately.

The lush green countryside passed by at a slower rate than Arlon would have liked. Betty's Kombi ran like an old woman with emphysema. Every so often, a cloud of smoke emerged from the exhaust, as the old car burned through oil to negotiate a small gradient. It was all Arlon could do not to overtake the ailing vehicle.

His late-model Prado wanted to break into a comfortable cruising speed instead of lagging back like a beaten dog.

He forced himself into a form of relaxation, where he allowed his mind to wander and his body to function on semi-automation. He followed her for over an hour before she finally made the Maroondah Highway, where she sped up a little. The scenery was magical. The towering eucalypts and mountain ash created a tunnel over the twisting highway as they made their way farther along the Black Spur Drive.

Arlon lost her momentarily as she disappeared behind a sharp bend. No major arterial roads branched off the highway in the immediate vicinity, as far as he was aware, so he wasn't overly concerned. Only, when he rounded the bend he had seen her take, he could no longer see her car on the straight stretch before him. At her speed, he determined that it would have been impossible for her to have proceeded farther than he could see up the bare road. He was unaware of any roads they could have passed.

Arlon stopped his vehicle one kilometre from the tight bend. He managed to locate a wide enough space to perform a U-turn. The thick vegetation on either side of the narrow highway revealed no passages as he drove slowly back toward the bend. A light rain trickled through the leafy roof of the natural tunnel. The vibrant greens of every hue, intermixed with varying shades of russet and orange, told of the forest's rich and fertile heritage.

Arlon drove back and forth along the same kilometre of highway, perplexed by his inability to find where Betty Payne had turned off. He knew she could not have eluded him by remaining on the highway. Her vehicle was just too slow for that. Had she finally made out her tail? Was it possible that she had played him for a fool? The questions vexed him, no matter how unlikely. He knew he was not infallible. He'd made many errors of judgement in his career.

Frustrated, Arlon parked his vehicle off the road on the wide verge, where he had turned his car several times now. The moment he exited the warm interior of the car he felt the biting cold seeping through his inadequate clothing. He wore casual cotton slacks and shirt accompanied by a light semi-waterproof jacket. He was chilled to the bone before he walked ten metres.

No other cars were speeding by, no sounds could be heard other than birdsong from the thick forest. Either side of the road had steep drop-offs, as far as he could tell. The trunks of the mighty mountain ash rose from the forest floor below, to impossible heights far above Arlon, as he tramped down the road. The rainfall had ceased, but the droplets continuing beneath the thick canopy made it more uncomfortable for Arlon.

As he drew near the bend he had revisited several times, he became quite confused. There was no sign of his target or where she might have turned off the highway. He almost missed it once more and would have given up entirely. Only the merest hint of a disturbance in the leafy tree ferns' foliage indicated recent passage. The mouldy, damp, leafy detritus underneath finally revealed the impression of Betty's thin tyres. The track paralleled the highway for about one hundred metres before it veered off. The semi-graded track was impossible to make out from the highway unless you peered over the edge directly above it. It was a beautifully disguised track, in Arlon's opinion.

Had Arlon not been entirely convinced of its existence he would have missed it altogether. Indeed, he did not immediately find it, when he returned in his car. There was no verge, no dirt on the side of the asphalt highway. The track led straight in off the main road at such an oblique angle that Arlon would never have been able to find it had he not walked it first. The track angled down perilously once it changed direction away from the road. According to his detailed map, it was a forestry track that didn't have a name, only a number; Rd 13.

Considering how slippery it was, Arlon wondered if his client could have made the journey in the old Volkswagen. It didn't seem possible. The rugged track twisted and turned as he wound his way through the misty gloom. It was early afternoon and already the fog was beginning to creep into the forest. Overhead, snow clouds made their way over the distant mountain peaks to dump well-needed powder on the popular ski fields.

When Arlon came to a junction he had to exit the vehicle to determine which fork to follow. The left fork descended farther. He assumed it to be Rd 22, according to his map. Rd 13 continued up to the right. He inspected the area and located her fresh tyre tracks readily enough in the soft leafy mulch covering the dirt road. It appeared he would have to ascend to the right. Despite witnessing evidence that the ineffectual Kombi had negotiated the steep slope, Arlon shifted his transmission into four-wheel-drive. He had no desire to slide off the track in his near-new vehicle.

Half an hour later, Arlon became lost. He couldn't remember leaving the track he was following, yet he could not advance through the thick foliage blocking his path. Once more he was forced to exit the comfort of his vehicle to scout the path ahead and behind. Mud squelched into his patent leather shoes, soaking his thin socks and numbing his feet instantly.

Pushing through the dense, wet foliage in front of his car soon soaked Arlon's upper body as well. He shivered with the cold as he inched forward. The fog had thickened considerably, making it difficult to see more than a few metres ahead. Arlon became concerned that he might miss a drop-off which would send him tumbling to the bottom of the mountain.

Instead, he banged his knee painfully into an abandoned and rusting ute which he did not see until the very last moment. The pale green colour of the remaining paint assisted the ute to blend in perfectly with its surroundings. The foliage had almost covered the vehicle. Arlon assumed it to be either a stolen and abandoned vehicle or a broken and abandoned vehicle. No way would anyone want to pay a tow truck to retrieve their worthless old ute from this location.

It was clear that Betty had not taken the track he was on. No way could she have made it around the ute. Arlon wasn't even sure why he had gone forward of his car's position in the first place. There were no signs of recent passage in the greenery. All the leaves and fronds were dripping with moisture, so could not been disturbed.

Arlon wasn't sure what made him decide to investigate the ute. Something in the back of his mind tickled his curiosity, urging it to recognise a connection. At first glance, there didn't appear to be any obvious signs of damage, other than normal wear and tear and the passage of time since the vehicle had last been functional. Another strange discovery was the fact that the car was locked. That denoted ownership rather than abandonment, in Arlon's view.

He pushed through the foliage to reach the driver's side door. Inside the cabin he saw the untidy remains of the ubiquitous McDonalds and KFC food packages littering the floor and bench seat. Everything about the vehicle and the circumstances advised Arlon that it didn't fit an abandonment scenario.

In his former role as a police officer, and then detective, he had been called to a few burned-out shells on remote roadways, all that remained of stolen vehicles. He'd even been called out to a suicide in a car once. He hoped never to have to attend another scene like that in his lifetime. The overwhelming stench sought to incapacitate him. Even thinking about it brought back the rising bile. He had to shake off the memories to forestall the inevitable.

As it was an older-style vehicle, with push-button locking knobs on the interior window sills, Arlon was confident he could unlock the vehicle to examine the interior. He retreated to his Prado, where he kept a toolbox full of different odds and ends to assist him in his investigations. Retrieving a hacksaw blade and a strip of plastic packaging tape, Arlon fought his way through the wet fronds once more to return to the ute.

With his hands shaking as the insidious cold crept into his bones, Arlon found it difficult to keep them steady as he went about breaking into the car. He folded the packaging material in two, creating a closed-end crease. He placed the hacksaw blade between the two layers, with one end snug up against the inside of the crease.

This gave a certain amount of rigidity to the instrument, while allowing enough flexibility to manoeuvre it into and around the window rubbers to get the material inside the car.

Once that was achieved he withdrew the blade, leaving only the tape inside the car. By pulling on one end of the tape from outside the window, an open loop was formed at the crease in the plastic tape. He hooked that end of the tape around and under the exposed locking button. With a swift upward motion he jerked the button up to unlock the car. The entire exercise took less than a minute. *Such was the safety of older cars left unattended*, thought Arlon.

He was presented with a stale, mouldy scent once the door was open. A few spiders and a couple of geckos had made their home inside the old car, otherwise it was relatively untouched. Before Arlon read the name on the registration papers in the glove box, he knew who owned the car. The memory that tickled his antennae was the make and model of the ute and the number plate. He'd recognised them from the reports. It was Noel Payne's car.

There was nothing else within the car to give any indication of what had happened to its owner. There were no signs of foul play or struggle, no blood or other evidence to indicate an injury. Arlon was careful not to disturb anything within the car, knowing that a full examination by the police would have to be carried out once he reported the discovery. DNA evidence and fingerprints would most likely prove the presence of Noel and his friend Harry in the car at some point. He replaced everything as he'd found it and relocked the door.

Then the lights went out.

CHAPTER FIVE

"Well, lookit what the cat drug in," stated Irma Cabbage as Arlon was coming round.

Through the fug in his brain, Arlon noted his unpleasant surroundings with less than perfect vision. His head ached abysmally where he'd been struck. As his vision cleared he saw the filthy owner of the declaration he'd heard, assuming that he was the subject referred to as what had been 'drug' in. Rightly or wrongly, he immediately formed an opinion as to the general level of intelligence of his captors, if that's who they were.

He was unbound, lying on a rug that reeked of filth. His skin crawled at the thought of what infestations may be inhabiting the worn and decrepit material long past its use-by date. Under the faded and threadbare rug were rough-hewn timber floorboards with cracks, allowing a cold draught to permeate the tiny cabin. Arlon smelled wood smoke coming from a potbelly cast iron stove situated in a corner of the tiny living area.

"Where'd ya find this city boy, Elmo?" asked Irma in the broadest Australian accent Arlon had ever come across.

The owner of that accent was a hefty woman in a voluminous, faded, filthy and shapeless floral frock about the size of a generous three-person tent. The unkempt mouse-brown hair hung limply around the broad face, which showed black stumps where there ought to have been teeth, possibly were at some point a long time ago. The round face with small, piggish eyes glared at Arlon like he was an alien or unwelcome vermin. Arlon assumed, rightly, that normal vermin were welcome in the household.

"Caught him sneakin' round our patch, Mum, out by the fork. By that old ute been there for a year now. He got a nice car, Mum. One-o-them swanky Jap jobs with four-wheel-drive, probably. Can't even buy good-old Australian."

"There aren't any good-old Australian cars," muttered Arlon.

"What was that? What'd he say? What ya say, ya dumb sack-o-shit? No good-old Australian cars? What about fuckin' Holdens, huh? What about them?" barked Elmo, kicking Arlon with a fleshy bare foot that stunk of rotting flesh.

"The company that started out as a saddlery in 1856 hasn't been owned by an Australian since 1931 when it came under the banner of General Motors in America."

"Ya lyin' mongrel..."

"Now, Elmo, he's right about that. Didn't know they wasn't bein' made here no more, though. That a fact, mister?" asked Irma, who stood over him like a mountain of smelly garbage.

From his position on the floor he was able to see up the knee-length sack she wore, past the fleshy knees, past the blubber-like thighs, to the hairy, filthy bush between her legs, which did not hide the prolapsed and putrid minge therein. Arlon quickly averted his eyes before he became ill.

"Stopped production here a few years ago and have now stopped selling here altogether. No longer made for Australians at all. Ford has closed down their local manufacturing as well. Imports only. I don't think any company is manufacturing here anymore. I can't be certain about that, though. Why was I clubbed and brought here?"

"Caught ya tresspassin'. Coulda shot ya legally for that," answered Elmo, with what Arlon thought to be an even broader accent, if that were at all possible.

"That isn't even close to being true."

"Yeah, how the fuck would ya know that?"

"I used to be a police officer and a detective. You can't legally shoot anyone in Australia unless you have absolute proof it was in self-defence. Even then you'd better have a licence to carry a weapon, otherwise you won't have a leg to stand on."

"Mighta knowed it. A fuckin' copper! Ya brung a fuckin' copper here, Elmo. Are ya stupid?"

"Well, if that isn't the pot calling the kettle black," said Arlon.

"If ya don't want me boy to give ya another kick, I'd be real careful about what ya say, copper," warned Irma, stepping even closer to Arlon, giving him another close-up view of her filth and another waft of an unholy pall. The disgusting mixture of stale urine, matted faeces in the pubic hair and in the huge cleft of her wobbling behind, as well as other fluids and exotic juices exuded by her womanhood, caused Arlon to gag.

"Don't ya go throwin' up on me good rug now," advised Irma in a stern voice.

Arlon didn't think she could be serious about the warning, and wondered what her less than favourable rug might have looked like. He decided to hold back any comments. With her fat son holding a smallbore rifle in the crook of his dirty elbow, it didn't seem wise to provoke these bumpkins.

"Listen, folks, I'm not a copper anymore. I left the force over three years ago. I am still a *private* detective, but I have no affiliations with the force. Whatever it is you folks are hoping to hide is none of my business..."

"Ya made it ya bizness when ya stuck ya nose inta it, mate. Now, tell us what ya know and what ya intend ta do about it."

"What is it you want me to divulge?"

"Eh? Ya bein' a smart-arse?"

"Wouldn't be difficult, but no, I'm not being a smart-arse intentionally. I wanted to know what you meant. I'm investigating a missing person, that's all. If you have nothing to do with that, then I'm not interested in anything else."

"Who?"

"Who's missing? The owner of that ute that's been out there for over a year," explained Arlon, harking back to what Elmo had mentioned earlier.

"Don't know nothin' bout that," said Elmo cautiously.

"Hush, boy. Don't pay to give him nothin'. We don't know nothin' bout no missin' boy, ya hear?"

"I didn't say it was a boy," whispered Arlon pointedly.

"Now don't go readin' nothin' inta what I said. Jest a figure-o-speech. We don't know nothin' and we don't like talkin' to no outsiders. We got our own ways out here. Been doin' it for a long time, too."

"Is there any chance I can get off this stinking rug?"

"Can't smell nothin'. Whatcha talkin' about?"

"I have asthma and this is beginning to affect me. If you don't want to see me suffer an attack and possibly die as a result, I suggest you let me at least sit up and get my face out of it."

"Ya gonna try anythin'?"

"You have me covered with a weapon. However, I give you my word I won't try anything."

"Maybe we should tie him up, Mum."

"He's a skinny little runt, boy, and you gotta gun. What's he gonna do? 'Sides, he's shiverin' so bad he might shake hisself ta bits. If he don't get up and get warm by the fire he's gonna catch the death-o-cold. Get some-o-that homemade, son. Need ta warm him frum the insides out, I reckon. Garn, get up then, mister. I warn ya, though. Slightest bit-o-funny stuff and I'll have me boy fill ya with holes. Sit by the table there," ordered Irma.

Arlon slowly peeled himself from the sticky rug, bearing the brunt of the pain in his head with stoicism as he rose. He made it to the rustic wooden table, where he sat on one of the bare wooden chairs, grateful for the fact it wasn't upholstered. He couldn't disguise his disgust for the unsanitary conditions he faced. On the table rested an array of chipped and stained enamel dishes with the residue of their last meal attracting a small squadron of blowies, buzzing about them noisily.

Irma Cabbage planted her enormous bulk on the groaning chair opposite Arlon. With her thunder thighs spread wide apart, Arlon was thankful he did not still have a worm's eye view of her nether regions. He was having difficulty unseeing what he had already witnessed. Elmo Cabbage took up station by the kitchen benches, keeping a keen eye on all of Arlon's movements, nervously fingering the trigger of the rifle. Arlon hoped the weapon did not have a hair-trigger. Judging by its worn and ancient appearance, he didn't think it would be a factor.

"Thought I told ya to get me some homemade, Elmo?"

"I can't guard him if I do that, Mum," replied Elmo in an annoying whine.

"If it's all the same to you, I'd rather not," admitted Arlon.

"What, you some sort-o-weirdo what don't drink nuthin'?"

"No, just someone who appreciates sanitary preparations where human consumption is concerned."

"Huh?"

"Not right now. I'm fine by the fire here," Arlon explained.

Arlon had to change tack. Although he usually blurted out pretty much anything that came to him, he was aware that antagonising these bumpkins was likely to end in more injury to him. His head provided a constant pounding where the youth had slugged him, probably with the butt of the rifle. His shivering diminished gradually as he warmed himself in front of the potbelly. His olfactory senses were in overdrive, attempting to identify, and then ignore, the assault. Leftover fat in the cast iron skillet, with bits of meat swimming in the gelatinous goo, competed with the body odours from the two inhabitants wafting in Arlon's direction. One look at the youth's black feet told the story of gross infections and fungus growth between the toes.

The greasy timber walls, hessian sacks for window coverings, liberally coated in dust and grime, exposed wooden roof rafters that were hairy with eons of accumulations, made Arlon's skin crawl. He was undecided about which medical condition would claim him first, after exposure to the filth in which the feral humans lived. The overall stench of human faeces and urine trumped the rest of the odours and was overwhelming in the cloying atmosphere of the small, rundown cottage.

"What we gonna do with him, Mum?"

"We'll let Daddy decide that. Where is he?"

"Tendin' the crops..."

"Elmo! Shut ya hole, boy," warned Irma, with fear etched on her features.

"He's not gonna tell no one, Mum. Daddy make sure-o-that."

"Don't ya be tellin' no one our bizness, anyway. Walls have ears."

"Never seen them ears ya keep warnin' me about," said Elmo sullenly.

"I don't give a rat's arse what you're growing out here. Doesn't take much imagination to work out you're dope farmers. I can smell it a mile away."

"Ya just signed ya death warrant, ya dopey prick!" exclaimed Irma. "See? See what ya done?" she accused Elmo.

"Like I said, he won't be goin' nowhere to tell no one. Stinkin' rotten, lousy copper won't make it ten minutes once Daddy finds out what he is. I'll be diggin' him a hole 'fore mornin'."

"Yeah, then you'll have cops everywhere. My wife will phone the manufacturer to ask them to locate my car via the transponder. They'll triangulate my car's position by satellite and this whole area will be crawling with more cops than you can count, though that wouldn't take many in my estimation."

"Bullshit! Ya talkin' crapola, mate. No way can they locate ya car in that lot out there. Can't hardly see nothin' for the trees and leaves. Bin hidin' out here all our lives and nobody found us," spat Irma.

"No amount of natural environment can block the signal unless it's under a mountain. Once the police or the insurance company is alerted they will locate the car easily. Most modern cars have it now as part of their security measures in case a car is stolen," attested Arlon.

"Then how come they didn't come lookin' for that other bloke's car, huh? Tell me that, Mr Smarty-pants," challenged Irma, with a look of smugness on her rotund features.

"Because that car's too old. They didn't have the technology back then when it was manufactured. I think it's an '87 model or thereabouts. Believe me, if it had been a late model vehicle, it would have been located the moment his mother reported her son as missing."

"What mother?"

"The mother of the missing boy...man. He was in his twenties, went missing around about a year ago, and that's what I was doing near the car, investigating, when this coward clubbed me from behind."

"Best mind he don't club ya again, talkin' about him like that. I've a mind to let him."

"Save Daddy the trouble if ya let me do it, Mum."

"Leave the thinkin' ta the adults, Elmo. If ya do him before Daddy has a chance ta question him, yiz'll be in deep shit. Now, I axed ya before ta hand me some homemade and I won't axe again."

"Where'd ya hide it this time, then? Daddy finds out ya hidin' the hooch from him he's gonna go off like a rocker."

"Listen to ya. It's either he's gonna go off his rocker or go off like a rocket. Ya can't mix-n-match em, dummy."

"He won't care about mixin'-n-matchin' when he finds out about it."

"You fixin' ta tell him, boy? After all I done for ya?"

"Ya never done nothin' special for me. Bloody dogsbody I is. Fetch this and do that all bloody day 'cause ya too fat and lazy ta do it yaself."

Irma gave the boy a long hard stare through her piggy, squinting eyes. Arlon could almost see the steam whistle about to erupt as the flush began in her fat cheeks. Mt. Vesuvius was about to blow, in Arlon's opinion. Just as quickly, the tension subsided, as a creepy smile emerged on her dirty face.

"Just fer that, ya don't get what ya thought ya had comin'," she announced with relish.

A look of absolute dread suffused Elmo's features. His body

almost caved in on itself as the realisation of the statement seeped through to him. His face collapsed into a pathetic look of pure desperation.

"No, Mummy, please. Not that. I, I'm sorry, I'm sorry I said that. It aint true. Ya good ta me, Mum, I swear. Please don't hold out..."

"Shut ya hole, ya ungrateful bastard. Shoulda done away with ya after yiz was born like Daddy wanted. Damn near killcd mc pushin' your fat arse outta my sweet tiny hole. Never been the same after that. Ruined me downstairs for good, ya did. Daddy don't want me anymore 'cause-o-what happened. Insides all comin' out like, and can't hold me water no more. Piss meself if I cough or I laugh. Don't even bother wearin' no pants no more. Waste a bloody time. And ya have the hide ta say I don't do nothin' special for yiz. Well, ya done it now, Elmo. Garn, fuck orf ta ya room-n-stay there. And don't ya let me hear no blubberin', boy, or ya won't get none termorra neither. Now git!"

"He might not survive cold turkey in his condition," Arlon suggested, after Elmo exited and the silence dragged on.

"Ya don't know what the fuck ya talkin' about. Now shut it."

"Doesn't take an Einstein to figure out you're all smackheads."

"Ya full-o-shit, mate, and I warned ya ta shut it. Haven't had me a pussy-lickin' in a long, long time. If ya don't shut it like I said, I'm just as like to sit on ya and have me a face-fuck. Last bloke had the pleasure-o-that ended up with his head all the way up there. Daddy had to pull that fucker outta there when he got stuck and died. Couldn't breathe no more. Ya wanna taste, pretty boy?"

"You grow dope mainly to pay for your habits, and the rest goes on necessities like food. The tracks make it pretty obvious, and I can see your shakes starting already, just thinking about the hit that's coming when your husband returns. I've been around junkies long enough to know the signs of addiction."

"I'll get me some-o-that bakin' grease from the pan over there and slap it on ya head ta make it nice and slippery, I will. Tole ya ta shut it. Don't know nothin' bout no tracks. Elmo knows enough ta cover his tracks so nobody can follow."

"On your arms. Needle tracks. Your boy probably has Hep C or worse, maybe AIDS from using dirty needles. That's what makes him so sickly-looking and fatigued. You think he's lazy and he said the same about you, but it's the illness making him like that. He needs treatment. You as well, most likely."

"What's that?"

"Hep C? Hepatitis. A bad illness that can kill you eventually if left untreated. Not sure if they have a cure yet. Probably not. AIDS, though, that's the nastiest one. "

"Well, we all gotta die somehow."

"Some of us sooner than necessary, perhaps. None of my business, though. You're right. You want to kill yourselves, you go right ahead."

"Ya sure are makin' me horny with all this talk about death, pretty man."

"You can't frighten me. I have no emotions. My condition prevents it. Otherwise, you would see the disgust on my face from what you're proposing. I might even be puking a little in my mouth right now."

"Ya sick, are ya? Maybe it'll be yaself what goes first."

"No, not sick. A condition. Part of...oh, never mind."

"Nah, that's right, us dumb folks wouldn't understand, would we?"

"First intelligent thing you've said since I've been here."

"Ya don't know nothin', mate."

"I know that's a double negative."

"Ya got a big mouth, ya know that?"

"Not as big as your...hairy gash!"

Irma Cabbage was stunned first, then shook with the tremors of mirth that soon transformed into full-blown, roaring laughter, which descended into a bout of phlegmy coughing. She slapped her fleshy thighs as she tried to contain the hacking emphysema overwhelming her. Elmo stuck his nose out from the loft bedroom at the sound.

"Ya okay, Mum?"

"Elmo Cabbage, ya little shithead, get back in that room 'fore I smack ya one," threatened Irma, once she regained a modicum of control.

"You're both sick. Probably your husband as well. You need to get treatment from a hospital."

"Fuck ya, and fuck them hospitals, too," spat Irma.

"Charming. Missed some of those elocution lessons as a child, did you?"

"I didn't get no lectrocution lessons. What the fuck are ya talkin' about? Got taught ta keep right away from the lectric stuff. Daddy got us on that solar power here so we don't mess with no lectric-city."

"E-lectricity, Mum! Jeez, no wonder he thinks we're stupid," Elmo yelled from his room.

"Shut ya hole, ya little shit. Don't make me come up there," she warned fiercely.

"Ha! As if ya can get up that ladder, Mum," Elmo replied smugly.

"Gotta come down sometime, fuck-face, and I'll be waitin'. Kids, no respect," said Irma to Arlon, as if he might somehow side with her on the issue. "Won't get no supper now, neither, ya little shit," she added, nodding her head.

Arlon shook his head in amazement. He shouldn't have. His head began to throb again. He would have asked for mild pain relief if he didn't think it would most likely cause more damage than the headache. They were just as likely to hand him an acid tab or ecstasy if they deigned to give him anything at all. On second thought, he didn't think there would be anything of a mind-altering substance left in the house, with the two junkies left on their own most of the day.

Arlon saw the tremors in both of them. They were waiting for their next fix from the husband and they weren't taking the waiting well. The rotten teeth were a dead giveaway for a heroin habit, too.

The addiction could often lead to a dramatic increase in high-sugar food consumption. Coupled with a lack of oral hygiene, it made a long-time addict recognisable by the condition of their teeth and gums. Not that Arlon required that to determine their condition. The needle tracks, tremors and volatile personalities were sufficient for Arlon to draw the obvious conclusions, just as he'd been taught in the police academy.

"What's ya name, pretty man?"

"What difference does it make?"

"Gotta call ya somethin' while ya still breathin' me air."

"Air I would much rather not be breathing, by the way. My name is Arlon Grey."

"Dumb-arse, if ya not breathin', ya dyin'."

"I didn't say any air, just not the stink in here. Making my toenails curl."

"Ya full-o-shit, mate. Nothing wrong with the air in here. I'm Irma. Irma Cabbage. Ya already met Elmo, me boy."

"Cabbage? Should have stuck to your maiden name, I reckon."

"What's that?"

"What, your maiden name?"

"Yeah."

"How would I know?"

"How would ya know what?"

"How do you expect me to know your maiden name? I haven't a clue."

"What's a bloody maiden name?"

"Really? It's your family name before you were married."

"Not married. I always had that name."

"Have you ever been out of here?"

"Once. Had the chickenpox and had ta go ta hospital in Melbourne. Daddy took me in."

"You must have been fairly old to get chickenpox."

"I was only a little tacker, 'bout five, I reckon."

"How could you possibly have known your partner when you

were five?"

"What partner? Make some sense, would ya?"

"The boy's father. How could you have known the boy's father when you were only five?"

"Knowed him all me life, ya dumb cunt."

Realisation slowly dawned on Arlon as he stretched his thinking beyond the accepted norm. He was in a very strange household, where normal conventions were ignored. He'd read accounts of hillbillies in the backwoods of America in similar circumstances, where meeting anyone new was a rare occasion. Laws unto themselves, and mostly spurning conventional society, they lived out their entire lives in isolation: bootleggers and moonshiners making their living on the edge of the law.

Irma Cabbage and her son weren't that different by making their living from dope. How they managed it in the middle of a forest he couldn't imagine. They didn't seem anywhere near sophisticated enough to be farming underground, with solar power to generate the growing light and the warmth the crops required.

Arlon wondered if perhaps they had utilised an old mine shaft instead of getting the equipment they needed to dig a field underground. It couldn't have been in a clearing to have lasted this long undetected by police. It had to be an underground installation. It would have taken her father too many years on his own to manage that, which gave more credence to Arlon's theory of utilising an abandoned mine shaft.

There were plenty of old gold mines in Victoria: a big one at Woods Point, not too far from where they were, if his memory served. He thought he had read recently that they were going to reopen that one with the price of gold soaring, making it a profitable proposition again.

"Look, Mrs...er...Irma, I have no interest in what you folks are doing out here. I'm only concerned about trying to locate the missing lad. His name is Noel Payne. His mother is worried to death about him. You can understand that, surely? Being a mother yourself?"

"Ha! If Elmo went and got hisself lost I'd be one happy woman, I can tell ya."

"Bullshit! I know ya'd miss me and come lookin', Mum," shouted Elmo.

"Dumb prick. I wouldn't. Worst thing ta ever happen ta me, havin' that ungrateful shit. Ruinin' me woman parts so's Daddy don't want me no more. Elmo, if ya don't shut it and butt outta my talkin', I'm gonna take a branch ta ya fat arse next time ya come down. Now shut the fuck up!"

"I'm sorry if I was trespassing on your property, Irma. It wasn't intentional. I won't say anything..."

"Ha! Like hell, ya won't. Won't do no good ta make no promises ya can't keep, Arlon Grey. Specially ta me. I wasn't borned yesterdee."

"Well, how about the boy, then? Do you know anything about the boy who owned that old ute?"

"Witch got him for sure!" yelled Elmo.

"Elmo, ya got dirt in ya ears, boy? What'd I say not more-n-a moment ago?"

"Mum, I can hear everything up here and I can't sleep. I'm sorry 'bout what I said, okay? Ya good ta me, Mum. Wouldn't be who I am if ya weren't good ta me."

"And just who is it ya think ya are then?"

"Elmo Thomas Cabbage, son of Colin...don't know his middle name, Cabbage, and Irma May Cabbage."

"Soon ta be deceased Cabbage if ya don't shut that hole," Irma muttered with a grin. "Come on back down, ya no good scallywag. Never could stay angry at ya for long, could I?"

"Nah, yiz a good mum," said Elmo, as he climbed down the ladder.

"What did you say about a witch?" Arlon asked, as Elmo took a chair at the table.

The front door suddenly swung open and slammed against the inside wall. Standing in the doorway, filling every centimetre of space within the frame, stood a huge man wearing a very old-fashioned and threadbare, pinstriped brown suit.

"What's goin' on here and why is there a bloody stranger sittin' in me chair?" thundered the man, whom Arlon assumed to be Colin Cabbage.

CHAPTER SIX

"So ya thought ya should bring him 'ere?"

"Couldn't have him snoopin' round up there, Daddy. Mighta found his way here," answered Elmo, trembling with fear.

"Elmo, ya got no brains, that's for sure. How the fuck was this little twerp eva gonna find his way 'ere? How many times I told yiz that no one's gonna make his way through the shit out there ta find our plot. Jeez, blimey, fuck!"

"It doesn't have to be a problem, sir. I have no reason to tell anyone what I saw here, which was nothing, by the way. I'll simply finish investigating the missing boy, if you return me to my car, and that will be that," offered Arlon weakly.

"Yeah, not bloody likely. We let ya go and the cops'll be all over that bloody car and everywhere else as well. Still don't think they'll make it 'ere, but ya can't be too careful."

"Shoulda done the witch when you said, Daddy."

"Elmo, yiz a Burk, ya know that? Now ya gone and tole him about her. Anything else ya'd like to divulge, ya moron?"

"What's that word?"

"Divulge? Look it up like I taught ya, ya ignorant prick! Garn, right now-n-be quick about it. Get the dickonary and look it up."

"Aww, Dad," he whined.

"Don't ya bloody 'aww, Dad' me. Do as ya tole. Up ta ya room-n-stay there before I gives ya me boot."

"Ya brung it, Daddy? Ya brung what I need?" asked Irma.

"Quiet, ya bloody dickhead. More friggin' divulgin' goin' on round 'ere-n-we may as well give up ta the coppers now! And I tole ya ta cut out callin' me that. Call me by me name."

"Why, Daddy?"

"Coz, that's why."

"Coz why?"

"Jeez, the both-o-ya. Dumb as horseshit. Wouldn't know ya arse from ya elbow."

"And you're surprised by that?" whispered Arlon.

"What?"

"Nothing."

"Tell me what ya said or I'll..."

"Or you'll what? Shoot me like that gutless boy of yours was going to do before? No one man enough to stand up to a runt like me in a fair contest? Are you all cowards, then?"

A deadly silence descended on the cottage. Elmo halted climbing his ladder mid-rung. Irma sucked her breath in and held it. Colin Cabbage stood behind the chair Arlon had earlier vacated, his face turning a deep shade of crimson. Arlon could almost make out the steam coming from his ears. If it wasn't quite so comical Arlon might have been more concerned.

Colin Cabbage squared up his massive shoulders and straightened his spine to stand at his impressive full height. A mean glare twinkled in the eyes of the brute, who seemed ready to take up the challenge. Just as Arlon was sure he'd suckered the man into a contest where he figured he had a better than even chance of winning, Colin deflated like a spent balloon.

"Nah, too tired after a bloody long day. I'll knock ya head in termorra. Elmo, get back down 'ere and make sure ya tie him up good for the night," ordered Colin.

Elmo obeyed by reversing the climb up to his lofty bedroom, while Colin relieved himself of his suit jacket, walking behind Arlon towards the curtained-off bedroom on the ground floor. Arlon was disappointed, chiding himself for not succeeding in luring the man into a fair contest. Too late, he saw Irma's little piggy eyes fly wide open as she witnessed something occurring behind Arlon.

The stunning blow to the side of his head would have rendered him unconscious, if not dead, had Arlon not managed to bring up his hands to either side of his head to deflect or lessen the blow. It still had enough power to knock him flying, landing heavily on the reeking rug once more.

Under normal circumstances Arlon would have rebounded to his feet in the blink of an eye. However, the blow left him feeling groggy. On elbows, he attempted to shake off the fug in his mind. That only succeeded in making his headache worse. When his hearing and sight gradually returned to normal, he could hear Irma and Elmo cheering for their father and egging him on. The steel-capped toe of the booted foot landed square in Arlon's gut, taking the wind out of him and possibly breaking a rib. The mighty kick lifted Arlon several centimetres off the floor, twisting him over in mid-air so that he landed painfully on his back.

Arlon could see that the children were rousing their father to insane levels of adrenaline, inducing further rage within the large man. If Arlon did not act quickly he would breathe his last on the dirty floor of the miserable hovel in the middle of the forest. He used the opportunity, while the big man wallowed in the cheers and praise from his children, to recoup his energy, to focus on recovery and implement an offensive strategy.

Utilising his powerful legs, Arlon thrust himself up from his prone position to land expertly on the balls of his feet. The cheering subsided. Colin blinked in confusion. No one had ever risen from a beating delivered by the big man. He almost laughed at the pathetic individual standing before him, poised in some Asian-style fighting stance. Arlon stood alone, defiantly against the man as he advanced. Colin Cabbage towered over Arlon, stopping in front of him with his legs spread wide to give him the support he required for the haymaker he was set to deliver.

The man was quick: Arlon had to credit him for that. Arlon was quicker. He kicked the man in the groin so hard he felt sure he had ruptured one of his testicles. As Colin Cabbage began doubling over in the exquisite agony only males know, Arlon brought up his knee to connect with the face of the big man. Placing every ounce of strength he could muster into the rising knee, Arlon broke Colin's nose in several places, causing it to erupt in a torrent of claret. The man fell to the floor, where he remained curled up in a ball with hands clutching his groin. Anyone else would have been rendered unconscious by the well-placed knee.

An awkward silence fell on the interior of the little cottage. Irma and her son had seen their father in several brawls and knew he could not be defeated by any ordinary man. In the volatile and dangerous occupation they had designed for themselves, Colin Cabbage had had to defend himself many times, when others believed that they could either muscle him out of his share or take advantage by overpowering him with superior numbers. Irma had never seen her father bested in all of her years.

Incensed by the humiliation visited upon her father, enraged beyond control, Irma May Cabbage rose from her chair to bear down on Arlon like a rampaging bull. Arlon kicked her in the same place as her father, knowing how vulnerable she would be in that area. He had witnessed the prolapsed vagina first hand, and knew that the purple and pink innards protruding through the labia would be extra sensitive to a stunning kick. He followed up the kick with a savage cross to the side of her head with his fist as she was going down.

The report from the rifle shocked him, but did not prevent him from hurling himself into a flying tumble toward the boy, holding the rifle at an awkward angle. Arlon was thankful for the panicked shot from Elmo, as the slug landed in the wood panelling directly behind where Arlon had been standing.

Coming out of the roll, just as Elmo was hauling back on the bolt to inject another round into the breach, Arlon lunged at him with a kick to the chest that sent the young man flying backwards. Coming to rest hard up against the kitchen cupboards, Elmo sank gradually to the floor in defeat, the rifle thrown away from him in surrender. Arlon walked casually over to retrieve the rifle.

Elmo watched in horror as Arlon advanced on him. The rifle was clutched in his hands by the barrel, ready to swing it like a club straight for his head. Instead, the rifle smacked hard against the kitchen benchtop beside Elmo's head, splintering the wooden stock and severely bending the hardened-steel barrel. Arlon bent down to glare directly into Elmo's eyes, daring him to make one false move.

"Do you know how to make coffee?" Arlon asked eventually.

"H-huh?"

"Coffee. Real coffee. I see you have a stovetop espresso pot. Can you use it to make a decent cup of coffee or not?"

Elmo nodded his head.

"Good. Get some boiling hot water in that sink, wash a cup for me with detergent and dry it on a clean cloth. Then pour me a cup of strong black coffee in that once it's finished percolating."

"Y-y-yep, okay. I can do that, I reckon."

"I'll believe it when I see and taste it. Make bloody sure that cup is clean or you'll be wearing that boiling hot coffee," Arlon warned.

Irma and Colin lay on the filthy rug moaning and clutching their groins. He was unsure about how to proceed with them. They were dangerous to leave unrestrained, yet he had no right to bind them. Arlon believed that they had information that would be beneficial to his investigation. He needed their cooperation and some trust. He would have to conduct a brief search of the cottage to locate any more weapons they might own.

"Do you own any other guns?" he asked Elmo, who was madly washing away the built-up grime from an enamelled tin cup. His hands were smarting from the hot water he'd placed in the sink from the kettle that remained permanently on the combustion stove.

"Daddy usually carries one on him when he goes ta town, and Mum's got one in her bedside drawers," answered Elmo.

Arlon went to the jacket Colin had discarded on the end of the king-sized bed behind the curtained area. He found the revolver in the pocket of the limp and reeking garment. After checking both laminated bedside drawer cabinets, Arlon located the second revolver. Both of the .38s, with freshly-blued barrels, were fully loaded. Arlon could tell they were prized possessions in the Cabbage household, as they seemed to be the only items given meticulous care and maintenance.

He placed both revolvers in the waistband of his belted trousers. He made sure that Elmo was doing as he was instructed before turning his attention back to the pair writhing on the floor. If he had emotions, Arlon would probably have been feeling guilt for harming a female. As he didn't, he wasted no time thinking about it.

"Do you have ice in the fridge?"

"Ice?"

"Yeah, you know, frozen water? That sort of ice?"

"Maybe, depends if the solar charged the batteries or not," Elmo answered sullenly.

"Now that you've got the coffee going, see if there's some ice and make up a couple of bags for your parents. Bags of frozen peas would probably work if you don't have ice. Get them to place the bags on their groins. You'd better clean up your father's nose as well. I'll get my coffee when it's done. Oh, painkillers."

"Huh?"

"Something for my headache. I'd like you to find me something relatively mild and in its packaging. No loose pills. Have you got all that?"

"Uh, what ya want me ta do first?"

"Pills and ice. Then clean up your father."

Arlon sat at the table drinking the coffee. It was a little bitter for his taste but passable. He still wasn't sure if the cup was clean enough for his liking. His skin crawled as he looked about the small living and kitchen area, silently wishing that all the germs and greeblies stayed away from him.

Despite being a big, dumb klutz, Elmo eventually saw to the chores he'd been ordered to perform, while keeping a close eye on the stranger.

"Did you see Noel Payne the day he drove his car up here?"

"Nuh," answered Elmo without hesitation.

"If you don't want to end with your nuts in your throat like your father...grandfather...him, then I suggest you take a little more time to answer my questions as truthfully as possible. For the last time, I'm not here in any law-enforcement capacity and don't care what crops you happen to be cultivating. I don't even give a rat's arse how much junk you all shoot up your veins. We'll talk about the thing I am concerned about in due course. For now, I just want to know about Noel Payne."

"Don't know nuffin 'bout him."

"How did you know his car was there?"

"Um..."

"See? I know you're lying. You heard or saw Noel Payne arriving in that car. What happened to him?"

"Dunno."

"Did you find those aspirin or something similar?"

"Nuh."

"Who's the witch?" Arlon asked, to change the direction and the pace of the questions.

Arlon sipped his coffee as he watched the interplay taking place in Elmo's head. He was weighing up very carefully what he should reveal or not. Colin began to stir and raised himself on his elbow.

"Don't tell the fucker nothin', son," he managed with a grimace.

The report from the revolver was very loud in the confines of the small cottage. Irma ceased her moaning with a start, rolling onto her side to determine the direction of the sound. Colin froze when he understood that the bullet had been aimed millimetres from his position. He saw the small hole where the slug had entered the wooden floor through the rug. Elmo produced a wet patch on the front of his dirty jeans.

"Here's what's going to happen now, seeing as you lot are just too plain dumb to know what's good for you. I'm going to finish this coffee in peace and quiet. Then Elmo is going to take me back to my car. You two are going to do nothing until he returns. If I see any sign of either of you, if Elmo falters or attempts to lead me elsewhere, I will notify the authorities about what's happening here. I can see that you think I could never find my way back here. Think again. I've planted a device in here that will pinpoint exactly where you are when I give the police the frequency. Won't take them long to identify the location."

"And if we follow ya directions?" asked Colin, still cradling the bag of ice to his crotch.

"While I can't promise the cops won't find this place on their own when I give them the position of the missing lad's car, I can promise that they won't learn anything about your set-up from me."

"Don't sound like much of a deal ta me," he grumbled.

"You won't like the alternative if I divulge everything I know. If you go to prison for the crimes you committed here, I don't like your chances of surviving once the other inmates find out what you're in for. Feel free to ignore my advice. I *hope* you do something stupid, so I won't be held to my promise."

Colin glowered at Arlon, who continued sipping his coffee. The revolver aimed at Colin never faltered from its target. Irma resumed her moaning.

"You need to get her seen by a doctor. She probably requires surgery."

"She'll be Jake, mate. We tend to our own in these parts," spat Colin.

"You mean there's more of you yokels out here?"

"Got us a community of good folks all lookin' out for each other, we have. Don't need no outsiders to tell us what for."

"Yeah, you do. You *really* do," said Arlon, with a shake of his head in disbelief. "All right, you've made up my mind for me. You can't be trusted to do what I ask after I leave here. Elmo, find me some cord to tie them up with."

"Ya can't tie up me family!" Elmo barked.

"You're right, I can't. You'll be doing it and I'll be checking to see you've done it properly. Now move! You two, get up and sit in a chair each. Come on, I haven't got all day," Arlon ordered.

Colin and Irma gradually stirred to make their way to a chair, each nursing their groins. Irma especially seemed to take on a pallid hue. Arlon feared he had caused her a greater injury than intended. When Elmo returned with some hempen rope, Arlon ordered him to bind his father first.

"No, leave her for a moment," said Arlon, as Elmo was about to bind her. Go get your car ready to take me out of here and don't do anything stupid. Matter of fact, don't think at all..."

"Not goin' in no car," muttered Elmo.

"What? You mean we have to go on a motorbike? Like a trail bike or something?"

"Nuh. Got ta go by Jessie," Elmo said with a smirk.

"Who or what is a 'Jessie'?"

"Only way ta get around in here is by horse. That's what I brung ya here on."

Arlon frowned at the information. He reached into his jacket pocket for his mobile, only to find there was no signal. That didn't surprise him. He watched Irma getting paler as she sat at the table, her face contorted in agony. If the worst were to happen in her case, he would be hard pressed to prove he had acted in self-defence when he kicked her. While he might escape conviction for manslaughter, at the very least he would be accused of having used excessive force to subdue her.

"How far is it?"

"What?"

"Don't be bloody dense. The cars, my car, how far by horse or on foot?"

"Coupla hours," Elmo replied.

"Your mother is in a very bad way, Elmo. Do you understand that? If we don't get her to a hospital very soon, she may die."

"Bullshit!" barked Colin.

"One more word out of you and I'll have him gag you as well. Elmo, I'm no medical expert, but I can see that she's unwell. Any idiot can. Are you willing to risk her life on his say so?"

"Whatcha wanna do?"

"I want us to take her out of here. If you take us to my car I can get her to a hospital."

"Be dark soon and the fog'll roll in. Can't see nuffin' then. We won't make it."

"I'll just bet you've been out there in the dark before. I can understand you want to delay me hoping your old man will find some way of getting you all out of this predicament, but your mother is gravely ill. Look at her. Ever seen her that pale before?"

"Mum? How ya feelin?"

"Ooh, I'm hurtin' boy, real bad. I feel awful, just plain awful," Irma managed breathlessly.

"Not gonna sit a horse feelin' like that, is she?"

"Nothing else we can do unless you have a car we can use."

"We gotta car but it won't get us ta where ya wanna go."

"Why not?"

"No roads from here ta ya car."

"In that case, why don't we use your car to get us to a hospital to drop off your mum? After that, we'll drive to where my car is. You can return here in your dad's car."

"Can't drive the car on the road. Got no licence."

"That's your problem, not mine. I'll drive us out of here, to the hospital and up to my car. After that, you're on your own. I don't give a shit if you're picked up for unlicensed driving, under the influence or any other damn thing. The sooner I'm out of here and rid of you lot, the better. You'd better work it out because he won't be happily tied up like that for very long."

"Still gotta walk."

"Thought you just said you had a car?"

"At the end-o-the road. Have ta leave it there and walk the rest-o-the way on foot."

"How far?"

"Dunno, 'bout a mile."

"Shit!"

"Tell me about it. Try walkin' it every day."

"Why on earth would anyone choose to live out here?"

"Reckon we could grow our crops in the city, mate?"

"Still, you're pretty isolated out here."

"That's the point, aint it?"

"Fair call. Okay. Nothing for it but to put your mother on the horse as best we can and walk out of here to your car. Is it driveable and less smelly than in here?"

"Brand new-n-clean as a pin. Daddy don't let no one muss up his car."

"You put one scratch on her and I'll hunt ya down till me dyin' day," warned Colin.

"Gaffa tape."

"Huh?" said both Elmo and his father.

"Bloody duet, no less. Gaffa tape, Elmo. Cloth-backed tape? No household should ever be without at least one roll of it."

"Sure, got some-o-that in the cupboard here," agreed Emo enthusiastically, going to the cupboard.

"Ya dumb bastard! Shoulda dropped ya on ya head at birth, ya miserable shit. When are ya..."

Colin didn't finish the sentence. Arlon placed a wide swathe of tape over his mouth, winding it around his head several times. The man's hair was so dirty and greasy that Arlon wasn't concerned about the tape sticking to it too much. It wasn't until he was close to the man that Arlon realised he smelled just as bad as the other members of his family.

"What is it with you filthy people? You all allergic to soap and water or something?"

"Only got enough in the rainwater tank for drinkin' and cookin'. Not big enough to hold water for showerin'," admitted Elmo.

"Not sure how the nurses in the hospital will feel about admitting your mother the way she is. They'll be a bit wary about head lice and other nasties. I'll probably have to shave my head as well, after being exposed to you lot. Douse myself in disinfectant or something. No way will I expose my family to whatever I may have picked up in here. We'd better get going. The sooner we leave, the sooner you can get back here to release your father."

CHAPTER SEVEN

It was a gruelling night for Arlon. He turned up at Betty Payne's house around midnight, exhausted, cold, and hungry and his head still aching abominably. He'd had himself checked at the hospital when he dropped off Irma Cabbage. The doctor told him he might have a mild concussion and required an X-ray to rule out anything more serious. He convinced him to give him some strong painkillers, with the promise he would go directly to bed after taking a couple and return in the morning for an X-ray.

He lied to the doctor and nurses. After swallowing a couple of the pills he drove the brand-new V8 Lexus sports utility vehicle with the all-leather interior to the site of his Toyota Prado. Immensely relieved to be free of the cloying, reeking atmosphere within the vehicle shared by Elmo Cabbage, Arlon sprinted for the comfort of his car the moment he pulled up behind. He did not wait around to ensure the boy was confident enough to drive his father's luxury car, which had a modified engine producing incredible horsepower. There had been several scary moments, when Arlon had applied only gentle pressure to the accelerator and the car had lurched forward as though rammed from behind.

He drove carefully through the dark forest, discarding the two firearms he'd confiscated through the window along the way, to the main road he had taken during the day. He had to stop many times to ensure he was on the right dirt track. In the end, he surprised himself by finding the connecting road that allowed him to make his way back to Yarra Junction.

The door at the rear of the house was unlocked. Arlon heard movement within, so wasn't concerned with being quiet as he entered. He didn't understand why she would be expecting him, as he had told her he would be back in the morning.

"I'm in the kitchen, Mr Grey," said Betty. "Make sure you leave your shoes in the laundry. Don't want mud on my clean floors."

Arlon had to back up into the laundry by the back door to follow her instructions. He didn't like taking his shoes off. He suffered from acute foot odour and didn't want to make the woman uncomfortable. Fortunately, right beside the laundry tub stood a can of deodorant for just that purpose. He sprayed his socked feet liberally before moving down the hall to the kitchen.

"I've made a stew. I hope that suits?" she asked as he entered the kitchen.

"Smells good. Why are you expecting me? Especially at this late hour?"

"Was told to expect you."

"By whom?"

"A very dear lady whom I have known for many years now. She's a bit of a clairvoyant. She's the best one I've ever met. Everything she has told me has come true or been true."

"And she told you that Arlon Grey would not be meeting with his family at Lake Eildon tonight? That he would be making his way back to your place at around midnight?"

"She didn't know your name, of course, but yes. She told me exactly that. She told me to make sure I have some aspirin for your headache as well."

"Hmm, not sure I'm comfortable with the notion that someone has intimate knowledge of me without my ever having met her. If what you say is true, however, then I am at a loss as to why you wouldn't simply ask her where your son is."

"Funny thing that. I did, and it was the first time she couldn't answer me."

"Couldn't or wouldn't?"

"Same thing."

"No, not at all. Someone may have the information and not be willing to share it."

"Sit down. I'll fetch you some stew and fresh bread. I hope the house is warm enough? I sold some of my poultry and managed to do a bit of shopping this afternoon, and paid for the wood delivery."

Arlon was famished. He sat down at the end of the table closest to the combustion stove, where he was immediately warmed. The delicious smell of the stew simmering on the stovetop made him salivate. Betty Payne placed a wine glass in front of him, which she filled with a cheap red. She placed two tablets beside his elbow.

"I'll have a look at that head once you've finished eating."

"No need. The nurse at the hospital checked me out earlier."

"Oh, you were at the hospital?"

"Didn't your clairvoyant tell you that bit?"

"She can't tell me every little thing, silly."

"Don't see why not. She seems to have told you a fair bit. She knew about me being hit on the head, did she?" asked Arlon as he took a mouthful of stew.

"She just told me that you'd need some painkillers for the head and nothing more. What happened?"

"Got knocked out cold after I found your son's car," said Arlon simply.

He didn't hear the sudden intake of air from Betty, who stood just behind him. She had brought a hand to her heart and her lips trembled as she digested the information. She naturally feared the worst. She was also incensed that the man was about to tell her that Noel was dead, and he acted as if nothing out of the ordinary was happening.

Arlon slowed his eating when he sensed an unnatural stillness about him. Betty wasn't moving or even breathing, as far as he could tell. When he turned to face her, he started at the paleness she exhibited.

"Is everything all right? What is it?"

"Y-you found his..."

"His?"

"Him?"

"No. Not him. I only found the car."

Betty slumped into a shell once more, exhaling in relief. She moved stiffly to the other end of the table, where she sat down heavily and reached for a glass of wine.

"Was it an accident, then?" she ventured after a moment, with great sadness in her voice.

"No. At least, not at first glance. No sign of injury or foul play at this stage. I'll alert the police to the position of the vehicle tomorrow morning. I want to go back out there and have a bit more of a poke around."

"Where, where did you find it?"

"Same place you went today," said Arlon, with a slight lilt in his voice to indicate that he knew she had absconded.

"I, I went to town."

"Before that."

"Sorry?"

"Don't play games with me, Mrs Payne. I followed you into the mountains today and up that dirt track through the Black Spur Forest. I did manage to get myself lost, and ended up finding your son's car in the spot he must have left it when he followed you a year ago. The same place you went to today. Probably to your clairvoyant? You go there for a little tea or palm reading, do you?"

"I don't believe you. Noel knew nothing about..."

"No, he probably didn't. That's why he wanted to find out. He must have known you were going that way, and decided to follow you to find out what you were up to at the same time each year. This is a very good stew."

"You're saying...I'm to blame?"

"Did I? You're very quick to take on guilt. You may be the reason he was in that area, but you can't possibly blame yourself for anything that may have happened to him. Are you going to tell me now what you were doing there?"

"I vowed never to reveal that to anyone," said Betty quietly.

"Is it the witch?"

"Shush, don't say that."

"Is your clairvoyant this witch that I heard about from a bunch of Aussie hillbillies living like feral pigs in that neck of the woods?"

"Nobody lives near there," she stated unconvincingly.

"Wrong! There is at least one lot of filthy, semi-human beings living near there. It was the son who walloped me on the head and took me to their hovel in the middle of the bloody forest. I may have to shave every hair off my body and delouse myself from head to toe after being there. They admitted that there were others."

"They must be the ones..."

"Mrs Payne? They must be the ones...what?"

"They're the ones that caused a lot of trouble."

"For whom?"

"Can't say."

"See, there's that difference again. You *could* say but you won't. You're protecting someone, your 'clairvoyant'?"

"Please don't ask me again. I can't say anything about..."

"Her?"

Arlon remained silent while he finished eating his meal, sopping up the gravy with a thick slice of homemade bread. While he was wiping his mouth with a napkin he cocked his head to one side, concentrating on something.

"What a coincidence, you seem to have a new rooster," said Arlon.

"You couldn't know that."

"Not that difficult. It's a totally new sound compared to the others I heard. Very distinctive call and not present earlier. I have a very good ear and an even better memory. It may well be part of my autism. I haven't been diagnosed as a savant, but it may be that I am somewhat gifted in the area of memory and auditory detection. Sharper since my last case, that's for sure."

"What happened?"

"Oh, I just suffered a traumatic episode that had some lingering effects. The doctors all seem to agree that it's temporary. Quite disconcerting at times. I have, on occasion, heard thoughts."

"Thoughts?"

"Yes. Now and then I can hear what people are thinking, especially the people closest to me, my family."

"That's not something you should be admitting to strangers. You might be taken as a bit of a nutter," warned Betty.

"This, coming from the lady who travels into the middle of a forest to consult with a clairvoyant and collect her prizewinning bantams every year at the same time?"

"That is not..."

"Of course it is. Rumour has it you don't breed your birds, Mrs Payne. The fact that one magically appears every year at the same time, after your little sojourn, lends credence to the theory that you obtain your birds from that person you are protecting.

"Listen to me. It doesn't matter to me whatsoever where you get your birds or what the rules of the competition are. From what I can tell, it's a grey area, at any rate. There doesn't appear to be any specific rule against it. At least, I haven't found one, if there is. Either way, it doesn't concern me. You are hiring me to find your son and that is the extent of my interest.

"Your son followed you last year, presumably to find out why his mother disappears every year and suddenly reveals her next show cock soon thereafter. He was curious. Your husband was never overly interested in your activities or your strange assignations?"

"No, he only cared about his own activities, work, church and lawn bowls. He hated my birds. He hated that I spent more time with them than I did with him. He hated our son because of the way he turned out. He was ashamed of us. When I wouldn't give up on doing whatever I could to find our Noel, he finally packed his bags and left. Haven't spoken to him since. Good riddance, I say. Pious arsehole!"

"So, tell me."

Betty Payne took a long while to gather her thoughts and ponder the consequences of revealing her secret, while Arlon sipped his wine. She had made a solemn vow to protect the source of her prizewinning birds. It was a mutually beneficial arrangement between two people who shared a passion. However, far more was at stake than just identifying her source. The show birds were the very least of the reasons she'd held to her promise for nearly thirty years.

"Do you want me to find your son, or not?" asked Arlon, when it became apparent that she needed prompting.

"If you tell me what I owe you, I'll pay your bill and you can leave," offered Betty.

"You're willing to sacrifice that much to keep the secret?"

"Some things are beyond selfish purposes. Some things are worth keeping from the outside world. What I know, what I've been told first hand, should never become public knowledge. It would mean a very tragic end to a wonderful and magical event. I can see now that I have inadvertently aided in risking that. You asked if it was worth sacrificing my flesh and blood. I foolishly led my boy there and he paid for my sins. If he followed me then he paid the ultimate price. The secret won't be revealed by me or his death will mean nothing."

"You don't know me very well. You don't quite understand how tenacious I am. I'm like a dog with a bone when it comes to my investigations. With or without your help, I'll continue to try and unravel this mystery. I'm far too invested now to quit. Besides, I have some unfinished business with a certain family that I aim to bring to justice."

"I'm begging you to leave it alone, Mr Grey. I should have known. I should have figured it out by myself. It's all my fault, and I won't see any more damage done as a result of my selfishness and stupidity. Your life will be in very grave danger if you persist with this."

"Oh, and why would that be?"

"There are persons who would do anything, anything at all to uphold the pact made so many years ago."

"You mean the other families living in that forest?"

Betty's eyes grew wide with concern and near panic.

"Don't bother denying it again. I found out from the Cabbages."

"We've had trouble with them for as long as I can remember," said Betty, sadness etched on her features. "There are quite a few more like them as well. We, we do what we can to get along...mostly."

"We?"

"We call ourselves the forest folk. Born and bred in the depths of the forest over a couple of generations since the logging contracts and concessions dried up. Others, mostly from the city, drifted in from time to time to indulge in all manner of illegal activities and other...abhorrent acts. The forest folk have been battling their kind ever since they first arrived. They are evil, Mr Grey. Just as evil as evil can be, and the Cabbage family are possibly the worst."

"You're a part of the forest folk?"

"Was," she admitted with a nod.

"Was?"

"I don't live there anymore, obviously. Not since long after my parents died under suspicious circumstances, possibly even connected to those horrible Cabbages. I *was* born there, though. It was a simple life without modern conveniences. I didn't even see my first TV until I left. That was when I was nearly twenty. My aunty would insist on taking me to church once a month despite the hardship in doing so and the danger of discovery. I met and fell in love with my husband in that church. He was being groomed as a preacher at the time. It was the biggest mistake of my life, agreeing to become his wife and leaving my roots behind."

"I don't understand something. Why was it so important to remain hidden from society? Was it like a religious cult or something?"

"Some would probably see it that way. We guarded our lifestyle and our secret zealously, but it was never anything to do with religion. It was a calling, though. You had to be a very special breed of person to survive in the wilderness of that forest. If the cold didn't get you, then there was the constant threat of fires or sickness brought in by outsiders."

"I thought you said you couldn't tell me about your secret?"

"I haven't. There's nothing clandestine about the people who live there. Although they are very reclusive, they do go to town for the basics, they do have to attend doctor's appointments and such."

"So, there's something else going on? Something to do with a witch? Your clairvoyant?"

"Her existence is not such a big secret, either. It's just, well, there is something quite remarkable that began over a hundred years ago and the ritual has been carried out ever since. I won't tell you about that and you will never hear about her location from my lips. It goes with me to the grave. And others will do anything in their power to protect her and the secret. And then there's her. A formidable presence and an indomitable spirit. She knows almost everything without ever leaving her home."

"And your son?"

"If he followed me that day, he's gone. I realise how that sounds. Makes me out to be very callous. I'm not. I still grieve for him."

"But you won't do anything more to find him?"

"I don't have to. I know what would have happened. My family never really knew about my past. I invented a whole story just for my husband and followed that up with Noel. I don't think I ever succeeded properly with Noel, though. He knew that something was amiss. He may not have been a very intelligent boy but he had good instincts. He could smell a lie a mile away, probably because he was such a good liar himself.

"Not many of the original families are left out there now. My legacy is gone with my only boy. Pretty soon they'll all be gone and there'll be no one left to carry on the..."

"Tradition?"

"Yes, tradition. Forest folk will be gone and everything will be left to fend for itself. The forest, the creatures..." whispered Betty wistfully.

"Might happen sooner once the police are notified by me about the car I found."

"I've already told you your help is no longer required. No need to inform the police." Betty looked worried.

"If a crime has been committed then it's my duty to report the finding of evidence in that crime. I could have my licence revoked if I was caught withholding information in an official investigation."

"But it isn't, is it? Not ongoing, I mean. They threw it out or simply forgot about it. They practically told me they dismissed it as a runaway and not a missing-person case."

"No point in trying to muddy the waters. I have a clear duty to follow and I won't be swayed by opinions to the contrary. I'll be going to the police first thing in the..."

Arlon found it impossible to stifle a yawn that came on rather quickly. Within seconds he felt himself becoming lightheaded and lethargic.

"Yes, I thought you might," said Betty, smiling.

CHAPTER EIGHT

The ute was gone!

Arlon scratched his head while he contemplated how foolish he must have appeared to the two detectives who had vacated the site moments ago. While it did not bother him much to appear foolish, it didn't sit well with him to know he'd been duped. His head was still quite foggy from the previous evening. He found it difficult to recall how he had wound up in bed.

Through the fug, he recalled parts of his conversation with Betty Payne. He remembered eating his meal, drinking the... Arlon shook his head. He dismissed the idea immediately, despite it making a lot of sense. Though his mind kept returning to the thought, he continued to dismiss the notion that he'd been drugged.

He woke later than he'd preferred, to find his travel clock beside the bed had had the six o'clock alarm deactivated. That wasn't entirely odd, because he didn't even remember climbing into bed, let alone activating the alarm. He was wearing only his underpants. His clothes were cleaned, dried and neatly folded over the back of a chair, as he would normally have done. He hadn't yet brought a change of clothes with him, as he had told Betty Payne he would.

There was no sign of his client when he entered the kitchen. The fire in the stove had all but expired, and he shivered with the biting cold. Despite never having been a Boy Scout or familiar with camping, Arlon managed to get a reasonable fire going in due course. There was a bowl of cereal and a bottle of milk left out for him on the kitchen table, along with several slices of bread and a range of homemade jams. Arlon placed the slices in the toaster, noting that the electricity had been turned on again.

Hours later he found himself standing alone on the isolated track, once the two detectives had left, staring at the bare patch of dirt where Noel Payne's car had been for over a year. There was only one explanation and he chided himself for not suspecting her sooner. It was obvious to him by then that he had indeed been drugged by Betty Payne to give her sufficient time to alert her forest folk community to remove the car.

He had lost any credibility he may have had where the detectives were concerned, by dragging them out on a wild goose chase on a dead case. It had taken his considerable powers of persuasion to convince the detectives that he had located the missing youth's car. He then had to insist that they follow him on the long journey to the site.

They were mightily pissed off with him when they were shown a bare patch of earth where a car had once been. It took a concerted effort to convince the officers that he hadn't meant it as a joke, that he was serious. They were neither convinced nor placated. They did, however, warn him that they would place him in detention if he should ever show up at their station house again, and advised him, in no uncertain terms, to leave the case alone.

When he heard the sound, Arlon could not be certain of the direction from which it came. It was somewhat muted by the forest, which disguised the direction and cause. That it was a rifle report became abundantly clear only when Arlon noticed that he was bleeding. Luckily, it was merely a scratch. Someone was either a highly skilled marksman, wanting to warn him, or inept, and failed to produce a killing shot. Not wishing to stand about to find an answer to the question, in case the latter was true, Arlon dropped to the ground.

"I think ya got him, Daddy. I seen him go down," shouted Elmo.

"Shut up, boy. I only winged him. He's playin' possum. Gone ta ground like a scaredy-cat," warned Colin Cabbage.

"What're we gonna do, Daddy?"

"What ya gonna do is shut the fuck up, boy, and leave the thinkin' ta me. Yiz'll give our pozzie away if ya keep up the jabberin'."

Arlon slunk off into the undergrowth on his stomach while the conversation took place. The damp and the cold eked their way into his bones as he made his way along the wet mulch beneath him. A dusting of snow began in the frigid air above. A few flakes made it past the canopy far overhead, turning into water soon thereafter. Arlon had had the foresight to bring a knee rug with him that belonged to Betty Payne, when he left the house earlier that day. The Afghan rug, wrapped around his shoulders, at least kept his top half warm in the dismal atmosphere.

Finding a trail of sorts, Arlon slithered forward, away from his vehicle and the road. Judging by the aromas emanating from beneath him, Arlon guessed he was following a game trail, possibly made by deer. He desperately hoped they weren't feral pigs. He'd had enough of pigs to last him a lifetime. His shoulder stung where the slug had grazed him. The bleeding seemed to have halted, though he couldn't be sure. Crawling through the forest could not be good for his wound. Becoming infected with whatever lived in the foul mud beneath him did not bear thinking about.

He stopped periodically to catch any suggestion of where his attackers might be. He heard movement through the wet foliage, but detected no further conversation to ascertain their range from him. He believed he was travelling away from them. He hoped that was the case. He continued to crawl along the muddy trail, getting filthier and wetter by the minute.

As a Queenslander, Arlon was acclimatised to the balmy weather of Brisbane, which seldom reached temperatures below 10 degrees Celsius. The bitter cold invading his body threatened to immobilise him. He was almost convinced he could feel frostbite attacking his extremities.

Gunfire and shouts behind him interrupted his thoughts. The raised voices didn't seem to belong to the Cabbage males. Arlon ceased his movements to concentrate on the sounds. While he couldn't be positive, it seemed that his pursuers might also be targets. Although it appeared too good to be true, Arlon remembered what Betty had told him about different factions within the forest communities, and that she knew of the Cabbages by reputation.

He was stuck for a decision: crawl forward to no known destination, or retreat into possible danger? He couldn't remain where he was or he would suffer hypothermia before too long. The thin rug he had borrowed did little to repel the invasive cold. His teeth chattered uncontrollably. It sounded so loud in the quietening forest that he was sure he would give away his position to his attackers.

Just then a string of strange sounds emanated from a source nearby. Arlon could not begin to determine what made the sounds. It was as if a chorus of different birds and, maybe, other animals were standing in a circle, taking turns to voice their particular calls. When he managed to locate a definite direction within the echoing ravine into which he had slithered, he noticed a single bird standing atop a fallen giant of the forest. On the massive trunk stood the lonely lyrebird, with its splendid tail plumage, cycling through a complex range of calls. Some Arlon recognised, such as the kookaburra, a raucous sound imitating laughter. Then came the distinctive and harsh caw of the crow, followed by the carolling of a butcher bird or, possibly, a magpie.

Arlon watched in fascination as the lyrebird continued to mimic, perfectly, every bird or other creature that made sounds it had encountered in its lifetime. There were a few that Arlon could not identify, including one distinctive yipping, like a puppy. Arlon decided it probably belonged to a fox. He knew that foxes were a prolific pest to the local fauna since being introduced by the British to continue their arcane tradition of the fox hunt in the new colony. It was either the sound of a fox, not that Arlon had ever heard a fox, or perhaps a domestic dog, a puppy in someone's back yard close by the forest.

Arlon broke off his observation during a reprise. He had crawled a fair distance since leaving his vehicle, mostly downhill. The trail, if it could be called that, continued into the undergrowth farther downhill. He thought he could hear water in that direction. His mouth salivated at the thought of a drink. He had been crawling for hours, and all other voices and the gunfire had ceased long ago.

The alarming speed of the fading light suggested that the sun had begun setting. The mountainside on the eastern slopes was the first to be bathed in shadow, and the air grew colder by the minute. Arlon knew he would probably not find his way back to the car in the dark. He was so chilled now that he could not contemplate fighting gravity as well as the cold to return uphill. Staying still was not an option either. He needed to find a warm place to hole up for the night.

Where the path would lead, he couldn't know. The only thing he was confident about was the presence of flowing water somewhere ahead of him and downhill from his current position. He was thirsty, and that was the only factor in determining his decision to proceed. That was what he told himself, at any rate. In truth, there was a tickle in the back of his mind urging him onward. If he were forced to explain the sensation he would be at pains to accurately describe it. It was almost a subliminal nagging, an insistent urging from an unknown quarter.

He'd experienced similar presentiments, if that's what they were, on his last assignment. On that occasion, they escalated to the voices of his loved ones, received as clearly as though they were standing next to him. Currently, he was unable to make out voices, only a deep-seated need to move forward along the animal path.

Night advanced and the temperature dropped alarmingly. Arlon began to feel the first signs of hypothermia in his lethargic limbs, and his eyelids threatened to close. The gurgling of the brook could be heard clearly as he inched his way toward the familiar sound. The darkness became an all-pervasive entity about him, almost tangible to the touch. His mind played tricks on him the longer he laboured downhill. He imagined the lyrebird nearby, mimicking the yipping sound once more.

Through the thickening fog came the tramp of many hooves in

his direction. It thundered in Arlon's ears, though in reality, it was merely the gentle walking movement of several deer making their way along the path. Arlon lay perfectly still as they neared his position. The fog prevented the deer from discovering him as he lay face down in the mud. Arlon winced as he felt several of their sharp hooves tromping heavily on his back.

He knew not to startle them by revealing himself. Deer had a reputation for lashing out with their hooves in self-defence when cornered or threatened. Arlon did not think a contest between himself and half a tonne of freaked-out muscle and flesh would favour him in the least, not to mention an antler rack that could be used as a weapon during such an encounter. He suffered in silence as the last animal, snorting and breathing heavily, crossed over him. Just as he was about to raise himself he froze at the sound of another movement in front of him.

Appearing through the thick fog came a bloody great lump of fur attached to four thick, squat legs. Arlon stared at the creature incomprehensibly; barely visible in the blackness, it stared back. Nose to nose with the wombat, Arlon was unsure as to how dangerous it might be. He knew wombats possessed long claws for digging and rooting around in the soil for their dinner, but was unaware of any evidence that they were used for defence. The animal was unfazed by the presence of an obstruction in its path, opting to mount and traverse Arlon's back to continue its journey.

Relieved to be free of a confrontation with a dubious adversary, Arlon crushed his pessimism into a small corner of his mind and continued. The compunction to move, the compelling need to persist in moving forward, dominated every breath and his desire to simply quit and go to sleep. The frigid air seared his throat and lungs as he struggled on. When he finally arrived at the stream he wasn't sure whether to be glad or worried.

While taking a mouthful of the delicious and refreshing liquid coming straight from nature, he pondered how he might proceed from that point. The welcome quenching of his thirst did not decrease the obstacle the creek presented. Having experienced the arctic taste of the water, he knew he could not contemplate crossing the stream, no matter how narrow it was. Having slithered and crawled that far, he wasn't even sure he could stand long enough to walk across the stream at its narrowest point.

He opted for the only conclusion possible in the circumstances: he continued to crawl along the creek bank, which had the luxury of being drier than the track. Though litter-strewn and soaked by the insistent snowfall above, which turned to sleet and slush below the canopy, it was infinitely better than sliding through the freezing mud and shit.

The debilitating cold eked its way through to Arlon's bones, causing him to slow down until he was barely moving at all. In his mind, he was moving fast. In reality, he was slowing considerably, nearing the end of his endurance. Only an infernal urge pushed him beyond that. The urge gradually evolved into a voice. A wise and kind voice, full of hope and courage, filled his ears.

"Not far now, my friend. Just a little farther and you will find what you're looking for. Push now, keep going. I know how strong-willed you are, how powerful you are in mind and body. You have friends to help you. I will help you if you dare to keep moving."

The voice continued to nudge Arlon's tired and aching body, inch by inch, along the bank of the gentle stream. He thought he detected the birds again, or the single lyrebird making the sounds of the other birds. The yipping and the other weird oral emanations crowded in around him, confusing him as the mercury plummeted. Knowing that if he stopped once more he would stop for good, Arlon forced himself onward. He had no idea where he was going or why. He had no reason to believe there could be anything of value ahead of him or behind, no help, and no salvation from his dire predicament. He crawled on, despite knowing that he could die that night.

His hands were blocks of painful ice at the ends of his arms, his stockinged feet inside his inappropriate town footwear were next to useless. His trousers had holes in the knees from the long journey, allowing the cold to seep in, adding to his discomfort. He assumed the rug had long since been taken from him by the clutching fronds of the ground ferns through which he'd travelled.

His head ploughed straight into a curtain of stringy, grainy material. Had he not immediately discovered a warmer atmosphere beyond the curtain he might never have found that last essential spark of energy to push through the web of intertwined organic threads. A greater darkness than anything he had ever experienced embraced him the moment he struggled through the barrier. Sensing a welcoming warmness ahead, Arlon edged forward on his elbows and knees, as his hands and feet were no longer responding to his commands.

He was blind to his environment, but Arlon sensed earthen walls on either side of him. The farther he crawled, the warmer and more insulated it became, until he suddenly came to a larger section with a soft floor beneath him of warm, dry leaves. When Arlon attempted to bring his legs under him to sit, he discovered the rug. It had merely descended to the back of his legs, with one corner caught in the waistband of his trousers. Protected by Arlon's body for most of the arduous and sodden journey through the mud, the rug remained remarkably dry.

Arlon hugged the blanket close about him as he shivered his way to warmth several hours later. His eyes closed and he fell into a troubling sleep. He dreamt he was huddled between warm furry bodies purposely keeping him warm.

CHAPTER NINE

Voices, indistinct, mere murmurs, softness and warmth crowded Arlon's mind as the morning light penetrated the inky blackness within his cocoon. He became aware of the aches and pains assailing his recovering body as the dreams and the voices retreated. His extremities had regained movement, albeit with agony as the warm blood coursed through them. He could not identify any discolouration to them when he held his fingers in front of his face. He sighed with relief.

Blinking back the sleep from his eyes, Arlon began to peer around his place of refuge. It was little more than a hollowed-out chamber in the dirt beneath the roots of a tree. Looking at the curtain he had passed the previous night, Arlon registered the fine hanging roots as the web-like covering to the grotto he crawled through. In the dimness within, he made out bits of hair and fur belonging to whichever animal had used it for a birthing or hibernation den, possibly the hairy-nosed wombat he'd encountered.

There was no sign of the animal and the recollection of his dreams faded. His clothing was still quite damp and he was far from being out of the woods, literally and figuratively. He would need to get somewhere warmer very soon, and a change of clothes was imperative. He berated himself for not having planned his investigations better. Clarice would no doubt admonish him, deservedly, when she became aware of his lack of forethought. He'd drummed it into her often enough to be prepared for almost anything. She had mocked him often for the safari suit he wore to aid in his investigations into bushland, which he now wished he had worn.

Arlon crept stiffly to the entrance of the grotto. Parting the curtain of fine, interlaced roots, he was immediately stung by the bitter cold. He estimated the temperature to be well below freezing. Peering upward through a crack in the leafy canopy confirmed his suspicions, as flakes of snow drifted downward, dusting the fronds of tree ferns higher up the slope. The picturesque alpine scene did little to lighten Arlon's mood. The sight of snow had the psychosomatic effect of making him feel colder than the actual temperature decreed.

Arlon knew he needed to move, not only to return to his car and civilisation, but to get the blood flowing through his body to maintain a level of warmth to survive. He emerged from the grotto, wrapping the damp rug about him tightly. The stream offered a refreshing and thirst-quenching reprieve, as well as clearing away the staleness from his mouth. He hadn't brushed his teeth or flossed in over twenty-four hours, and his mouth felt disgusting for it. Arlon was nothing if not meticulous about his oral hygiene.

He stood up tall to assess the situation and orient himself. He admitted to being utterly lost, with no idea in which direction to proceed. He tossed a mental coin in the air to decide on upstream or down. He wasn't able to cross the stream as it was too wide. He couldn't proceed behind him because of the dense foliage blocking his path. He had only the choice of left or right. He chose left only because it angled downhill slightly.

"*STOP!*" came the unsounded warning.

Arlon obeyed, if only to determine who or what had warned him. He hadn't heard a sound, yet received the warning clearly. There was nothing around him other than the giant trunks of mountain ash and a smattering of sundry eucalypts, palms and other flora, steeped in an unearthly quiet. Time stood still while Arlon wondered if he was going insane, hearing voices. He even postulated that he might already be dead, and was experiencing some existential passage from one realm to another.

"*Wait,*" came the message in his mind.

"Mr Grey?" an audible voice from the other side of the stream.

"I'm here," stammered Arlon, as the chill of more than just the temperature invaded his being.

"Mr Grey, my name is Alex, and I'm not your enemy, not a Cabbage nor any of their mates. I'm coming from the other side of the creek. You'll be able to see me soon enough. Please don't move until I get there."

Arlon saw nobody on the other side of the creek. Not that that was surprising, because he could see very little through the tree fern foliage and ground ferns occupying both banks of the creek.

The loud report ripped through the crisp morning air, sending a shower of droplets from the foliage as the slug tore through them to strike Arlon's left arm, twenty centimetres lower than the last time. The impact swung him around and caused him to stumble forward a step, placing his foot squarely on a steel-jawed animal trap. He fell back against the bole of a tree that towered above him, his knees buckled and he slid to the ground

"Thought you said you weren't my enemy?" asked Arlon breathlessly.

"That bullet didn't come from me, Mr Grey. More or less guarantee it came from the others, Cabbages and their friends," claimed the voice from the face poking through the ground ferns on the opposite side of the creek to Arlon. Alex winced when he spied Arlon's foot caught in the evil-looking trap. "It will have been them that planted that trap we tried to warn you about as well."

"I, I don't understand. Who's we? I, I heard a voice...only, I didn't."

"Yeah, she sent me to get you."

"She?"

"Never mind that now. We have to get you out of here, see to your injuries and get you warmed up. I'm coming across..."

"No, no, you'll be exposed."

"I expect they're gone by now, but I have my cousin out there searching. He'll be sure to get their attention to give me some time."

"Who..."

"Alex, like I said before."

Alex Granger rose from his position to an impressive height of well over six feet. He was very broad with a thick black beard. Kind, laughing eyes shone through the fringe of wavy brown hair. He was dressed in a thick lumberman's jacket of check design with a warm, sheep's wool lining. He wore jeans of a coarse denim material, tucked into knee-length rubber boots.

Alex frowned with concern at the trap gripping Arlon's ankle in its toothy jaws. Using his walking stick he manipulated the jaws open until Arlon was able to slide his foot free. Before Arlon knew what was happening, the big man had thrown him easily over his shoulder in a fireman's carry, then reversed his direction back the way he came, through the creek and over the bank.

The intense cold had the effect of numbing whatever pain Arlon might have felt from his injuries. He knew that time would remedy that situation. The way he was being jostled about on the big man's shoulder would only add to the multiple strains and agony to come. Arlon's lightweight body did not slow down the man in any way, though Arlon was unable to distinguish a track or path to indicate where he was going.

With unerring ease, the man made his way through the dense growth near the creek until he was through into the relatively clear understory of the temperate rainforest, with only the trunks of the large trees to detour around. Alex increased his pace while he was able. Arlon grunted and moaned with the jolting and jarring effect on his wounds. He was grateful that he heard no further shots from his attackers. He was still unsure whom to trust, but he was left with little choice.

Somewhere along the brutal journey, he blacked out with the pain. When he woke, he found himself in another wooden cottage similar to the Cabbage residence, only a million times cleaner. For that alone, he was immensely grateful. Through slitted eyes, he made out a handsome woman tending to his injuries. Her gentle movements caused him no alarm nor further pain. The interior of the cabin was blessedly warm. Arlon was seized by pins and needles in his limbs as his body warmed.

Somewhere to his left he made out a familiar female voice, but couldn't immediately put a name to her. She was talking to the man who had rescued him. Their words were mere whispers, barely intelligible. He made out the word 'car' once or twice when the volume rose. Arlon broke out in occasional shivers as the woman removed his shirt to tend to his bullet wound.

"Mr Grey, you're a lucky man. The bullet went right through at a shallow angle. You'll have a scar but no other lasting damage. I redressed the other graze there as well. The leg is another story, though. I think the trap may have chipped the bone. You'll be hobbling for a few days and you'll have to have a tetanus booster as soon as possible. Watch for any infection. I've done all I can with what we have, which isn't much, I'm afraid."

"Th, thank you...?"

"Dorothy Granger, Dot. It was my husband, Alex, who brought you here. I'm sorry, Mr Grey, I think we may be partly responsible for what happened to you. You see, Alex and I moved that car before you got there with the police. If we'd left it where it was then this probably wouldn't have happened," explained Dot with a look of guilty concern.

"Now, Aunty Dot, you shouldn't be blaming yourselves. If anyone's to blame, it should be me. I was the one who asked you to move it," admitted Betty Payne, as she stepped into view.

"Mrs Payne?" acknowledged Arlon in a husky voice.

"I'm very sorry, Mr Grey. I know this must seem very strange to you after I hired you to look for my son. I can assure you that I have good reasons, honourable reasons, for what I did."

"Ah, honourable intentions. The catch-all phrase to justify almost any action. Save it, Mrs Payne. I'm not much interested in whatever your excuses are. They nearly got me killed."

"Let's not get into that now. Mr Grey, if you can manage to stand, I think you should have yourself a nice long, steaming hot shower, then get dressed into something warm. Don't suppose anything of Alex's will fit you, but you might fit something of mine," suggested Dot.

"Not sure how I'd look in a dress," answered Arlon wryly.

"Aren't you a one? I haven't worn a dress since my wedding day. Help him up and into the shower, Alex. Wrap some of this plastic around his bandages so they don't get wet," ordered Dot. "We'll have a nice big breakfast waiting for you when you get out. You'll be starving by now, I expect."

Alex did as he was bid. He assisted Arlon to stand, then supported him to the bathroom, where he saw to the wrapping once Arlon had undressed. The pins and needles went to town when Arlon stepped under the steaming hot water. He felt like a boiled lobster after ten minutes of luxuriating under the strong jets. He stepped from the shower to find a clean towel and dry clothes hanging on the rail for him. A checked flannel shirt, long thermal underwear, moleskin trousers and a pair of sheepskin slippers all fitted him to a tee. He finished off with a sheepskin jacket.

When he re-entered the kitchen it was awash in the mouth-watering aroma of frying bacon, toast and eggs. On a place setting in front of him was a plate brimming with everything he could smell and more. Without waiting to be asked, Arlon sat down before the meal.

"I don't suppose you have any coffee?" he asked indelicately.

"Coming right up, Mr Grey. You go on and eat now. Don't mind us, 'cause we already ate," instructed Dot in a motherly tone.

After seasoning it well with rock salt and ground pepper, Arlon tucked into the food with gusto. He hadn't eaten since the previous morning and it showed. Hash browns, toast, eggs, bacon, baked beans and coffee disappeared in short order, while the others watched in fascination. Dot was beginning to wonder where on earth the man was putting it all, worried she may have to begin all over again with a second course. She was relieved when Arlon finally pushed the plate aside, with a small bacon rasher remaining to indicate he was full.

"Would someone mind telling me exactly what's happening around here? I do think I've earned that right," suggested Arlon with a wince, as he moved his shoulder in the wrong direction.

"Aunty Dot?" asked Betty.

"Up to me, is it? Well, you'd better make us all another pot of coffee. Alex, come sit, you can help with some of it," instructed Dot with an authoritative air.

"You warm enough?" asked Alex before he sat down.

"A little too warm. I might just take off this heavy coat, if you don't mind?"

"Let me help," said Betty, who stood behind him.

"Where to start?" mused Dot rhetorically. "We, the Granger family, have been here almost as long as anyone else. We call ourselves the forest folk. I was born and bred in here and I wouldn't be anywhere else in the entire world. Met my bear of a man in here, Alex, when I was only a little tacker. We took in Betty when her parents suffered a tragedy. We think it was caused by them Cabbages, but have never been able to prove it and not much we could do about if we did."

"We do have the police force, you know? People trained in this kind of thing, believe it or not," noted Arlon drily.

"You sure don't mince words, do you? Alex did risk himself to rescue you," Dot admonished.

"Now, Aunt Dot, I told you he was a queer fish. He claims he has no emotions, some sort of condition," explained Betty, after serving everyone a fresh brew with some scones and homemade jam.

"That right, Mr Grey?"

"Yes, you shouldn't take offence at anything I say. As I have no emotions, there is never any malice intended. I was born this way and you'll most likely take offence, anyway, so why not just get on with it. Excellent jam, by the way."

"Thank you. I harvest the wild blackberries and blueberries myself. We're pretty self-sufficient in this forest; have to be to get by. Now, as I was saying: there are more or less two factions in here, which can be described as good versus evil. Even though we are all descendants of the original lumbermen hereabouts, it seems we can't escape the no-goods who want nothing more than to deal in the underbelly of life, drugs and alcohol, mainly. Bad people who were brought up bad and don't know any better."

"I've had the misfortune of making the acquaintance of one of those families. My skin is still crawling from the filth I experienced in that place."

"Yep, those Cabbages are just plain evil. Started with their great-granddaddy and kept going. They may live in squalor, but they have lots of money for fancy cars and by now they have new guns. We understand you broke one of theirs and discarded a pair of handguns?"

"How could you know that?"

"We get to know everything that happens in here, Mr Grey, everything. That was a very nice thing you did for that poor girl, Irma."

"That is possibly the vilest one of the lot," remarked Arlon.

"Well, she has every right to be confused, Mr Grey. Hard to reject what you've been taught from birth. She doesn't know any better. I feel very bad for those children. It turned out to be a very bad day when their mother passed away. Hung herself is what we heard."

"How many families are here?"

"Ten of us original families and two new ones. It's about an even split as to which side everyone is on."

"And you know exactly where everyone lives?"

"We all grew up in here, of course we know."

"Why haven't the bad ones tried to get rid of their opposition?"

"We walk a very fine line in here. They can't afford to have the authorities come in here in earnest. So they mount a skirmish every so often, but it never comes to outright war with us because they know we'll get the police involved if it comes to that."

"Why hasn't that happened already?"

When Dot hesitated, Arlon noticed the other two stiffen as well. It was evident to Arlon that it was not all cut and dried as to who belonged to which faction, or maybe everyone had something to conceal.

"Seems to me, if what you say is true about you lot attesting to be the good guys, that you would've done everything in your power to alert the authorities by now."

"Not everything is so simple to explain, Mr Grey. Just because we cherish our privacy doesn't mean we're tarred with the same brush as the other lot. You have no idea what's at risk here."

"Then why don't you enlighten me?"

"Don't do it, Aunty Dot, we can't," warned Betty.

"Here we go again. So far you haven't told me a thing about what's really going on. You! Your son died in here most likely and you're trying to cover it up. If that isn't downright evil, I don't know what is. You should all be ashamed of yourselves for your participation in that. You're failing to convince me that you are any better than the Cabbages, just cleaner!" Arlon claimed quietly to a deathly silence.

"There are some things larger than we simple folk. Some secrets worth dying for," said Alex with sincere sadness.

"Unless you're talking national security, terrorists or something, I don't accept that. As I see no connection to that sort of need for secrecy, you lose all credibility."

"What about a form of eco-terrorism?"

"You would have to explain what that is, at least, in your perception of the term."

"What if we are protecting something so fantastic and unique that the loss of it would cause everlasting and tragic consequences to our environment?" asked Dot in a whisper.

"So someone is looking to spoil this pristine environment you live in? Loggers have been doing that for donkey's years. Someone is endangering the forest by threatening to burn it down? Nature has been at that far longer than humans. There is nothing about a bunch of trees that is worth losing your son over, or any life, for that matter. I hold life more sacrosanct than you lot, apparently."

"Maybe we aren't talking about the flora."

"Oh, give me a break. What are you talking about: the black-faced squiggly flying possum or some such creature that only lives in this little neck of the woods? Maybe a yellow-striped humpty-dumpty frog or the green-eyed Bogan bat? And you think that's worth the taking of a life? Grow up! You people have been living your lies for too long. You're starting to believe them."

"Humpty-dumpty frog and the bogan bat?" asked Alex incredulously. Dot and Betty broke out in laughter. Alex soon joined them.

Arlon was startled by the levity. While he knew he was plucking silly names out of the air, he had never before caused anyone to laugh. He'd been told once by a very dislikeable man that he should take up comedy, with his straight face and deadpan voice. He didn't take it seriously and still didn't. He supposed the Grangers were releasing some tension that had been building. He drank his coffee while the others regained their composure. His wounds ached and he was in no mood for anything other than the truth. It didn't seem likely that he would achieve that goal.

"Should we take him?" asked Betty, when the uncomfortable silence had dragged on for too long.

"You think?" asked Dot.

"Already a connection there," Betty responded cryptically.

Arlon was baffled by the new line of thought, then had an epiphany.

"Her! You're thinking of taking me to her? She...spoke to me, I thought. I may have been imagining it," he confessed.

"Most likely you weren't. She gets inside our heads from time to time when the need comes," explained Alex reasonably.

"Can you tell me about her?" asked Arlon.

"No, no, we can't do that. We can only take you to her and if she decides to tell you anything, that'll be her decision."

"Hmm, very mysterious. So much for my insignificant missing person investigation. Do you have mobile reception in here or a landline I can use? I need to call my wife to tell her I'm still alive."

"Nope, none of us has one of those mobile things and we don't have a home phone. We don't have anyone on the outside we need to talk to urgently."

"Hospital, doctor?"

"Nope. If we can't fix it ourselves, we go on in. Never really had an emergency and if we did, it would be easier for us to get out than for a stranger to get in and find us."

"Do you even have electricity? All I've seen so far are hurricane lamps and candles. You have a combustion stove and I assume you have a gas heater for the water?"

"We live simple lives in here, Mr Grey. We mostly grow our veggies and don't eat a lot of meat. We trade for the little we do get, usually a haunch of venison from a sick or injured deer or the occasional wild pig."

"You don't have any children?"

"When we took in Betty Boop here, we thought she was a handful enough for us. Her mother, my sister, meant the world to me. It was my privilege and honour to raise her child as my own. Then Alex had a fall one day and messed up the plumbing a bit. Doctors told us it wasn't likely he'd father any children. We're content with our lot. We have ah...other children to worry about now. The children of the forest."

"Huh?"

"Well, the forest itself and all that it comprises is our responsibility now. It has been ever since I was old enough to listen to the stories handed down to me by my parents. Alex was promised to me almost at birth. He is a very distant cousin or something, which isn't ideal but hardly illegal or as wrong as the others. We'd hoped Betty's boy might come into the fold eventually, after he'd rid himself of those outsider ways, when he'd matured some. You about ready to come back, Betty?"

"I think so, Aunty Dot. I had no idea that Noel followed me here. I should have guessed, though. I blame myself for what happened and everything that followed, including what happened to you, Mr Grey. I love my boy more than you could ever know and that's why I hired you to find him. Knowing what probably happened in here, I couldn't let your investigation bring the police in, even if it meant never finding out for certain about Noel. You wouldn't understand and I don't expect you to. There is something here worth protecting from the outside world. They must never know and we have sworn to keep the secret, to protect it with our lives."

"I didn't," said Arlon simply.

"Beg your pardon?" asked Betty.

"I didn't agree to protect the secret with *my* life. I have a wife and child whom I would very much like to see again. I have no intention of joining your reclusive brethren in their sacred mission. I'd just as soon be on my way to join my family, if you don't mind?"

Another awkward silence befell the small gathering. The fire in the stove crackled, the candle on the table flickered, and the collective breathing and sighing triggered grave misgivings in Arlon's mind.

"If you're thinking about holding me against my will, I would think again if I were you. Not only would I be able to hold my own against you once my wounds healed, but you also have no idea how tenacious my wife is when it comes to me. She'll leave no stone unturned to mount a search for her missing husband."

"*If* we wanted to hold you here, no one would ever find you, believe me," warned Alex.

"Wrong! Something very strange and unnerving happened to me on my last assignment, something that remained with me. I retain a special connection to my wife and daughter as a result of that. A connection that will lead her here. I can guarantee *you* that. I did hear your person in my head while I was escaping those two maniacs, the Cabbages. I heard her just the same as I hear my Clarice and Tara if I relax and allow it. She led me to that grotto, that animal den. She saved my life. For that fact, and that fact only, I will assume that you don't wish to hold me against my will."

"Will you agree to see her? Please?" asked Dot with sincerity.

"If I say no?"

"We won't keep you against your will. You're right about that. We'd be no better than the others if we sink that low. You'd be free to go," said Alex carefully.

"Oh, I see. I'd be left to my own devices, I take it? Technically, I'd be free, but I'd have to find my way out of here and risk being found by the Cabbages. Very clever. So much for your high opinions of yourselves."

"As I told you, this is bigger than us. Your opinion of us doesn't matter when it comes to the higher calling we have."

"Oh, right, I know already that Betty is some kind of God-botherer. Is that what this is about? Some ancient sect, a cult?"

"While we all go to church when we can, we aren't members of some secret cult. We don't hold ceremonies in the forest dressed in long robes at midnight, making sacrifices to the gods or anything as arcane as that, Mr Grey. We say our prayers and we try to live Christian lives. We also have a calling handed down to us by our fathers and those before. It all started just over a century ago, and that's all I'm going to say about it. If you want to know the rest, you'll have to agree to meet her. She'll decide how much to tell you if she chooses to do so," said Dot.

"You in there!" came the amplified voice from outside.

"Who's that?" barked Alex.

"You know who it is. That bastard hurt my Irma, put her in hospital, and I want him. He's mine, ya hear me?"

"The whole world can hear you with that bullhorn, Colin," answered Alex.

"Well, send him out and we can go our separate ways. No need ta drag this out between us. We always abided by each other...mostly."

"Well, now, that wouldn't exactly be the truth, Colin, would it? You lot have been trying to make war with us for more years than I can remember. I'm sorry about your Irma, Colin, I am. She's a...was a...sweet girl...once."

"Hand him over, Alex, or I swear I'll make ya pay, all-o-ya."

"Been threatening that ever since I was a little tacker, Colin, but you know it does no good. If you bring us down, you only bring yourselves down as well. We won't have any choice but to bring in the police. Seems to me, you might have more to lose if that happened."

"Reckon ya wrong about that, seeing as ya care so much about the bloody secret and the witch. Maybe ya got more ta lose, eh? He's an outsider, Alex. Not one of us. He's not worth fightin'-n-dyin' for."

"Colin, we've had this argument so many times I'm getting bored with it. It doesn't matter which side has the most to lose. Everyone loses if the cops come in. You lot would probably end up in jail if we told them about your shenanigans, and we would if it came to that. Are you willing to take that chance over a lousy outsider?" asked Alex, with an apologetic smile toward Arlon.

"Reckon you won't be getting no chance to tell the cops anything when you're all dead. I have guns and you don't."

"You sure about that, Colin?"

"Buncha goody-two-shoes ya are. Ya don't believe in guns, Alex, ya told me that yaself," insisted Colin.

"Might be I changed my mind, Colin. Are you willing to take that chance? Besides, we have other means of protection."

"The witch? She's not gonna be no help ta ya this time. And if she moves one step outta her house, me boy Elmo has instructions ta shoot. Told him ta make sure it's right between the eyes, too. If ya thinkin' I come here alone, ya better think again. Got Billy lookin' at ya back door ta make sure none-o-ya chicken out that way."

"Colin, this is madness. Let it go and we can go back to the way it's always been, as unsatisfactory as it is for us."

"None of ya need ta get hurt if ya turn him over. He done harm ta mine and we aim ta make him pay."

"What are you going to do, stay out there all day and night and freeze to death?"

"Might be we'll get us a fire goin'. A nice big one with your rotten little shack in the middle of it."

"Yeah, sure. That won't attract any attention, will it? One phone call from us and it will all be over for you and your crops."

"Can't fool me, Granger. I know ya can't get no signal in here."

"Not on an ordinary mobile phone, no. This fellow has one of those satellite phones that don't rely on cell towers, Colin. Heard of them?"

"He don't," came the unsure reply.

"Go ahead and test us then. Won't take but a moment to make an emergency call. In the meantime, I can use you and Billy for target practice with my new rifle. It needs sighting in."

"He's right. I don't have a satellite phone. I only have this new mobile that my wife purchased at the same time as she bought one for our daughter. Half of the time I don't even know how to use it. All the latest in technology and modern apps, most of which are completely alien to me," said Arlon quietly.

"I know that and you know that, but he doesn't. As long as I give him pause, I can keep this stalemate going," proposed Alex.

An explosion nearby startled them all.

"That was a small one. A shot over the bow just ta let ya know what's what. I give ya five minutes ta send him out or I blow yiz all up ta kingdom-come," warned Colin.

"Seems like it's a war between us," said Dot in a whisper.

"Time to go, I reckon," suggested Alex.

"You going to hand me over?" asked Arlon.

"We would have done that already if we were going to. You need to trust us a little, Mr Grey."

"That goes both ways, Mrs Granger," countered Arlon.

"Well..."

"Now, Dot, let's not get into it. We need to leave while we can.

If anyone is going to know whether this man is trustworthy or not...?" Alex left the suggestion in the air.

Dot nodded her head reluctantly.

"Best we move then," she said.

"Move? Move where? They have both exits covered by men with weapons. Do you have any?" asked Arlon.

"We don't need them. We aren't going out of those doors," Alex said, stomping his foot on the floorboards.

Arlon watched as Alex moved to the living room, where he tilted a small roll top desk that seemed to be hinged to the floor. When he pushed aside the rug, Arlon was able to identify the trapdoor.

"Dot, go get our emergency packs. Mr Grey, I need to take you down first. I don't think your arm or foot will be well enough to climb down the ladder."

"Going down into a cellar won't help us much if he blows the place up on top of us."

"Not a cellar; tunnel. I'm betting Colin won't be dumb enough to blow the place up. He may blow a door, though, and come storming in. When he does, all he's going to see is an empty house."

"I imagine his crops are underground, Mr Granger. The first thing he'll think of when he discovers the house empty is an underground escape. Once he finds the trapdoor, he'll simply follow us."

"Once we're all down there, I have a system that pulls the rug back in place, then tilts the desk back on top with a steel rod. See this, attached to the desk and going through the floor? Underneath, I fix that steel rod to an anchor point and latch the door from below. It's reinforced with inch-thick steel plate. He'll have to rip up the entire floor before he comes close to finding the tunnel. If he does, we'll be long gone, and I have a few other measures in place to cover our retreat."

Dot returned with two backpacks.

"I put in some extra clothes for him and Betty and enough food so that we won't be a burden."

"Good one, Dot. You're a peach. Now, over here if you will, Mr Grey? Hop on my back as best you can. I'll go down with you, then come back up. I have to be the last one down to put everything back in place. Now hurry, we don't have long."

Arlon winced as he draped his good arm over Alex's shoulders, wrapping his one good leg around the man's torso. Alex descended the ladder with little difficulty. He placed Arlon on the dirt floor before climbing the ladder once more. Betty descended next, followed by Dot. Alex handed down the backpacks and lanterns one by one before joining them.

He lowered the trapdoor. In the dim light, Arlon watched as Alex pulled on some twine extending through the trapdoor which was attached to the edge of the rug above. He then pulled down on the steel rod protruding through the door, which lowered the desk with a heavy thump. He latched the end of the looped rod to a hook anchored to the floor, then threw back the heavy bolt on the underside of the steel door to secure it firmly.

"Right then. Mr Grey will have to lean on me for support. You two will have to travel in front with the lanterns to light the way."

"Umm, I don't mean to sound pessimistic, but just how far do we have to travel? I mean, I can't hobble for long," admitted Arlon.

"Only about a hundred metres or so before we come to a junction. From there, we have an easier way to travel. We need it because the tunnel gets much smaller and we have quite a way to go," answered Alex. "Pity it's the last time we can use this escape route," he said wistfully.

"Oh, why's that?" asked Arlon.

"Once we're at the junction, I'll collapse this portion of it. No one will ever be able to follow us or know in which direction we're heading. Even if Colin is stupid enough to lob a few sticks of dynamite around the area above, we'll be long gone."

"Alex, he's bound to know where we're heading, though," remarked Dot.

"If he takes it that far then it's an all-out war between us, anyway. Time for this to finally end one way or the other. Hurry up now," urged Alex.

The tunnel walls were supported by hefty wooden beams every second metre or so. Now and then the tunnel would veer sharply to the left or right. The tell-tale signs of an extensive root structure, appearing suddenly through the walls of the tunnel, revealed the reason for those dramatic directional changes. Whoever had constructed the tunnels did not want to kill off a tree by brazenly cutting through the roots to continue the tunnel in a straight line.

A slurry of claylike mud had been plastered onto the walls to prevent cave-ins of the loose, rich forest soil. Dot led the way along the tunnel with barely a stoop, but Alex had to bend painfully at the waist under the low ceiling. He struggled with supporting the limping man while maintaining a brisk pace to keep up with the others.

Behind them, they heard nothing of what was occurring back at the house they had abandoned. The distance they had travelled, and the dampening of all the acoustics by the surrounding earth, prevented any normal sounds from reaching them. No doubt they would hear any explosions, though.

Just when Arlon thought he could go no farther, the light ahead of them disappeared around a bend.

"Hold up there, Dot. I have to take a moment to rest and set up the fail-safe."

"Fail-safe?" asked Arlon.

"If, by any quirk of fate, they manage to find the steel rod attached to the desk and disconnect it, when they tilt the desk it will activate a connection that will blow the tunnel supports all along the section we're leaving. With any luck, the whole damn house will collapse on them. I doubt it, though. Built it too strong, I did."

"I'm exhausted and I don't think I can go much longer," said Arlon.

"Won't have to. We have an old mine cart around the bend, with rails running all the way to the end. I have a line set up overhead, which I'll use to haul the cart along the rail. None of us will have to walk. We wouldn't be able to, at any rate. The ceiling is too low."

"How did you manage to do all this?"

"Wasn't just me. Three generations of us helped to construct this. I'm probably the last of the line. Lucky for us it's complete."

"And this leads where?"

"Relative safety and maybe some answers for you."

"The witch?"

"Not a term we use, Mr Grey. A downright disrespectful name for a veritable saint in our time, if you ask me. Now, just let me put you onto this cart. I cut the sides off the original ore cart with an acetylene torch to produce this flatbed. Won't be all that comfortable, but it's better than walking."

Alex hefted Arlon's lightweight body onto the cart easily, then beckoned the two ladies to climb on. He reached for two exposed wire ends protruding from the last timber support at the junction of the two tunnels. He swiftly twisted the two ends together, ostensibly to complete the circuit, which would be given an electrical current once activated by tilting the desk.

"Where did you learn explosives?" asked Arlon.

"All lumbermen are trained in basic explosives for removing stumps and other obstacles to a logging operation, especially one where reforestation is essential. Can't have all these huge dead stumps taking up valuable real estate where a healthy tree could grow to replace the fallen ones. We were trained to blow them out of their holes and burn them before planting the new trees. Those areas wouldn't be touched until the new trees were fully mature. Usually, the next generation got to chop them down again."

"I thought forest conservation was relatively new?"

"Not to the real loggers. We aren't so stupid as to cut ourselves out of jobs by destroying the forests. Our men used to go in and hand-select the trees beyond their prime and ready to be felled. We'd go in and direct each tree to fall in a particular direction to avoid collateral damage. We don't harvest an entire mountainside in one swoop, as that would never be able to regrow as it once was. That just wouldn't make any sense.

"Of course, that all changed over the years, when greed and speed killed the old-growth forests to near extinction along with most of the animal life depending on it. I dedicated my life to protecting the forests and the animals, but I was finally told my ways no longer fitted the modern logging concepts. No longer profitable to do things the old way, I was told with my last pay cheque."

A series of distant and muted thumps began to march their way down the tunnel from which they had exited.

"Damn! Didn't think they'd work it out that fast. We'd better get going," urged Alex.

Heaving on the overhead line, Alex strained to get the ancient ore cart moving along the rusty rails. The loud squeaks from the protesting cast-iron wheels revealed how long it had been since they last rolled. Grunting with the effort, Alex eventually forced the cart to move slowly along the rails. The squealing and groaning of the rusty bearings settled into an acceptable mouse-squeak as the cart advanced along the track.

Arlon could not be certain, but he imagined a slight declination to the tunnel in which they travelled. It was possibly the only reason that Alex was able to move the cart at all. Assisted by gravity, the cart gained a little speed as it clickety-clacked over the rail joints. The progressive series of percussive blasts, eliminating the supports in the previous shaft, forced a billowing cloud of choking dust into the forward tunnels, enveloping the retreating ore cart.

Alex ordered Dot to distribute any material she might have to help them keep the dust out of their lungs. She placed a towel in each person's hand, which was gratefully accepted. Arlon offered to keep one to Alex's face while he hauled on the rope with both hands, but was unable to do so and keep a towel to his own face at the same time. His injured arm simply wouldn't allow the strain. Betty saw how he struggled and took over from him.

The rolling dust cloud almost obliterated the light cast by the two lanterns, making it nearly impossible to see much beyond the blurry halo within the cart. The occupants coughed and spluttered with the reduction of breathable air. Exposed roots clawed and clung to the vulnerable humans as the cart passed beneath them. As Arlon lifted himself to gain a more comfortable position with his injured leg and arm, one large root hanging lower than the rest knocked him clear.

With no means to communicate his immediate stress to the others, as the wind was knocked out of him, Arlon soon found himself in complete darkness as the cart trundled on without him. He supposed the others were either too busy, or simply couldn't see well enough in the swirling dust, to recognise his absence.

Arlon rose unsteadily to his feet, only to knock his head painfully on the exposed root that had snagged him from the relative safety of the cart. The total blackness around him was suddenly transformed with the twinkling of stars as a result of the heavy knock. He shook his head to clear his vision of the annoying sparks. The billowing dust made breathing an extreme chore.

If not for the injury to his leg he might have been capable of catching up to the cart. Unfortunately, that was not the case and he had very little choice other than beginning to make his way down the track. He hoped they would return for him once they discovered his absence, though Alex might lack the strength to reverse the direction. The incline was only gradual, yet existent. Arlon could easily sense the slight declination as he hobbled forward painfully, holding to the side of one wall to steady himself and maintain orientation.

He paused several times as he simply couldn't muster the breath he required. The pain and the difficulty of movement had him gasping for air. He decided that continuing was out of the question. The only option he recognised was to sit and wait it out. The energy reduction would diminish his urgency for air. The dust would settle soon enough and he could then continue. He held the terry-towelling cloth tightly to his face, tempering his breathing as he'd been taught, relaxing and meditating to pass the time.

The totality of the blackness around him would have caused a lesser mortal, with a full set of emotional capacities, panic and fear. For Arlon, it was nothing. It would only be a concern if the collapsing tunnel in the other branch triggered further cave-ins. He had not detected any further deterioration of the tunnels other than the initial concussive blasts taking out each support beam domino-fashion.

The silence was broken by a few skittering sounds around him, probably insects or lizards, possibly geckos in search of prey, disturbed by the commotion. At some point, Arlon wondered if he was hallucinating. He could have sworn he'd seen a pair of eyes peering at him from a distance. He listened carefully but could not hear any movement other than the very light disturbances he'd heard earlier.

"Don't be alarmed, Arlon Grey, they are your guides."

"Who said that? Where are you?" Arlon shouted into the darkness.

"Shush, you'll frighten them," explained the voice inside his head. A kindly, elderly voice, full of compassion and patience.

Arlon had heard the voice in his head before, but believed he was imagining it. He still wasn't certain he wasn't dreaming. With no way to tell if his eyes were open or closed, he questioned if he had fallen asleep. If Arlon were capable of being comforted, he assumed he would be relaxing at present. The voice was not threatening in any manner.

Arlon shook his head to clear it. He thought he could still be suffering the effects of his previous assignment, where he was able to hear others' thoughts. He did not like the break from his normal existence, experiencing emotions or hearing people's thoughts. He was uncomfortable with the notion that someone could talk to him through the ether. He especially did not like the idea of a witch communicating with him.

"Not a witch, Arlon Grey. Only an old woman who has developed other means of coping without one of her senses."

Arlon refused to answer, either out loud or in his head. It wasn't logical to do so and went against everything he'd come to believe. An old woman was in his head and it unsettled him profoundly. Alone in the cloying shroud of absolute nothingness, Arlon was unaccustomed to feeling entirely helpless.

Periodically, a pair of eyes appeared through the velvety curtain to assure Arlon that he was not alone. It did not ease his discomfort. Judging by the height of the eyes relative to his sitting position. With his back against the dirt wall of the tunnel, he surmised the creature to be larger than a domestic cat, yet perhaps smaller than a large dog.

He remembered the Cabbages talking quietly about a bunyip during his captivity. He passed it off as yet another ridiculous quest by humans to manufacture legends and myths around something perfectly natural and explainable. Similar stories had surrounded the sightings at Allies Creek on one of his previous assignments. Clarice had researched the stories and found all manner of speculation about brief sightings of hairy monsters, a Yowie, Australia's equivalent of Big Foot, or a Yeti. Arlon had passed them all off as pure hogwash, and his investigations supported that opinion...to a degree.

The furtive movements by the unseen animal suggested a restlessness, an indication of some urgency, perhaps? The dust seemed to have settled in the interim, which may have prompted the increased activity about him, marshalling him to resume his journey down the tunnel. Sighing, Arlon raised his weary body from his seated position, making sure to avoid rising too suddenly. Bracing himself for the arduous task of moving on, he steadied himself against the left-hand wall to move forward.

Within only a short distance, he found he no longer required the use of the towel as a mask. He was able to breathe relatively freely again, albeit with a dank and musty quality invading his nostrils. Ahead of him, at an indeterminate distance, the eyes glowed with an unnatural sheen. It didn't seem logical that eyes could be seen in the absence of all light, yet there they were, defying his notions, leading him, it would seem, in the direction the cart had taken.

Unknown to Arlon, who remained close to the left-hand wall, the tunnel branched off to the right at several places. Had he been stumbling about without the periodic glimpses of the haunting eyes, he could well have blundered down one of those alternate branches for many hundreds of metres until halted by a dead end. They were not always tunnels with no destination. Over the years, the network of tunnels had been drastically reduced at the behest of the families entrusted with the safekeeping of the secret. Some of the tunnels had been discovered by their adversaries, and it had become necessary to abandon all but the most important.

His leg ached and his upper body felt as though he had been in the wars, which he supposed he had been to a certain extent. He had no idea in which direction he was headed. The disorientation he felt, in the deepest darkness he had ever experienced, pressed in on him. He could not feel fear, yet he became more unsettled the longer he remained in total isolation from his usual sense of sight and space. He felt close to being buried alive.

Arlon struggled on gamely, despite a growing sense of despondency creeping into him. His emotions, or lack thereof, had become a shield of sorts for him over the forty-odd years of his life. Since his last assignment, where he'd had a taste of those raw emotions that everyone else on the planet takes for granted, he'd experienced relapses at different times. He was unaccustomed to the alien responses of his brain at those times. It was almost debilitating to an extent. Depression: he'd read about it, of course. His current thoughts came dangerously close to that.

He fought it off, concentrating on placing one foot in front of the other. He pitied the rest of humanity if they had to cope with such feelings on an everyday basis. He preferred his former existence. He was able to cope with that. It was an ordered, logical life, without emotional problems plaguing him at the oddest and most inconvenient times. He hoped it was temporary, that the lapses would cease with time.

"*Do you honestly believe you are without feelings?*"

"I don't have to believe or disbelieve. It's a fact. Proven medically," Arlon announced to the darkness without wanting to.

"*No one is ever truly devoid of emotion, Arlon Grey. Just ask Clarice and Tara.*"

"How do you even know about them?"

"*The mind is a wondrous thing, Arlon. With enough practice, almost anything is achievable, utilising an instrument as powerful as the mind. Take away distractions, one or two other senses, concentrate, and other worlds begin to open to the perceptive and accepting.*"

"If you believe in that sort of thing."

"*Who are you talking to, then?*"

"Probably myself, my conscience, my questioning and deductive mind, making conversation with myself in the absence of several sensory factors."

"*You're honing your skills in the absence of sight, just as I've done. Only you are proceeding at a greater rate than I thought possible. I sense strange patterns to your brainwaves, disturbing confluences and alien structures within the network of thoughts and configurations.*"

"You didn't answer my question. How is it you know the names of my wife and daughter?"

"*They are foremost in your thoughts and your heart, Arlon Grey. You have a deep and abiding love for those two humans, despite your assertions and denial. The tidal wave of information and emotions I detect from you for those two females is quite the force.*"

"Something...something happened to me on my last assignment, something I'd hoped would have faded by now. It altered my condition somehow, allowed me to experience emotions for the first time in my life. It was unpleasant, disturbing and not something I would like to go through again."

"*I sense such goodness in you, Arlon Grey, that I sincerely doubt you would welcome the complete absence of those emotions again. Not in a flood, as they first came to you. That would overwhelm the strongest of individuals. A gradual introduction to milder emotions, building to full sensations of a positive variety, would be more ideal.*"

"No. I disagree. I would welcome back my previous disposition with open arms."

"*Only because you are unused to anything new. Given time and a gradual introduction, I feel sure they would not be the burden you see them as currently.*"

"The sooner they're gone, the better. How much longer...?"

"*You're here.*"

CHAPTER TEN

"Open your eyes," suggested Betty.

Arlon was unaware that his eyes had been closed. When he glanced about him he saw that the others had waited for him at the end of the tunnel, where there was a bare bulb giving off dim light within a large area the size of a living room.

"Where are we?" he asked.

"She wants to meet you," answered Alex.

"She told you that? Won't the others know where we've gone and simply arrive here sooner or later?"

"We have to assume that Elmo is here already. They won't do anything here, though. Too much risk involved in that."

"Risk?"

"No matter how bad Colin and his mob want something, they won't risk the police coming here. They have far too much to lose. They could lock him up 'til kingdom come for all the stuff he and his cohorts are up to," explained Dot.

"We'd best get up and out of here. She'll be anxious to see us and get a good look at our guest," ventured Alex.

"I didn't think that was possible," said Arlon.

"Not in the literal sense, perhaps," admitted Alex.

Alex led the way through a trapdoor arrangement similar to the one they had exited not so long ago, though it felt like a lifetime to Arlon. Once more he was reduced to riding on the big man's back to ascend the ladder, and wait above as the rest took their turns to rise through the floorboards.

Arlon peered about him in the gloom of the room in which they found themselves. Mouth-watering cooking aromas wafted in from under the door. There was still a modicum of natural light entering through the window, informing Arlon that it remained daylight outside, albeit muted and shadowy. The room, a sewing room or spare room by the look of it, was chilly. Arlon shivered despite being well rugged-up in his borrowed clothing.

"Go on through, Mr Grey, though you might find it dark as she doesn't need lights blazing," urged Dot.

Arlon found himself gravitating toward a source of warmth once the door was opened into a short hallway. He noticed an orange glow at the end of the hall to his left, indicating the direction he felt he should take. He didn't notice that the others weren't following.

"C'mon in, Arlon, don't be shy," suggested the elderly voice, full of warmth and kindness.

When Arlon spied the centenarian seated in the wooden rocker by the open fire, he felt he knew her intimately. He formed an immediate fondness for the woman, despite never having laid eyes on her. He moved forward to a wingtip chair at her side, where he sat with a small grimace escaping him as his ankle brushed against the leg of the chair.

"Nasty business, those animal traps. Should be outlawed and melted down to nothing but slag; all of the evil things. Dot fixed you up, did she? Not too bad now, I hope?"

"No, er...."

"Call me Hildy. Name's Hilda Haggerty but most everyone always calls me Hildy."

"Pleased to meet you, Miss Haggerty. I'm still confused by...all this, but I suppose I have you to thank for being alive?"

"Yes, most folks would be plenty confused by things they haven't experienced before, even though most everyone probably has these abilities if they train themselves. Of course, some do, like the Indian yogis and other practitioners of deep concentration and meditation. Early humankind had to rely on many of their other senses to avoid dangers, Arlon. Is it so hard to accept that modern man is all that different, if placed in a position to develop those abilities through necessity?"

"I find it very difficult to accept things like that. I am a natural sceptic of anything I'm unable to explain with pure logic and science," admitted Arlon.

"Yet your last assignment had you expanding those parameters rather broadly, did it not?"

"I, I have no way of understanding how you could know about that or to what extent."

"Mr Grey, I practically know everything about you. Possibly more than you, or that you are willing to recognise. I can see inside your mind as easily as opening a book to read the contents. I see past all those barriers you present, all the hurts and the tearful memories of your troubled existence from the moment you were born. Terrible the way your parents weren't able to accept you for the wonderful human being you are. They pushed you further and further into yourself until you almost started to believe you didn't exist at all. Sorry if that sparked a sadness in you."

"That-that's not possible. I don't feel..."

"Nonsense. You were born with a condition that prevents you from displaying emotions but not necessarily from being affected by them. They have eked through to your inner person, anyway, because they shaped the man you are today. That small window of opportunity you experienced so recently, to feel and express emotions, though overwhelming at the time, proved how deeply you can communicate on an emotional level. I have felt the powerful love you have for that beautiful wife of yours and that delightful child. What I'm about to tell you will probably shock you. Your wife and child are in danger. I believe that the Cabbages are off to find them at this very moment. I fear they know where they are at Lake Eildon. Betty must have told someone and that got to them, somehow."

"In that case..."

"There is nothing you can do at the moment. In another hour or less it will be completely dark, and there is no way to get out of here after dark. That trap you stumbled into is only one of the hundreds out there just waiting for an unsuspecting soul to suffer the consequences. Believe me, there are worse ones than the steel trap that injured you. Betty lost her son to one of those other traps, though I wasn't aware who it was at the time. When I found him, he was past any memories I might have investigated to discover his identity. I never knew he had an interest in the forest or our ways. Seemed he didn't in the end. He was following his mother to work out where she went every year. My fault that he died. I should have opened my mind to the possibility."

"I can't possibly stay..."

"Mr Grey, I know you are a strong man with great courage, but there is nothing to be done about your family at the moment, and neither I nor my friends could guide you out of here safely. I wouldn't allow them to risk their lives for such a foolish errand, in any case. Besides, I think you will hear the voice of your wife before the cock's crow tomorrow morning."

"Are you saying what I think you're saying?"

"Not at all. I'm talking literally. That you will hear your wife's voice first-hand in the early hours of tomorrow morning."

"What do you mean by that? I don't..."

"I'm not infallible, Mr Grey, my gift isn't total sight. I sometimes get only snippets of a person's mind and I can tell you that some minds, like that of Colin Cabbage, are a minefield to explore. If I delve too deeply into that evilness, I find myself becoming tainted by what I hear and see. It is abominable that that man should even exist, let alone be permitted to perpetrate unspeakable acts upon innocents. My heart cries out for Irma and Elmo, even though they are capable of despicable acts as well. Had they the loving and nurturing of a different environment, they would not have grown into what they have become."

"Had I the ability to sympathise..."

"Why else would you have insisted on taking her to seek medical treatment? You keep contending that you are emotionless, but prove yourself wrong at every turn. You have great compassion and understanding for the less fortunate in this world, the underdog, and the victims. You are their champion, Arlon Grey. Your actions alone saved the world from a possible calamity, did they not?"

"An exaggeration."

"Your modesty is unnecessary here, Arlon Grey. You shun accolades for your great achievements solely because you are unable to cope with them at present. You often utilise that persona of yours to shock people with harsh truths as a coping mechanism to avoid emotional proceedings."

"What's the big secret, then? I think I have a right to know that, at least, if you won't tell me about my family or let me leave here," stated Arlon sharply.

"I understand your consternation, Mr Grey, but it will do you no good to transplant blame or guilt upon me or my friends. You're free to leave if that is your desire. You won't get very far and I will not allow the others to leave here with you. It's simply too dangerous. By morning everything will change, at any rate. There is no need for you to go. As I said, you will hear your wife's..."

"Yes, you already said that twice and I still don't know what it means."

"You don't know what hearing your wife's voice means? Even a less intelligent person would consider that to mean that your wife will be here tomorrow morning, if I say you will hear her."

"You didn't say that."

"You didn't hear it, but it was implied."

"You're saying that my wife will be here?"

"Assuming, not guaranteeing."

"Small comfort."

"Really? Have I not demonstrated my friendship and extended my assistance to your betterment so far?"

"I don't know. Was it you I heard? Were those your eyes in the dark?"

"Of course not. Look at me, could those eyes have been mine? I have been here all along guiding you and...my helpers."

"Helpers?"

"Not yet, Mr Grey, not yet. I'm not convinced of your allegiances at present, and not willing to divulge everything until I can be sure that you will act in a certain manner. Once I have that assurance I will reveal everything to you. Meanwhile, you will be tested by the unfolding circumstances in our little forest. You will need our assistance and we risk everything by supplying that aid. Before that occurs we need to bring the others in and have a bite to eat and some strong coffee, which I brewed especially for you."

Arlon peered at the elderly woman for a long time, taking in every detail of her and the scene. He was anxious about escaping the confines of the claustrophobic cabin and the forest. He yearned to be with his family. He felt it way down in his bones, a desperate urge, an all-encompassing need to be with them after hearing of the imminent threat to them.

Hilda Haggerty sat calmly with an almost Cheshire cat grin on her face. She was dressed in a threadbare cotton dress with a faded floral pattern; homemade, certainly. She wore no jewellery or other accoutrements. Her long grey hair was clean and styled neatly into a bun resting at the back of her head, tucked into a near-invisible net. Her colouring suggested a life well away from the ravages of sun and wind; pale and spotted, though belying her actual age. Her swollen ankles were restrained by clean, white medical stockings, her feet tucked into sheepskin moccasins.

"How long do you have?" Arlon asked quietly.

Hilda started at the question, but quickly regained her composure.

"I've been alive for more than a century. I don't suppose I have that long, Mr Grey."

"I want to know how long it will be before you succumb to the illness."

"You cannot possibly know anything about me or my health, so the question..."

"...is perfectly legitimate, Miss Haggerty. While you delve into others with that...gift of yours, whatever you may call it, others may explore or become aware of certain aspects of yourself in the process. A little piece of you remains, becomes embedded in the recipient of your explorations. It isn't as crystal clear as your investigations, I assume, but capable of interpretation, nonetheless. Didn't you know that?"

"I..."

"Never wondered why your nemesis out there always managed to know most of what was transpiring between you and your minions?"

"But..."

"It's a two-way street, my dear. While the mind is open to probing another it is vulnerable to the same examination. Oh, I doubt your Cabbages and the others were aware enough to properly identify that connection. It was more likely transplanted into their subconscious, where it leaked out slowly over time. I imagine my previous experience has amplified my ability to a certain degree, which is why I can positively conclude that you are unwell, with very little time remaining."

Arlon's deadpan voice created an ominous air within the confines of the small area. Hildy stared straight ahead with unseeing eyes, tasting his words with her unique talents, testing their veracity and his sincerity. What she discovered unsettled her. All the years of the feud between the two factions of forest folk might have been avoided to an extent if she had not exposed her mind to them in return for the information received. She had never once entertained the notion that it was possible. It made some sense, however. A few incidents in her past suddenly became clear in the new light of the strange man's words. She took a sudden intake of breath as a realisation dawned on her.

"Yes, that's right. Your...secret became known to them only through your...interference, your meddling. Impossible to avoid a bit of backwash, Miss Haggerty."

"It, it can't be true. They couldn't know," she murmured uncertainly.

"Oh, they don't know the details, that's for sure. I overheard them talking about a bunyip, for goodness sake. They do know you are protecting something, though, something they perceive as having value to them."

"Yes, yes, I know they think that. They've been laying those traps and others around my property for years now, hoping to profit from the results," admitted Hilda.

"Is that how Noel Payne came to grief? Did you know about that?" asked Arlon after a moment.

"I warned Betty about her trips to visit me every year. I knew it would arouse suspicion in time and eventually someone would follow her if she weren't careful. I didn't know who it was when I was...alerted to the fact that someone had been caught in a trap. I buried the poor soul; what was left of him after a week in the forest. I made the connection only recently, when Betty came here to tell me about her missing son. I didn't have the heart to tell her."

"She told you all about me? She told you where I intended to go before returning to her place?"

"She..."

"It was you, then. It's your fault that my family is in danger. You managed to impart the knowledge of my family's whereabouts to the Cabbages while you sought to divine their intentions. Colin Cabbage is more astute and aware of his mind than you were led to believe. He figured some things out, such as how to interpret the messages arriving in his subconscious. He sees your thoughts and memories to a certain degree."

"I understand that now. I'm sorry, Mr Grey. I have done you a grave disservice. I think Colin Cabbage intends to kidnap your family and bring them here to make a trade-off or to deliver retribution for what occurred to his daughter. You won't know this, but she passed away a few hours ago."

"And you know this because?"

"I sensed Irma's presence at the hospital, then she was gone soon after," said Hilda reluctantly.

"This has to end here, tonight. This invasion into people's minds ends at once. You are interfering with dangerous persons, possibly encouraging their hostilities and aggression with your meddlesome antics. I want to know what this is all about, everything. If you don't volunteer the information I will bring the authorities down on you like a ton of bricks. I will reveal everything I know. If the police no longer believe me I'll go to the press. I'll blow your little secret wide open and you will have hordes coming in here to spoil your dream. Your...'bunyip', will no longer be a secret..."

"Okay, okay, Mr Grey. You have made your point. I understand your pain and frustration. I guess you have a right to know. Not *just* you, though. My friends have a right to know, even more so than you."

"I thought they were all a part of it?"

"They know only vague facts that I have drip-fed them through the years to gain their cooperation. They are fiercely loyal and extremely protective of me and the miracle I preserve."

"Miracle?"

"Nothing less, Mr Grey, nothing less, as far as I am concerned. Please bring the others in so that we can have something to eat and drink before we settle down to have the conversation you demand" pleaded Hilda in her gentle and reassuring tone.

Arlon moved back to the room at the end of the hall reluctantly, shaking his head in frustration and impatience. He was very worried about his wife and adopted daughter.

CHAPTER ELEVEN

Clarice could smell it the moment she stepped outside the caravan. The pungent odour that smacked of unwashed bodies, of accumulated sweat and filth, lasted only a brief moment before it wafted away on the gentle chilly breeze drifting over the serene lake. Dressed in many layers of clothing, including an under-layer of thermals, Clarice almost waddled in the bulky outfit as she battled with the frigid southern Australian conditions.

Moments ago she had ordered Tara to evacuate the camper, which the girl had stubbornly refused to leave, even briefly, for several days, citing the bitter cold. Being Queenslanders through and through, both females were finding the arctic conditions, especially the southern breezes, intolerable. The rain had persisted in a steady and annoying drizzle for much of the few days spent there. With signs of the clouds departing and their first glimpse of real sunshine, Clarice was determined to extract as much outdoor use as possible for herself and Tara.

She regretted having finagled Arlon into accompanying him on his latest assignment. The fact that Arlon had failed to contact her as promised caused her further concern. Although she had not expected to see much of him during their holiday/business trip to the southern state of Victoria, he had promised to keep in touch via the new mobile phone she had purchased for him and a visit or two if he could.

While she and Tara had bonded further while sharing their enforced company as they awaited a break in the weather, it became a chore after days cooped up together in the miserable cold with inadequate heating facilities. They were rugged up until they looked like versions of the Michelin Man, unable to easily navigate the tight confines of the pop-top camper. She was pleased that she did not have to share the camper with another adult as well. It suited them that Arlon would be forced to be based closer to his client.

She could not immediately locate Tara when she stepped out of the van onto the moist grass. The picturesque Lake Eildon stretched before her, sparkling with tiny diamonds as the sun rose in the east. The wind had died and the air began to warm ever so slightly. Clarice was not overly alarmed at being unable to see her daughter, for she knew Tara to be a resourceful and resilient child who had shown maturity beyond her nine-years-going-on-ten. Clarice was relatively assured that Tara would not have ventured too far. In all likelihood, she had meandered down to the water's edge and followed it to explore the next bay.

Clarice grabbed a lightweight folding camp chair, which she carried down to the edge of the calm water. She intended to soak up some of the sunshine before it disappeared behind the building cloud bank. In short order, the area would be subjected to more of the miserable drizzle they had experienced for the duration of their holiday. Spying an abandoned fishing rod laying nearby, Clarice scanned the area to look for the young girl whom she adored beyond all expectations.

It was odd for Tara to leave a fishing rod with the line extending into the water, presumably baited. Arlon had demonstrated to her carefully how to thread the worms onto the hook and cast the line out, set the drag and place the rod in a holder. He had warned her about the size of some of the carp caught in the lake, capable of snatching a rod and taking off with everything if left unattended.

A sudden tingle made its way up Clarice's spine to the base of her head. She made a connection between the foul aroma when she stepped out of the caravan, which had no place being there in the pristine environment, and the absence of her girl. It was a connection that did not bode well for either of them.

Her tomboy upbringing, surrounded by five brothers who roughhoused with her daily, ensured that Clarice did not break down immediately into a helpless and quivering mass. She was made of sterner stuff, able to withstand far more than her peers at school. She had often found herself siding with the boys when her friends broke down and bawled at the slightest remark or rebuke from a boy.

However, it took all her inner strength to push back the panic she felt welling up inside her. The tears were threatening when she thought of her precious daughter in any sort of danger. Arlon and she had managed to talk their way into adopting the delightful child after their last assignment. It was an instantaneous bond between the girl and them, even for the non-feeling Arlon Grey.

Instinctually, Clarice knew that something was amiss without understanding the exact nature of it. Someone had her daughter, of that she seemed certain. The whiff of bad body odour, mixed with the essence of urine and human excrement, indicated an unsavoury character close by when she exited the van. The odour was transient; long gone. To Clarice's investigative mind, something that seemed natural since being in Arlon Grey's employment, she intuited that to mean that Tara and her abductor were no longer in the immediate vicinity.

Clarice gave no outward indication that she was aware of anything untoward in case she was being observed. She did what she believed would be natural. She peered casually about for a sign of her daughter, as any parent would in the same circumstances. Without displaying signs of panic, she swivelled about through a three-hundred–and-sixty-degree arc to ostensibly find her daughter, when, in fact, she took note of every single detail that might be out of place or to indicate the path taken by the intruder.

If someone had taken her daughter, they would have been sure to leave the area straight away unless they had certain...designs on the young girl that didn't bear thinking about. At the moment, Clarice could think of no logical reason for anyone to simply take a child unless that were the motive, as disgusting and troubling as that thought was.

There was nothing to see in any direction. She wasn't sure what she hoped to find in any case. A trail of breadcrumbs? She wasn't thinking straight. She tried to determine what her husband would do in the same circumstances. *That calm bugger would probably shrug and go get his bloody safari suit on,* she thought unjustly. He would stage a search grid in an infuriatingly logical manner, to find the slightest shift or break in a blade of grass to determine which way the abductor exited the area. Clarice didn't think she could do that.

Besides, she had something far better at her disposal, something she had investigated and implemented without the knowledge of her husband or daughter. She rummaged around in her voluminous clothing to locate the device she sought. She knew it was secreted somewhere on her person, she just couldn't be positive of its exact whereabouts.

She eventually found what she was looking for in the inner pocket of her parka. To display the look of an unconcerned person for the benefit of any observer, Clarice sat on the camp chair. Shielding her hands and the activity from behind, she laid the device in her lap while her fingers frantically tapped out the password. After several failed attempts she finally remembered the proper entry code. Then she typed 'findtara@clarice.BAM'. The glowing dot appeared on her screen, which was displaying a map. The dot appeared to be moving, relatively slowly, away from her location. Once Clarice had herself oriented properly, she understood that the dot was moving towards the large car park for day trippers to the lake at her rear.

Arlon had paid the admission fee to the rangers for the site the van occupied presently. That token fee paid for the upkeep of basic facilities in the campsite, such as the ablution block, the BBQs, tables and benches, as well as bins scattered throughout the area to keep it clean of litter. Anyone travelling to the area for a day trip did not have to pay the fee. Only campers staying longer than a day were charged.

Clarice, no longer worried about being observed, was unsure how to proceed with the information she had. Arlon had their car, so she was unable to follow the trace if they entered a vehicle in the car park over a kilometre away. She wasn't concerned about losing the tracking symbol because it worked by satellite. She had installed the app on their mobile phone when she upgraded their business package a few months ago.

She hastily tried calling Arlon, urging him to answer while the tone rang. When the message bank kicked in, she cried out in frustration. Arlon had been out of range for days, or he had forgotten to charge his phone, as was his custom. She suddenly had another light bulb moment. She swiped the screen to retrieve the tracking app, typing in a new set of instructions, 'findarlon@clarice.BAM'.

The new dot gave Arlon's location relative to Clarice. She was surprised to find that he was not that far away, at least, not as the crow flies. It was puzzling, however. Peering at the map on her screen she could not understand what Arlon was doing in the middle of nowhere. She could understand why there was no signal for her to reach him. She swiped the screen blank to revert to Tara's trace once more, after typing in the appropriate code.

The dot was moving faster than before. Tara was now in a vehicle, she assumed. Clarice was feeling the first vestiges of panic creeping into her demeanour and a solitary tear escaped her eye. She swiped at it angrily. It was not the time to be feeling sorry for herself, she admonished. It was time to act decisively without histrionics and useless tears. Apart from calling the police with some lame, female report of a lost child after only a few moments of her going missing, Clarice wasn't sure what else she could do.

According to her tracking app, Tara and her phone had been taken and placed in a moving vehicle. It was the only explanation possible for her disappearance and the evidence before her. On an impulse, she split her screen in two and applied the code to bring up Arlon's trace again. Arlon was unaware that Clarice had ordered the software to keep track of her family members. She had hoped it would never be necessary to employ the device.

Oddly, the dot representing Tara was almost headed in Arlon's direction, though by no means in a straight line. Clarice tried to picture the topography around her from the way Arlon had described it and on their way to the lake. Twisting mountain highways ran through thick forests and stretches of verdant valleys and peaks. It seemed one mighty coincidence that Tara was heading toward Arlon. Of course, she could have that completely wrong. After all, there weren't that many exits out of the area. Nothing about anything that was happening made much sense to Clarice.

She tried Arlon's number again. It went straight to the message bank after the requisite number of rings. No signal. Clarice wished she had purchased a satellite phone for Arlon while she was upgrading their communications. There weren't too many places on planet earth not covered by a satellite.

There was only one thing for it. Something she fervently wished she didn't have to do. She swiped the screen clean and brought up her list of contacts. When she found the one she was searching for, she hit the green telephone symbol to initiate the call.

CHAPTER TWELVE

Hilda Haggerty closed her eyes momentarily, while the others gathered about her in a state of heightened anticipation. No one knew the exact nature of the miracle, only that it was of vital importance to retain its secrecy and protect it from all outsiders. The evening was drawing near and bitter winds blew against the exterior walls, periodically lifting the galvanised-iron roof sheeting noisily. Inside the cabin, the fire crackled, warming them all with its comforting glow and heat.

Everyone had partaken of a full meal, and now sat with a steaming brew of coffee in their hands while they waited for what Hilda would reveal. She sat rocking in her wooden chair, seemingly compiling her story. It would be the first time she had spoken of it to anyone other than her dear father, whom she missed desperately.

When Jason Haggerty was a young man, he came across an injured animal one cold winter's day. Jason lived with his parents in a small worker's cottage, not far from the section of forest being felled by the lumber company he worked for. His parents would be the first of the legendary forest folk to remain in the area long after timber operations ceased. A few other scattered families stayed on, forming a tight-knit community dedicated to upholding a tradition among themselves and displaying fierce loyalty to their friends and kin.

While honing the edge of his axe to razor perfection, Jason heard an odd sound from the vicinity of the rear yard. In the tool shed at the rear of his parents' cottage, Jason diligently performed the necessary maintenance on his beloved tools of the trade. It became an extension of his arm during the day, when he lost himself in the zone of hard labour. The giants of the forest would crash to earth with a thunderous explosion of sound that would shake the ground beneath his feet, yet Jason Haggerty was oblivious to almost all sound during his labours.

A great lump of a lad at an early age, Jason grew to his father's large proportions and more as he aged. Few of his fellow workers had the stamina or speed to match the youth when it came to felling a tree. No one other than Jason's father, Conroy Haggerty, had the gift when it came to the precision required to select the right tree to fall in the exact position to allow free movement around it. All too often a tree was hung up on the bough of another during the work shift, calling for the felling of a secondary, unprofitable tree.

Conroy and Jason worked together since Jason had been old enough to bear the weight of an adult-sized axe. Conroy's axes, though, were larger than those of an ordinary man. He forged his own, weighing in at approximately double that of a normal axe. He wielded a forge hammer as easily as the mighty Thor, glistening in the fires of the forge as he laboured to make the instruments from the finest steel available. His meticulous ministrations with the raw material saw the finished product able to keep its razor edge for the better part of the day, while others were swapping or honing their axes many times a shift.

Conroy instilled in his son the intrinsic gift of near-instant value recognition beneath a tree's rough bark, and this caused Jason to rise in the ranks quickly, admired by his fellow workers. Any crew led by the Haggerty family saw double the profit of crews sporting many more workers. Careful selection and pinpoint precision of the felling process, taking in the angle of the hillside, the lean of a particular tree relative to the incline, the prevailing weather and soil conditions, all played out in the profit margins at the end of each day.

Conroy would scout ahead of his crew, days in advance, to indicate each tree with his customary pink ribbon marker. Jason would then follow, deciding where to make the first cut after studying each tree carefully against all the conditions. These men were not paid by the hour, but by the cubic foot of wood secured. It had to be clean wood, free of imperfections made by any number of natural causes. When considering a tree that stood over three hundred feet tall and as thick as twenty feet in diameter, it was of the utmost importance to gauge the health and profit of the tree accurately.

Conroy could be seen on any given day shinnying up a tree to the very top if necessary, to identify any imperfection not visible from below. Half a tree's unusable wood, because the top half had been reduced to worthlessness by a lightning strike or disease, was a waste of human effort and time. Many a time lesser mortals worked diligently for most of a day to bring down a forest leviathan, only to find the wood spalted and spoiled by water or other. Though highly prized by woodcarvers and speciality craftsmen, the wood failed to pass muster where quality construction or furniture timbers were required.

Thus, Jason could be found at the end of every working day, and often the remainder, hunched over a whetstone or the grinding wheel in his father's workshop behind the cottage, attending to the tools of his trade with meticulous care. Working its way through the pleasant haze of sound and reflection accompanying the repetitious task, came the plaintive sound that had Jason pondering its source.

The Haggerty family were well-versed in all the flora and fauna of the Victorian temperate rainforests, having lived among the rich and vibrant foliage all their lives. The heady scents and mouldy aromas of a healthy rainforest, breaking down the multitude of fallen leaf matter into usable nutrition and energy for the giants therein, was the elixir of life for the reclusive family. Jason had been schooled in all things pertaining to the land by his semi-naturalist, though traditionally-uneducated, father. Conroy's education came from the land itself and what his father had passed down.

Had he known the identity of the animal in question, he would have relegated the recognition to the back of his mind and continued with his preparations for the next day's labours. That he had never heard such a sound during his twenty years in the forest seemed impossible, and it diverted his attention from his precious axe.

He recalled something else that had registered in his mind earlier that day. Sunday, his one day off, had been spent in his usual practice of ensuring his equipment was in top order for the start of his shift on Monday morning. The distinctive sound of gunfire had penetrated the dense insulation of the forest to reach the ears of Jason Haggerty. He was incensed that a hunting party had found its way deep into Black Spur Forest.

The Haggerty family was almost religious in its endeavours to protect all wildlife, from the lowliest worm to the beautiful black cockatoos that were in great abundance during the early to mid-1900s. Jason's affection for all native fauna was inherited from his father, who was very active in the conservation of all animals and their natural habitats. It was yet another reason he made it his mission in life to be the one selecting the trees to fall to his axes. He always made sure they did not house some exotic, near-extinct avian or reptile species.

Jason heard only one or two rounds of gunfire before all fell silent again. By the time he decided he might venture out to locate the hunting party, he heard the neighing of horses and the sound of their hooves galloping away. Jason knew who it would be by the sound the horses made; heavy, thudding clomps. They were Clydesdales, by the sound of it, and only one family in the area had these large animals for pulling the ploughs through the soil on their land. It was the reason he did not go after them in the end. He knew exactly where the Cabbages lived.

Hours had passed while Jason concentrated on his task. It was only the introduction of the new sound that penetrated his subconscious. The prickles on the nape of his neck stood proud as he surmised what the sound might be. It had a distinctive quality of pain, an animal in pain. It was a sound he could not endure. One of the few things that brought tears to the eyes of the Haggerty menfolk was the sound of an animal in distress or suffering. Conroy and his wife were out of the forest on one of those rare occasions when food stocks and other essentials needed replenishing. So it fell to Jason to explore the area in an attempt to locate and provide aid to the injured animal.

The air was frigid outside the warm workshop, heated by the blacksmith's forge, as Jason stepped through the large double-hinged doors. It was the eve of the winter solstice and the daylight was fading fast within the ravine. Jason could no longer hear the sound that had sparked his concern. His heart sank when he thought about the most likely reason for that silence.

Bracing himself for the inevitable, he made his way toward the creek at the bottom of the clearing, demarcating his parents' property. He thought the sound had emanated from that direction. The previous night's frost had not fully melted throughout the day. Snow would be falling on the peaks surrounding the area. His breath formed clouds before him as he made his way down the cleared property.

The crystal-clear waters babbled comfortingly over the stones and boulders in its path downstream. Jason bent to take a mouthful of the refreshing water. Peering up and down the creek, he found no evidence of the death he expected to encounter. Beautiful dark brown rock wallabies frequented the area and would allow Jason to pet and hand-feed them without fear. Jason worried that he might find one with a bullet hole to tell of its demise. Wombats, lizards, fruit bats and birds of many varieties visited the Haggerty property, knowing somehow that they were welcome and safe. Jason and his mother would often feed the animals, including errant reindeer and the odd fox.

Jason concentrated by closing his eyes and blocking out all sounds. He could no longer hear the cause of his explorations. Tossing a mental coin, he opted to walk upstream for a distance, knowing of a game trail that crossed the creek a short distance away.

Once he crossed the border of his family land, he was immediately immersed in the dense foliage of tree ferns and ground ferns among the forest giants all vying for supremacy, attempting to gain as much sunlight as possible in the highly competitive environment. Every plant battled for its share of life-sustaining goodness from the sun. Without it, each was doomed to wither and rot, adding to the pungent richness nurturing the hardiest specimens to gain maturity.

Before he reached the small waterfall near the top of a ridge, he heard the whimpering sound once more. Excited that life persisted when he had thought it finished, Jason renewed his determination to find the injured animal. Within moments he located the furry bundle, whimpering softly, near its end, barely expanding its chest to take in new oxygen.

Jason recoiled in horror when he turned the animal over: a crossbow bolt was embedded in the creature's eye. It had to have been young Colin Cabbage who caused the injury. The gunfire afterwards would have come from his friends, to unsuccessfully complete the kill. Colin was never seen without his crossbow.

It was a juvenile of its species, that much Jason intuited immediately. What he could not discern as quickly was the species. He guessed a fox or a young dingo, perhaps, though he did not know dingoes were in the area. It may have been a domesticated dog that had given birth to a litter of pups in the wild. An elongated body presented Jason with doubts.

Without worrying too deeply about the creature's origins, Jason set about gathering the animal to take it back to his home. It was so near death that Jason firmly believed it impossible to rescue the poor thing. He raged inside as he carried the limp bundle in his arms back the way he had come. He seethed at the unnecessary taking of a life, any life. He was angered beyond words at the soullessness required to injure an animal and leave it to suffer needlessly. Somehow, he would make the Cabbages pay for the deed. He swore an oath to repay the callous and cowardly act.

For nearly a year afterwards, Jason had taken great pains to keep the creature alive. Several times it appeared as though it would lose the fight and perish, only to regain life at the last second; holding on tenaciously with Jason's assistance. Conroy and his mother knew nothing of the animal, which Jason kept hidden in a small corner of his father's workshop, later transferring it to a grotto beneath the roots of a large mountain ash, where the creek waters had washed away a portion of the soil.

Several weeks before the first anniversary of being rescued, it finally gave signs it might survive the ordeal, and was left to roam freely thereafter. That was when Jason finally decided to confront the perpetrators.

The Cabbages lived at the edge of the forest on a cleared plot of fertile farmland. Jason knew they were cultivating a crop that did not exactly fit with conventional farming practices. The local police turned a blind eye to the activities because they were handsomely rewarded for doing so. The ill-gotten lucre provided the Cabbages with enough protection to make them impervious to the complaints against them by neighbours and the like.

Roman Cabbage, the patriarch of the Cabbage clan and nearing the sunset of his years, was sunning himself on the rear porch of their rundown hovel, on a worn and rickety rocker. The best of his children had been given their orders to tend the crops until daylight was gone, a rule he enforced with a heavy hand. Roman was a hard man brought up rough by his lumberman father. The abuse he and his mother suffered under the tyranny of his father made him an angry man as he entered his teenage years. Eventually, he grew tall enough and tough enough to stand up to his old man.

That contest, which he won, was both the rescue and the undoing of the young man. The methodical inculcation of his mind with all the wrong life lessons became Roman's only means of communicating with his children, when the time came. Colin Cabbage, his oldest, already of an age when he could stand against his father as Roman had, showed signs of bearing the very same personality and mindset. They were born tough and lived rough, with nary a thought spared for anyone but their own. Their hatred for each other and everyone else ran deep.

Roman sometimes struggled with the actual relationships the family members had to one another. Roman was the product of a union between his father and a close cousin. His wife was a first cousin. His daughter, Emma, was showing signs of pregnancy. He knew his children played around that way, had caught them at it once. After punishing them severely for their sins, he made sure that he was the only one allowed that sort of access thereafter.

His wife spat out a bad one ten years ago, which put an end to his relations with her. That retarded lad could barely wipe its arse and drooled all day long. Roman made the boy a room over the shed, where he lived and ate the meals his mother brought to him. He wasn't allowed anywhere near the main house or in his father's sight. Many a time his mother had to rescue the lad from being taken out into the forest to be abandoned or shot, depending on how angry Roman felt at the time.

The sunlight was suddenly blocked out by something. Roman opened his rheumy eyes to stare with disdain at the intruder standing on the steps in front of him. The fact that the stranger was holding a rifle pointed directly at Roman was sufficient reason for him to put a lid on his initial outburst. He thought he recognised the large man, but wasn't sure. His mind raced quickly to discover how he might have wronged the man in their dealings. He didn't recall pulling any swift ones lately and wasn't sure what the man's beef was with him.

"Do ya for stranger?" he asked confidently.

"Kids-o-yours been poachin' me dad's land," replied Jason Haggerty.

"Who that be, son?"

"Conroy, Conroy Haggerty."

"You his sprog?"

"I'm his son, Jason, yes."

"Ya either a very brave boy or a complete an utter imbecile, ya know that? Ya know who ya talkin' ta, boy?"

"Probably Roman Cabbage, I reckon."

"Ya know that and still come here ta threaten me?"

"Come to offer you an ultimatum. Your kids done wrong by poachin' on our land and injuring an animal. That isn't right and a debt needs to be paid. Bible says "an eye for an eye" and I aim to collect on that."

"Ya daft. Me kids been nowhere near ya land today. They's all workin' in the fields, ya dumb arse!" spat Roman.

"Didn't say it was today. A time back now. Near enough a year, and that's the time it took me to care for the animal. Come good now, so thought I'd come to see that they pay for what they done."

"What ya threatenin' me with and what ya want as payment?"

"Leave the form of payment to yourself by way of punishment for the young folk. As for what you can expect if you disagree, I think I may be able to convince some federal police to investigate certain things hereabouts that aren't quite legit," stated Jason in an easy tone.

"Ya really wanna start a war 'tween us, then?"

"Nope, not at all. Doesn't have to go no further than punishment for poaching on our property. Injured an animal with that crossbow thing and didn't even make sure it was dead. Can't have that, Mr Roman. If you want to take it as a slight to your family and start a feud, then I can't stop you. I wouldn't like your chances of remaining here if the federal police come sniffing around, though."

Roman thought about it for a moment in silence, "I'll git ya what ya want, and ya family name will be mud by me and mine till kingdom come. Think ya can come here and threaten me, ya dumb shit? Think again. Don't never let it be said a Cabbage didn't pay his due. Ya wait right there," said Roman, rising from the chair swiftly.

"I hope you aren't thinking of bringing a gun into it, Mr Roman? I told me pops where I was going and what I was aiming to say."

"I'm no fool, boy. It was a Haggerty what brung a gun here, threatenin' me. Yiz remember that down the line. I'm not gettin' no gun. I'm gonna get ya what ya asked. Ya want me kids punished, that's what yiz get. Now just wait there and don't ya move."

Jason watched the rake-thin man, dressed in the filthiest set of dungarees he'd ever seen, march past him and down the stairs towards the shed at the rear of their property. Roman Cabbage ascended the exterior stairs two at a time, belying his age and fitness. Then came a hue and cry to send shivers up the spine. Jason had no idea what could be happening, but someone was copping the old man's wrath in full measure. The bloodcurdling screams were setting Jason's nerves on edge. He wondered if he should investigate.

The crashing and stomping in the room above the shed ended abruptly with a pitiful cry of sheer agony and torment, which lanced through Jason's heart. He began to dread what he had instigated, feared the result of his ultimatum. He knew it would not end well for whoever was involved in the mighty kerfuffle, nor even himself. He contemplated leaving and forgetting all about the mission.

The old man returned through the shed doors with a ramrod-straight back and a steely glare. Something was concealed in Roman's right hand, something bleeding. The old man marched up to where Jason remained on the rear porch of the house, and held his fist out for Jason to receive the contents. The man stood perfectly still, breathing hard, his arm outstretched, with blood seeping from between the fingers, dripping onto the wooden deck.

"Take it, ya mongrel, it's what ya asked for," Roman commanded in a deadly whisper.

Jason stared at the man, whose foetid breath blew directly into his face. Then Fay Cabbage came crashing through the screen door, whimpering with fear.

"Cory? Mama's com..."

She stopped still when she caught sight of her husband holding something bloody in his hand. She turned deathly pale.

"What ya done now, Roman Cabbage? Ya done it at last, did ya? I swear..."

"Shut ya gob, woman. Yiz can cuss me all ya want, but watch I don't backhand ya for it later. Now git back inside," Roman warned.

"I'm goin' ta me son and ya not gonna stop me, ya hear? If ya hurt him..."

"Yeah, what? What ya gonna do, woman? I'll do a bloody sight worse if ya don't git. This here is 'tween the mongrel and me. He come here with a gun and guv me a ultimatum he's gonna regret. He and his kind will rue the day they crossed a Cabbage by name-o-Roman T…"

Fay was torn between wanting desperately to see what had happened to her son and the fear she felt for the consequences if she didn't follow her husband's orders. She had made up her mind years ago to leave the savage bastard who abused every member of his family, but especially their youngest, Cory Cabbage. From the day the child was born, Roman had wanted to end his life. He declared the infant an aberration and a disgrace. He ended his relations with his wife from that day, and she copped his abuse tenfold thereafter.

Jason could see the defiant look fading in Fay Cabbage's eyes as the realisation set in that she could do nothing for whomever Roman had accosted in the shed. The cold hard stare that bore through her from her husband warned of her punishment if she should disregard his orders. Jason felt a pang of pity for the tiny woman, who seemed to shrivel into herself before his eyes. Her head dropped to her chest in resignation: she knew she was helpless to do anything other than what she was being commanded to do.

As Jason watched her leave, with her shoulders beginning to heave with heavy sobs, he also capitulated to Roman's demands by holding his hand under the old man's. Roman smirked with satisfaction as he slowly turned his fist upside down to release the prize into the waiting hand of his new enemy. Jason cringed as he spied the bloody eyeball staring back at him.

CHAPTER THIRTEEN

"An eyeball?" repeated Arlon, as if he couldn't believe what he was hearing.

"Yes, I'm afraid so," said Hildy sadly, shaking her head. "My daddy had tears in his eyes when he told me the story. He never imagined that Roman Cabbage would take him so literally when he demanded justice for the injured animal. Had my daddy known what Roman was capable of doing to his poor son, he never would have confronted him. He carried the guilt for that deed up to the day he died in a work-related accident."

"So how does all that fit in with what's going on around here?"

"It's complicated, Mr Arlon. I'm not even sure if I can explain it to you so it makes any sense."

"I think these folks might deserve whatever explanation you can give for all their troubles and loyalty over the years. And I would certainly like to hear the rest of it."

"Several days after it happened, my daddy went down to the bottom of our property around midnight on the eve of the winter's solstice. He was chewed up inside with the guilt and shame he felt. The winter air was freezing, but my daddy didn't feel a thing, he told me. He said he was just numb inside. He'd released the creature back into the wild after it had recovered sufficiently and hadn't seen it since. In Daddy's hand, he held the eyeball, which had kept reasonably well in the cold weather.

"The depression he'd been feeling had given Daddy thoughts of no longer living in the world, something he only admitted to me many years later. He thought he might just stay out on the tree stump all night and slowly freeze until life left him. He'd run out of tears for his part in the ruination of a young boy's face. He held on to that eyeball in the moonlight until he saw some movement at the edge of the clearing.

"The furtive rustling among the ground ferns continued while my daddy watched on. Several moments later, the creature appeared like a wraith from between the fern fronds, walking slowly toward my father. He knew it was the one he'd saved because one of its eye sockets was empty. Daddy didn't know how many others there were in the area, as he had never seen them before. Slowly the animal made its way to where Daddy sat on the stump. It stood in front of him with a curious look on its face. Then it approached his outstretched hand and gently took the eyeball into its mouth. Daddy said it gave him such a look, as if to say the debt had been paid and it was very grateful for everything that had been done to save its life. The creature then turned and left.

"That animal ended up saving my father's life a dozen times after that, and my grandparents' as well, alerting them to the presence of the Cabbages. The feud between us and the Cabbages grew into an all-out war. Several of the other forest families sided with us and others sided with the Cabbages. Somehow or, rather, someone always ended up losing their lives every year or so and Daddy would make sure the debt was paid on the eve of the winter's solstice, when that creature would miraculously appear to take the offering."

"An eyeball? From a dead person?"

"Yes. Those Cabbages have been laying down traps to catch the creature or us ever since. It didn't happen every year that someone died. It only had to happen every second year, and sometimes two people died in one year. There was never a shortage of eyeballs if the spare ones were preserved, or, later, frozen, when we had generators or solar power. The saddest thing I ever had to do was remove my daddy's eyes after he died. He passed on his secret to me when I was only five years old, and I went down with him to the stump every year after that. I am so very, very sorry, Betty, that it was your boy I found last year. I had no way of knowing. I had no connection with him because he wasn't born in our forest."

Hilda was shaking with grief, so Betty went to her side.

"You weren't to know, Miss Hildy. I never thought to bother you with my woes. He wasn't a good boy, I'm afraid. If the traps hadn't got him I think the drugs would have, or he would have ended up in prison. I'm, I'm sad about knowing, but not upset that he is now a part of the forest."

"So much sadness and suffering over one mindless incident. It hasn't been easy to keep matters from escalating beyond our sanctuary, I assure you. Though I suppose that may now be happening and it is probably all my fault. Oh, dear."

"Now then, Hildy, I don't think you should be taking all that guilt on yourself. Seems to me we've all been to blame for keeping this infernal feud going for as long as it has. We should've ended this years ago," argued Dot. "How about a fresh coffee, everyone?"

After receiving nods all round, she set about making a pot in the small kitchen.

"What is it, then?" asked Arlon during a silent pause.

"What is what?" enquired Dot.

"The creature. What is this miracle you're sacrificing yourselves for?"

"In a few days, you will see that for yourself. The rest of you, as well," answered Hildy quietly.

"Why wouldn't you simply tell us now?" asked Arlon.

"Seeing is believing, Mr Grey. I doubt very much that any of you would believe me one hundred per cent if you didn't see it with your own eyes," suggested Hildy.

"Why now, Miss Hildy?" asked Alex softly, suspecting the truth.

"You know already, Alex."

"Are you sure?"

"Positive," she answered flatly.

"Someone like to fill me in?" asked Arlon.

"You said so yourself, I'm a very old woman now and way past my use-by-date. I won't see another winter. It's high time I passed on my duties. I was hoping Betty might like to take over from me now that she's returned. I don't suppose there's much for you out there anymore, dear?"

"I, I'm not sure what to say," Betty stammered.

"Just say you'll consider it when the time comes. Someone has to. You'll get my house, the land and all the chooks. I'll even pass on my secrets for coming up with prizewinning bantams. I can't think of anyone better suited to the task than you, my dear."

"You folks believe that Jason Haggerty saved the life of a bunyip?" asked Arlon doubtfully.

"Whoever said anything about a bunyip?" asked Hildy, trying to keep back the laughter.

"That's what the Cabbages believe. I overheard them talking about it."

"You should know better than that, Mr Grey. There is no such thing as a bunyip, a drop-bear or a yowie. They're all fictitious. Why would you even consider it?"

"I didn't say I believed it. I just wondered whether you folks thought of it as a bunyip as well as the Cabbages. You seem very reluctant to reveal the identity of the animal."

"I know what it is, but I fear no one will believe me unless they see it with their own eyes. Once you've seen it, I'm sure you'll all agree that it is a minor miracle."

"And you control them?"

"Not at all. I 'see' them in my mind much as I see all of you. I can sometimes guide them to a task, or encourage them to take a certain direction, but that is the extent of it. Somehow they seem to know my mind better than I do theirs."

"How is it they've managed to evade discovery all this time? Surely one or two have perished since it all began? Why has no one unearthed bones or other evidence of their existence?"

"They are extremely shy creatures, venturing out of their dens only at night to hunt. If one of their kind is injured or dies, the rest consume the dead animal to leave no trace of its existence."

"I find that a little hard to believe," suggested Arlon.

"My daddy fed them their dead whenever he found one and it sort of imprinted on them."

"So, they're carnivorous?"

"Most definitely."

"Native?"

"You'll see," answered Hildy mysteriously.

They were interrupted by a yipping sound, accompanied by a host of other calls from around the cottage.

"Oh, it seems we have company," said Hildy.

"Elmo Cabbage and some of his friends?" asked Arlon.

"One of the Cabbages, to be sure. Maybe others as well."

"My wife?"

"No, not that I can tell. I'm trying not to extend myself, Mr Grey, for fear it may be used against us."

Just then a piercing and gut-wrenching cry of desperation reached Arlon's inner mind and Hildy's, causing them to cry out simultaneously. Arlon's reaction was more acute than Hildy's, though she shook and shivered with dread. The rest were totally beside themselves with concern as Arlon descended to his knees in some pain, while Hildy appeared to be in the throes of a convulsion.

"What is it, Hildy?" asked Dot, attending to her as best she could.

"It, it's Mr Grey, he's in terrible pain. Some-someone is hurting. A girl. His daughter, Tara. She's screaming for help. Frightened. Oh, the poor thing. It, it, no, I can't tell who has her just now."

CHAPTER FOURTEEN

"Ya little shit, I'll learn ya not ta bite me. How'd ya like me ta choke the livin' daylight outta ya? Huh? Like that, would ya?" shouted Colin at the girl, who had bitten the hand which he held over her mouth while they walked quickly toward the waiting car in the parking lot.

Her tiny teeth had bitten through to the bone, he was sure. Everything had gone well up to that point. He had managed to grab the girl right from under the nose of the stupid mother, who had sent her outside the van on her own. He had waited patiently in his car to ensure the mother did not emerge from the van before he decided to nab her.

The plan was simple. Once he'd learned the whereabouts of the wife and child from...well, he wasn't sure just how he came by that piece of information. It just suddenly came to him in a quiet moment, as though somebody had whispered it into his ear. He saw it clearly in his mind, the location, the pop-top caravan, the mother and daughter, easily found and captured once he'd thought it out.

The original plan was to grab both of them. Fortunately, the girl made it too easy for him to change his plans, enabling him to grab her without the mother knowing or seeing, which gave them a perfect getaway. The mother would have no way of knowing where they had gone, and the cops wouldn't be all that quick about conducting a search, until time had passed to prove the girl was missing.

The girl was busy with her fishing rod as he crept up behind her, making no noise at all on the soft green grass at the lake's edge. Though the kid struggled mightily and kicked like a mule, his strength was no match for the frail little thing. He clamped his filthy great hand firmly over her mouth and hauled her back the way he'd come, keeping some trees between himself and the caravan in case the mother peeked out of a window.

Just as they were parallel with the caravan, the bloody sprog bit his hand and it was all he could do to stop from yelling out and releasing her. Despite the debilitating pain as her teeth touched bone and the blood flowed freely, Colin Cabbage retained his grip firmly over her mouth to stop her from screaming and alerting her mother. It took an age to negotiate the kilometre or so back to the car park and his waiting car.

Once inside, where any noise would be too muffled to make a difference, Colin backhanded her savagely. After voicing his indignation and wrath at her, he proceeded to strangle the girl, allowing his foul temper to get the better of him. When the girl blacked out and lay limp on the front passenger seat, Colin quickly regretted his impulsiveness. He needed the girl alive or his plan would never stand a chance of working.

When he heard about the death of his daughter, Irma, he became demented with rage, tearing through the filthy cottage destroying everything not bolted down. Elmo cowered in a corner while the tornado ripped through the interior of their home, hurling abuse at anyone and everyone imaginable, God being given His fair share of the invective. Elmo knew his father to be an angry man at the best of times, having been a victim of his indiscriminate punishments and tongue-lashings regularly, but he had never witnessed anything on the scale of what he saw that day.

When the giant beast of a man finally settled enough to inform the boy in a cold, hard manner about the death of his mother, Elmo wept long and hard. His mother was sometimes the only safeguard between himself and his father. Though her admonishments and punishments were as frequent, they were by no means as violent or painful as his father's. He curled up into a tight ball on his cot in the loft while his father continued to mourn her passing, though hardly as a loved human.

What Colin Cabbage felt was the loss of a chattel, a thing he owned, akin to a favourite car or a pet dog. She'd served her purpose, and could be relied upon to have a decent meal waiting at the end of a long day underground, or after his business dealings on the long drive to and from Melbourne. He no longer maintained sexual relations with her because of her gross appearance and the 'stuff' she had hanging out below since giving birth to the simpleton of a son they called Elmo. He wasn't as bad as Colin's young brother, who had passed away a few years ago, not long after his mum, Fay Cabbage.

Colin recalled when his father, Roman, explained to him how Jason Haggerty had snuck onto their land and attacked his retarded brother in his loft above the shed for no good reason one day, removing his brother's eyeball in the process. Ever since then the bitter feud had escalated year after year, with neither side ever truly gaining the upper hand. No one wanted to bring their troubles to the attention of the law, beyond the sphere of influence the Cabbages held within the local law-enforcement community.

When Colin left home to set up his operation in direct opposition to his old man, whom he loathed with a passion, he located to a plot well within the forest, taking his crops underground, where they couldn't be found by planes overhead, the rangers or the errant forest explorers and workers, poking their noses around where they weren't wanted. Colin had caught more than his fair share in booby traps he set up around the perimeter of his property.

Disturbingly, many were missing eyeballs when he found and disposed of them. It made him believe Jason Haggerty played a part in the mutilation of the corpses, though quite how he managed to locate them as often as he did was a mystery.

Roman's sister, Amelia, came visiting young Colin on Roman's insistence a year after moving out, attempting to bring about a reconciliation between the father and son. Though older than Colin by some years, she stayed on to become his lover. Colin was very tall and powerfully built, even in his youth, attracting many a female with whom he came in contact. Their family relations being what they were, neither his aunt nor he had ever questioned the relationship. When Irma was born, and the warring began between the aunt and him began, even though she gave as good as she got on occasion, more often than not, Amelia ended up the poorer of the two.

Amelia took her own life when she began to suspect interference with their daughter. Knowing that she would be unable to prevent it or talk sense into him, she took the only way out of her private hell. She loved her daughter too much to witness her destruction and the possible result of any union between the pair. The incestuous family grew more brazen with each generation, and Amelia feared the outcome of such inbreeding.

Colin found her hanging from a large tree outside their shared cottage. He made the young child of their loins witness the outcome, snorting with the contempt he believed her mother deserved for taking such a cowardly way out. He left her hanging there as a reminder to anyone that paid a visit of his absolute power in all things. Not that anyone was unfortunate enough to be visiting with Colin Cabbage. The smelly corpse remained until it was nothing but a flyblown, maggot-ridden sack of bones, long past recognition as the beautiful lady she once was. When the rope finally rotted through to dump the carcass on the ground, Colin discarded the pathetic remains in a garbage bag, which he threw onto the public refuse tip some kilometres from the forest.

Elmo was born several years later.

Colin had built a substantial customer base for his product, which fetched the highest prices in the city of Melbourne. His contacts met him in the city at an arranged rendezvous, a different location every time, to exchange goods for cash. The business of planting, maintaining and harvesting the crops required much of his valuable time. The bagging and weighing of the harvest he left mainly to his daughter and then his son, when he became old enough to be of some help.

Irma managed to help out with the crops as well as cooking and taking care of other 'needs' as required. The family prospered monetarily, though no one would ever know that from the condition of their home, apparel or themselves. Only the latest in fast and powerful automotive transportation gave any indication of means.

Colin Cabbage roared down the scenic, tree-lined highway in his latest machine, always black, nursing his injured hand, while clutching the steering wheel with his good hand. The girl hadn't moved since he choked her and he wasn't overly confident that she had survived his attack.

He cursed his impetuosity and temper, believing he might have to retrace his path to capture the wife. Only the slightest indication of possible life in the girl kept him to the road toward his forest. The smallest sound of a cough bordering on a bark, earlier, alerted him to the fact that some life persisted, though for how long might be very debatable.

He had wrapped his aching hand in a dirty handkerchief to stem the flow of blood, which failed miserably. He could not afford to stop anywhere to administer further aid. The girl might come to at any moment, leaving him to deal with the consequences of the fierce brat, while trying to keep the car on the road and any travellers from witnessing a young girl in obvious distress in his car.

His balls were still the size of a melon, sporting any number of dark and vibrant hues from the kick he'd taken by her father. His groin ached intolerably and every movement of his legs was a lesson in new pain. The brat and her father would pay for the damage done to his family and himself. The taking of his daughter's life would be met by an equal measure as repayment. Only the brat's life would suffice and he aimed to make sure it happened. Her mongrel father would have to be played along to believe that she would be spared in exchange for him. Colin had no intention of allowing that travesty to occur.

They would both be required to pay the price for the pain and humiliation caused by that skinny prick with the deadpan voice, who reckoned he had no emotions. Colin was determined to have the man squealing like a stuck pig and begging for his life and his daughter's. He would see the man a blubbering wreck before the day was done, which reminded Colin to get a move on, as daylight was quickly fading in the canopy of the rainforest covering the road.

CHAPTER FIFTEEN

"She's alive," uttered Arlon, as he lifted himself from the floor.

"Yes, barely," admitted Hildy.

"Can we get to her?"

"I don't like our chances," suggested Hildy.

"What happened?" asked Dot, with great concern creasing her gentle features.

"It appears there's been a terrible accident and his daughter is involved. A crash, I fear, and she's in a bad way, calling out desperately for her father. The connection is strong between them and I'm picking up on that."

"I have to go to her," insisted Arlon.

"Not sure how you're going to accomplish that, Arlon, even if we gave you all the help you need," answered Alex.

"How, how far away do you think it is, Miss Haggerty?"

"I couldn't tell you for sure, and I do wish you'd call me Hildy."

"I've never been comfortable calling people by their first name, and right now I have no interest in attempting to change that."

"Now, now, no need for anger, Mr Arlon..."

"See? It's absurd to be calling me that, Mrs Payne, and I am incapable of getting angry..."

"Let's just all settle down a moment here. We appreciate your pain at this moment...Arlon, and we understand your need to be doing something. What we have to figure out is what we can do and how. It's pitch-black out there at the moment and too bloody cold to be traipsing about without a clear idea of how to get out," said Dot calmly. "Alex, could you find your way to the forestry road from here without them others seeing you?"

"Big call, but I think I could swing it if I had to. Have to dress in darker colours and be really slow about our movements initially.

Might be we could leave up the back through the chicken coop and swing around to the top of the ridge, then work our way downwards away from there. We could intersect the road somewhere around Old Mike's place. Might be we could use his place to warm up some and grab a quick cuppa before heading out again," he explained.

"That sounds feasible, because I think Elmo and a couple of others are stationed at the bottom of the property near the creek," added Hildy.

"Won't be long before they send someone around to the rear of the property to cut off our retreat," suggested Dot.

"Which means, if we aim to do something as crazy as that, we better do it quick-smart."

"I can't ask you to risk your lives for me," said Arlon.

"Already have, so it's a moot point, don't you think?"

"Can you do it, Alex?" asked Dot fearfully.

"Can't answer that with certainty, love."

"I don't want you wandering around out there getting lost, husband."

"I should be the one to take him; it's all my fault, anyway," admitted Betty. "Besides, you need Uncle Alex here to defend Hildy and yourself, Aunty Dot. The Cabbages aren't going to wait forever before they try something."

"You don't know the way, Betty," said Alex.

"I could guide her and send some help like I did for... Arlon," said Hildy.

"I have to go to my daughter, I have no choice. I'm not asking anyone to risk their lives. This is all on me, folks," said Arlon.

"My Betty knows this forest, or, at least, *knew* this forest like the back of her hand as a child growing up in here. It'll come back to her with Hildy's help. Is it the forestry road you're heading for?" asked Dot.

"Yes, back to the road where I left my car...if it's still in working order, that is. Who knows what they may have done to it after I was captured, though I doubt the young one is all that knowledgeable about modern automobiles. He may rip out a spark plug lead or similar, if he works out how to take the engine cover off, but not much else, unless he cuts wires and hoses indiscriminately. It seems like forever since since I left the car. All I know is, I have to try. I can't stay here to wait. My daughter is out there somewhere, in the dark and the cold, waiting for her daddy to come, and I'm not about to let that young girl down."

"You aren't wearing your original clothes anymore. Do you still have the key to your car?" asked Dot.

"No, but I have a spare tucked under one of the wheel arches in a magnetic case. I doubt they would have looked for it or found it. One thing troubles me though, Miss... er, Hildy. You said earlier that my wife was heading here, as a hostage, you suggested?"

"That was true at the time. Something changed, though I still feel that she's heading here. I can only tell what is happening in a mind at the time the image appears in my head. What I said earlier is what I picked up from Colin Cabbage and his motivations. I can't tell you exactly why or how that changed and what happened to your wife," explained Hildy patiently.

"And it was from you that Colin Cabbage was able to track down my family?"

"I am ashamed to say that may be the case, yes."

"I can't tell you not to interfere anymore because I'll need your help to get out of here. What I'll ask is that you limit the time spent in their heads before any more information is leaked to them."

"I'll do what I can, Arlon, I promise. Your little girl needs help right now and I have to send my little helpers to guide you and Betty through the forest. Follow the eyes, Betty."

"I have my rubber boots here from when I visit Hildy to inspect the next rooster in the coop out back. You'll be needing a pair or those moccasins will get soaked and your feet will start to freeze, Mr Grey," instructed Betty.

"Well, Alex's boots will never fit him, so I suppose mine will have to do," said Dot, as she bent to remove the gumboots she still wore, despite being indoors. "Didn't think to take them off earlier. Sorry, Hildy. I'll clean the mess off the floor we made soon as they're gone."

"Not like I can see that mud or dirt, Dot," Hildy chuckled. "There's one other thing you're forgetting, Arlon Grey."

"Oh, what might that be?"

"How do you think you're going anywhere on that injured leg, and with your bad arm to slow you down even more?"

"Shit, you're right! I wasn't thinking straight at all."

"I can help if you'll let me," offered Hildy.

"How?"

"I'm over one hundred years old. How on earth do you think I manage to get around each day alone in this house?"

"Well, I wouldn't know, would I?"

"You do know. You just refuse to acknowledge it."

"My aberration is only temporary, if that's what you're talking about," suggested Arlon doubtfully.

"Hah! Not likely. Whether you like it or not, you are very much attached to your wife, child and, more importantly, yourself. You may not have had the benefit of the many years of training I've had due to my failing eyesight, but I can assure you that it's there. You are a very lucky man, Arlon Grey, to be blessed with such a unique ability, no matter how you got it. It requires tweaking, though, instruction and guidance to achieve desirable and highly beneficial results."

"If you're talking about getting into other people's heads, I'll pass, thank you very much. There's been enough trouble from that already."

"You are quite dense and stubborn for a man who professes to have an advanced degree of acuity and intelligence, Arlon Grey. I'm talking about you, getting deep into your psyche, learning to manipulate the machinations of the mind to unearth the capabilities therein. You do know that humans generally use only a small fraction of their brain's capacity?"

"So I've read."

"Ah, ever the sceptic?"

"Something like that. The whole Bizarre and Mysterious Detective Agency was my wife's idea. I was never a true convert to the concept or the practice."

"Only believe what you can see or touch?"

"No, that isn't... Look, can we not get into this right now? My daughter is in trouble and by hook or by crook I will leave here and get to her."

"Don't go getting your panties in a knot. I said I'd help you but you need to be open to it, otherwise it'll fail. You say you want to help your daughter, but something as simple as opening your mind to me is too much of a burden for you? Not very courageous or noble, if you ask me," said Hildy.

"So how can you help me with my injuries by seeing into my mind?"

"I didn't say *I* was going to help you with your injuries. I said I was going to help you to help yourself."

"This is getting us nowhere. How long will this take?"

"Up to you," stated Hildy indifferently.

"Do as she says, Arlon. She knows," said Dot.

"What do you want me to do?" asked Arlon, after a long pause.

"Sit in front of me and shut up for a start. Then I want you to empty your mind of everything. Then, the worst thing of all for you; trust me, completely."

Arlon sighed heavily before hobbling over to sit in front of the ancient lady in the old rocker.

"You want to hold my hands?" he asked awkwardly.

"We aren't going courting, young man," said Hildy with a snicker.

She closed her cloudy eyes to concentrate while Arlon sat back in the chair.

It came first as a feather-light touch on his consciousness, just the fleetest brush of an image or a suggestion across his mind. Arlon did as he was told by emptying his mind of everything else, just as he did each day during his exercise and meditation routines. It wasn't long before he felt a heaviness within his essence, as another presence inveigled its way in. It was a little like having a dream begin while fully aware of it unspooling before your eyes.

The probing became more urgent, burrowing deeper and deeper, until Arlon felt himself losing control, unable to prevent the exploration and subtle manipulations. At some point, Arlon felt the ache in his leg and arm more sharply, causing him to wince inwardly. On the exterior, the others saw only that Arlon had fallen into a deep sleep, whereby he flexed a muscle here and there involuntarily, or an eyelid shuddered periodically.

Arlon did not see anything, nor did he hear a voice as before, when he was struggling along the creek. The sensations he experienced were more of an insistent pressure which examined, touched and insinuated itself into every fibre of his brain. The pressure released its influence along the innumerable neural pathways of his conscious and subconscious thoughts, memories and long-forgotten experiences.

Arlon then sensed warmth. A physical heat spread throughout his person, following a distinct path to the parts of his body that were injured. Gradually the heat suffused his limbs, rendering them free of pain or encumbrance. He felt his strained muscles, sinews and tendons around the injury sites relaxing, feeling rejuvenated and invigorated anew. After a while, for Arlon had lost all sense of time, he felt as though he could run a marathon on his injured leg and lift a record-breaking weight with his arm.

More importantly, Arlon sensed a knowledge being imparted to the nether regions of his brain: a set of instructions to guide him in the means to perform the functions of healing himself. It was planted in the subliminal recesses, where he wasn't sure if he or she was determining the strategies employed to bring about such blessed relief.

Not only was a physical repair occurring within his body, but a mental cleansing was also ensuing as he relaxed further into his meditations, allowing the invasion to take place with complete confidence in the advancing force. He trusted the presence implicitly to anoint his mind with the abilities and perceptions imparted therein. It would be simultaneously exhilarating and foreboding if Arlon could be attributed with such emotions. A lesser mortal might not have had the fortitude to withstand the invasive probe, succumbing to the often irrational and debilitating forces that emotions can produce.

As Arlon retreated from his deep meditative state he could not describe what had taken place nor begin to explain the process by which he could now control aspects of his body. It was knowledge entrenched in his psyche as though it had been imprinted there from birth, inherited through generations sharing their unique wisdom and guidance with him. He felt himself peaking physically, as if he had emerged from the other end of a rigorous and torturous exercise routine.

Arlon woke with a start to find himself entirely alone. He tested the strength of his injured leg by standing, gingerly placing his foot upon the floor. He found that he could place his full weight upon the foot without the slightest indication of pain. His arm felt equally unencumbered. Before he could step forward, the others re-entered the living room from a door that presumably led to Hildy's bedroom.

"We had to put her to bed after the effort of assisting you. She was completely exhausted by it," explained Alex.

"How long did it take? I mean..."

"About an hour. Did you think it was longer?"

"It felt like a week had passed," said Arlon in wonder.

"You sound different. Are you all right?" asked Dot.

Betty, standing next to her, nodded her head in agreement.

"Sound different, how?"

"More... animated. Not so..."

"Like a dead fish?" offered Arlon.

"That's it," agreed Dot.

"How are the leg and the arm?" asked Betty.

"Surprisingly good. I don't know what she did..."

"She didn't. It was you. She just gave you the right tools," said Dot.

"She's... given you those tools as well?"

"Some, whatever was needed at the time. We haven't been injured badly, so we didn't require what she gave you. I assume you're convinced about what just happened? Considering the evidence, you'd better be."

"Not entirely sure I know *what* is going on here. It goes against everything I am, everything I've learned and come to recognise as real and logical. This is so far out of the box for me that I can't take it all in at the moment. I *can* tell that my arm and leg feel ten times better. I know I just went through a profound experience and feel enlightened to an extent, but exactly what form that new knowledge takes leaves me confused and in the dark."

"Do you still intend to walk out of here?" asked Alex.

"Yes. Otherwise, it was all for nothing. I have no choice in the matter. My daughter needs me and I'm compelled to go to her. Can we leave immediately?"

"We have some boots for you and some other supplies by the back door. Elmo and his mates haven't made a move to get around the back yet because they probably figure its way too difficult to make it out that way uphill in the dark," said Betty, secretly hoping Arlon would change his mind.

"How is Miss Haggerty going to be of any help to us while she's asleep? I thought she needed to guide you?"

"She gave me all the information I needed while she attended to you. It's all up here, just as it is with you."

"Hmm," murmured Arlon uncertainly.

"Gee, I don't know what it's going to take to make a believer out of you, but I would have thought you might at least show some gratitude. She's a very old woman who suffered greatly from the exertion of helping you. She could barely walk with our help back to her bedroom."

"I don't show gratitude, just as I don't show anything else, Mrs Payne. The sooner everyone accepts that, the better."

"Well, don't show it, then, say it! Surely your parents taught you some basic manners? If you employed those courtesies from time to time, whether you felt them or not, it would help grease the wheels of acceptance a little more. Right now I'm more concerned for the wonderful old lady in there than you or your child. Nothing matters more to me than her, and if you want my help to get you out of here and keep you alive you had better learn to mind your manners. I'm no longer beholden to you, Mr Grey. My son is dead, and even though I only know that because of your investigations, it doesn't mean I owe you anything more than the remuneration we discussed, which you will receive in due course."

"Get me out of here so that I can get to my daughter and I will consider the debt paid."

"Oh, no. And have me feeling guilty for the rest of my life? No chance, Mr Grey. You will be paid the ten thousand I offered as a reward. Besides, you're probably going to need every cent of that to make sure your girl gets the care she deserves. I felt some of what you and Hildy were experiencing when she came into my mind. Your girl could be suffering right now. The only thing I will ask of you in return for our help in getting you to her is that you return here on the night of the winter solstice to experience the event for yourself. Hildy wants to share it with all of us so that we can carry on the tradition."

"Fair enough. I agree."

"Get going, then."

"Do we have any sort of weapon we can use if they catch up with us?"

"Sure," said Betty cryptically.

Betty moved past Arlon to the rear door of the cottage, where she doused the hurricane lamp, hanging on an ornate wrought-iron bracket from the door jamb, so as not to give away their position when they opened the door. Arlon swapped his inappropriate and ill-fitting sheepskin moccasins for a pair of rubber boots that fitted him better with the aid of thick woollen socks. Betty and he wore thick, fleece-lined, dark lumber jackets to ward off the biting cold. Woollen beanies in black completed their night camouflage and arsenal against the cold.

The moment the door was opened, the bitterly cold wind hit them squarely in the face, causing their noses to run. Betty told Arlon to lie on the cold stone path leading to the coop at the rear of the property. Arlon could see nothing beyond a few centimetres from his nose, but he could smell the distinctive odour of the chicken coop wafting his way. He dropped to the path with surprising agility, given the amount of pain and discomfort he was experiencing before his session with the old woman.

Arlon did not entirely agree with the tactic of crawling up the path, believing the night sufficient to mask their exit. He did not get the opportunity to advance his opinion, as Betty began to crawl up the path with stoic determination and hidden strength belying her age. Arlon reprimanded himself for that ungracious thought. He had to remind himself that Betty Payne appeared older than her years only because of the anguish she had struggled with for over a year.

The ascent up to the rear yard, though a chore, proceeded uneventfully until they reached the coop. Betty swung open the door, while remaining low on the path. She urged Arlon through by tugging on the collar of his jacket. Once inside the coop, they both rose to a standing position within the safety walkway, an area which ensured the birds could not escape when the exterior door was opened. Betty walked the two steps to the inner door. She knew the fowls would be roosting for the night and shouldn't be alarmed by the intrusion.

She was wrong.

Wincing at the cacophony raised within the coop by the hens clucking worriedly and the roosters sounding their ire at the invasion, Betty felt sure the gig was up. She expected the party at the bottom of the property would soon be making their way up to them upon hearing the commotion.

She was wrong.

When they exited the coop by the rear door, they could hear the forest all about them alive with the competing sounds of all manner of animals. The birds especially were raising a din that drowned out almost everything else.

"What's going on?" Arlon whispered.

"Hildy," she answered, expecting Arlon to understand.

He didn't.

Betty grabbed Arlon's hand to lead him farther up the garden path...figuratively speaking. They entered the thick forest at the perimeter just as most of the animal sounds diminished. The eerie silence descended upon them once more, as the first signs of fog drifted through the massive trunks of the forest giants about them.

Betty worked her way unerringly upward through the dizzying obstacle course, in and around the thick vegetation. Both of them donned woollen mittens when their hands began to succumb to the frigid air and the moist foliage through which they traversed. In the distance behind them, they heard a couple of reports; gunfire.

"Don't stop, Mr Grey. They aren't shooting at people...yet. They're being harassed by animals."

"I thought Miss Haggerty was asleep?"

"And so she is. She couldn't stay awake."

"Then...you?"

"Uh-huh."

"She passed it on to you? Just like that?"

"No, not just like that, Mr Grey. It nearly killed her. May have, actually. She may not survive the ordeal."

"I'm...sorry. That's not what I wanted. Not what I wanted at all."

"Hildy did what needed to be done. She didn't need your blessing or your permission, only your cooperation and trust. At least you had the decency to do that for her."

"Why are you so hostile with me at the moment?"

"I'm angrier at myself, if truth be told. I brought this terrible thing to her doorstep, and you, and now it looks as though we might all die as a result. We normal people have this thing called guilt to assist us in behavioural management. I don't suppose I'm going upstairs to meet the Almighty once I depart this earth, Mr Grey, but, while I have given up much of my faith, I still like to hedge my bets where eternal damnation is concerned. So I am using my guilt as a means of compensation for my selfish behaviour and the trouble I caused."

"That's a lot to take on your shoulders, Mrs Payne. I would have..."

"Can we do this some other time? I thought you were in a hurry to get to your daughter?"

"I'm being realistic, Mrs Payne. There is no way we're going to find our way in this. I can hardly make out the pale skin of your face mere centimetres in front of mine. We have no hope of traversing blindly through this thick rainforest," ceded Arlon reluctantly.

"Harrumph! You learned nothing from her, did you?"

"I don't feel any pain in my injured arm or leg, so I think I may have picked *something* up."

"Look past me, Mr Grey. Concentrate on the ground about ten metres in front of us," instructed Betty impatiently.

It took only a moment or two for Arlon to discover a pair of eyes, amber/yellow eyes, shining from the darkness, seemingly floating in the air. There was an air of expectancy about them, intelligence and trust, urging Arlon forward. He could not be certain, but he felt they may have been the same pair of eyes he had followed to freedom in the tunnel. The eyes glowed somehow in the pitch-black surroundings.

"Very well. Let's go, then," suggested Arlon.

Betty turned immediately, following the receding eyes. The eyes would disappear, then reappear several metres ahead each time. The going was steep, made treacherous by the rotting mulch underfoot that offered little in the way of decent traction. The ravine in which the Haggerty cottage was nestled had practically vertical walls on either side, continuing to narrow the farther they proceeded uphill.

Betty followed the creature in front with complete trust, understanding the route it chose to be approximately the centre of the ravine. It would eventually lead them to the top, where they would reverse their direction along the northern ridgeline, well past the property and the group of men holding the siege. They would make far better time by following the ridgeline, where the trees were sparser and the fernery less abundant.

Arlon heard the now-familiar rifle reports, followed by a faint howling from the vicinity of the Haggerty property. It had an unearthly, eerie quality about it. He could not conjure up a single notion as to the identity of the animal responsible. The only conclusion he could settle on was that of an abandoned domestic dog forced to go back to its wild nature.

The longer the journey took the more worried Arlon became, for he could feel his daughter's anguish and suffering.

CHAPTER SIXTEEN

Tara heard the enormous man mumbling to himself as the car drove on. She maintained the illusion that she was asleep or unconscious to better ascertain her position and her options. Overpowering the brute of a man was near to impossible without a mountain of good luck in her favour. Even then she supposed that she would be just too weak and small to achieve her freedom.

Tara found it difficult to breathe with her swollen throat. Swallowing her saliva became a nightmare. She entered a meditative state, as her father had instructed, to calm herself and lessen the strain on her delicate throat. She regulated her breathing just as she'd been shown, and found it working for her. Her daddy had taught her to employ cunning whenever her strength was insufficient. Anyone, even the smallest person, could topple another if intelligence and logic were applied, according to Arlon Grey.

Since the moment she had joined her new parents, Arlon had been instructing her in the basic martial arts, as well as street-fighting techniques that she could use against opponents of any size. Biting, scratching and head-butting were just a few of the methods at her disposal, where her diminutive nature against a superior challenger would cause an unfair engagement. Arlon drilled her relentlessly until her actions were almost instinctual, reflexive.

The stench of the man in the driver's seat was bordering on intolerable within the confines of the car. Every turn of the wheel in the twisting, turning road brought a nauseating waft of foul underarm odour from the filthy man. That was accompanied by many movements of the man's body as he attempted to find a comfortable driving position. It seemed to Tara that he might need to pee, such were the erratic shifting and shuffling movements of his pelvis.

Through slitted eyes, Tara could see the ugly brute wince with pain every so often, when he brought his legs closer together or when he was required to use his injured hand. Tara smiled inwardly at that, knowing she had struck a blow for the little people against the giants of this world.

Soon after the horrible man had placed his filthy hands over her mouth, she knew exactly what to do and waited for the best opportunity. She bit down hard on the disgusting hand, even though the taste of it made her want to vomit. Her daddy had explained how jaw pressure is of no small consequence when it comes to a person of any age. The amount of pressure a set of jaws can bring to bear can cause great pain and hardship to the recipient, which might even bring about an escape from a large man's clutches. Tara was profoundly disappointed that she did not achieve that goal when she lunched on the man's hand. That she witnessed his discomfort repeatedly as he drove buoyed her spirits immensely.

Intermittent flashes of her father's mind came to her as they drove on. She knew she was never truly alone anymore, not since the event on the island where she had lost her biological parents. The strange and mystifying occurrences on that island still played a part in uniting her and her new father. The enhanced mindsets allowed them an exclusive communication that was intensely gratifying for the young girl. It was not crystal clear by any means, but often enough it was a tangible picture or a simple idea planted in her head by her new father.

She shared some of his memories that came to her in fits and starts. The kaleidoscope of confusing images and emotions bombarded her at times when her father was experiencing distress or injury. Once was the time her daddy fought the man sitting in the driver's seat of the powerful car throttling up the highway with a burbling V8, making short work of the distance and gradient of the mountainous range. The final moment of that engagement became so clear in Tara's mind that she almost laughed when she first saw it. She had to control herself, for she felt she may have given away her dead-possum routine when she saw the man reacting to her movement and sound.

The plan she formulated was derived purely from that piece of worthwhile information. Tara belied her limited years in her courage and intelligence, a fact that did not escape her father's scrutiny. In the short time spent in her new parents' company, she had blossomed with the love and attention lavished upon her. Her previous parents had barely tolerated her existence. Shuffled off to endless camps and other venues as a convenient means of child-minding, Tara had led a sad and lonely life until she met Arlon and Clarice.

The bond she felt was instant and reciprocal. The previous year had been the happiest of her life. Her new parents always found time for her for any reason at all, even for an arbitrary hug or a smooch on the cheek. However, it was Arlon to whom she was drawn, heart and soul. The bond they shared was cemented long before the aberration that allowed them to share thoughts. The events on the island where her life was saved altered her father's mind and hers to a degree. Though far less pronounced than at first, it nevertheless remained, connecting the pair across the ether.

The profound connection they shared enabled them to communicate on a deeper level than either thought possible. When Tara saw into Arlon's mind and found the unconditional love therein, she realised for the first time in her life that she mattered, that she had a purpose and that she was appreciated for exactly the person she was, warts and all. What Arlon lacked in outward emotions, he more than made up for in his unwitting revelations while they explored each other's minds.

She knew instantly about the troubles his condition had caused as he grew. Without seeing it in chronological order, she understood the torment he suffered during his troubled childhood. She wanted to cry for him and protect the young boy she saw with all her little heart. She had been the victim of neglect and verbal abuse by her parents, so she empathised immediately with the odd man who loved her in his special way.

Clarice showered her with enough physical affection and demonstrative love to make up for what Arlon was incapable of displaying. In Clarice, Tara saw a mother any girl would dream of, and made sure her love was reciprocated in full. Tara did her very best to ensure she followed the basic rules of the house, of the...family. She always did her meagre chores on time and thoroughly to prevent the least disappointment. She made sure her homework was attended to every afternoon, revelling in the attention she received by way of assistance from her new mum.

She needn't have been worried. Clarice adored her adopted child and would never have thought to punish her for perceived neglect of the family rules. Chores and schoolwork were a form of disciplining a child to the rigours of adulthood, to instil good habits. They were never meant to be such hard and fast rules as to deserve punishment if a child forgot or simply had too much fun with friends to think of it. In Clarice's mind, childhood was meant for happiness and contentment. The rest would come at its own pace. Punishment in the form of admonishment only, and delivered in a kind and understanding tone, was reserved for the harsher infractions where her safety was concerned, such as crossing the road without looking both ways.

Clarice and Arlon also enjoyed their first year with their loving daughter, diligently ensuring that her health and happiness were paramount and that her education was the best their meagre funds could provide. Some of Tara's impressive inheritance had been utilised to pay for a private school; however, the balance would become available only on her eighteenth birthday. Arlon had ensured that Tara chose subjects that would enable her to responsibly manage her inheritance when it came into her possession.

Clarice had objected, claiming that a child in primary school should not be choosing dry economic subjects. She needn't have been concerned: Tara took to the specialised curriculum with verve. Tara not only hoped to please in everything she did, but she openly enjoyed her lessons in whichever subjects Arlon recommended. Anything he suggested she took to with great enthusiasm, knowing he had her best interests at heart.

When the holidays drew near, Tara measured how her new parents would treat her. She hoped beyond hope that they would not send her away to some camp or other to avoid being with her. She didn't honestly believe they would, but her former experiences had her fearing it, just the same. She was intensely gratified when Clarice mentioned that she and Tara would accompany Arlon on his new assignment. Although the few days spent at the wonderful lakeside setting proved to be rich and invigorating, and she enjoyed her time with Clarice immensely, she missed Arlon's company terribly.

It was for that reason that Tara rested quietly, feigning unconsciousness or sleep in the front bucket seat of the luxury vehicle, roaring around the sharp bends. With their innate connection, Tara sensed she was headed in Arlon's general direction. Intuition decreed that the horrible, smelly man in the driver's seat was somehow connected with Arlon's whereabouts. However, that sixth sense also warned her of the clear danger she faced from the huge man. A sudden and painful blow across her face confirmed that fact.

"Don't ya be tryin' ta deceive me, ya little bitch. I know yiz awake," grumbled Colin Cabbage, as he shifted about on his seat once more.

Stinging from the brutal backhand, Tara opened her eyes to glare at the evil man. Only his face could be seen in the shine from the bright headlights and the dim glow of the dash. He had a mean snarl on his features and foul breath exploding from his rotten mouth.

"Pretty little thing like yiz will come around soon enough, eh? Once I get that old man of yiz outta the way," said Colin, in a disturbingly disgusting manner.

Tara wasn't sure what the man meant by the comment, but she

knew it was a bad thing from the smirk on his face.

"My daddy is going to kill you dead!" spat Tara defiantly.

"That mongrel bastard is already dead, bitch. Only he don't know it yet. Yiz me bait and that idiot will just about do anything for yiz, won't he? It's him what'll be dead and then I'll have ya to meself and I'll teach ya a few lessons about life, ya little shit. Say that again about killin' me and I'll give ya another beltin' that won't be so soft next time."

After a moment to digest his words, Tara asked, "Why do you want to hurt me and my daddy?"

"Because he killed my daughter, that's why. We Cabbages repay our debts."

"Cabbages?" asked Tara, giggling involuntarily.

"What's so funny?"

"Vegetables paying debts," said Tara innocently.

"If ya don't want another smack in the gob, ya better pay some respect. My family name is Cabbage and we're right proud of it, so careful how ya speak."

"Your name is Cabbage? What's your first name?"

"Why ya wanna know?"

"Do I just call you Cabbage, then?"

"Smart-arse! It's bloody Colin Cabbage and watch ya mouth."

"I can't."

"Can't what?"

"Watch my mouth; it's impossible unless I have a mirror."

Colin went to slap her hard again, but Tara was ready for the blow, just as Arlon had taught her. She easily ducked under and deflected the swinging left arm of Colin Cabbage with her left arm, while bringing her right arm up quickly, making a fist that came smashing down into Colin's groin exactly where she knew he would feel it the worst, especially as her father had previously tenderised the area so expertly.

Colin screamed in agony and collapsed forward with the explosive torture to his delicate groin. His head hit the steering wheel and his foot pressed harder on the accelerator. The powerful V8 motor sprang forward with invigorated life toward a sharp hairpin turn in the highway. Almost crumpled inward, Colin Cabbage was barely able to keep himself breathing for the sheer agony in his crotch. His balls felt as though they were about to explode. The car bucked beneath him and, all too late, he raised his head to view the road.

Which was no longer there!

The car tore off the road at breakneck speed, straight into the treetops, with the forest floor many metres below street level. The soft treetops did little to expend the forward momentum of the speeding metal juggernaut, until gravity took over to send the vehicle plummeting. The car nosedived through the trees with a squeal of the motor as it revved way beyond the red line. Then it died as the sudden impact with the soil drove the motor through the firewall into the passenger cabin, where it ticked loudly. The sharp tang of petrol invaded the confined area. Tara, and the large man next to her, moaning pitifully, were soon covered in oil and fuel.

Tara found her legs trapped within the foot well, with the glove box hard against her legs, pinning her to the seat. The passenger-side airbag had deployed, and the only reason she remained unhurt was that she was too short to have received the full brunt of it.

Colin Cabbage was not so fortunate. His face had copped the full concussive blast of the safety device from the front and side, rendering his nose a bloody pulp, and his right ear rang loudly. In a couple of days, he would sport a pair of magnificent black eyes, making him look as though he had gone a few rounds with a pissed-off Mike Tyson. He would compare with any pugilist who had fought one too many fights during a long career in the ring.

Tara could hear him moaning. The collapsible steering wheel shaft had failed to activate as part of the car's safety features, causing the wheel to press hard against the man's sternum, making breathing difficult. The petrol fumes within the car made both their eyes sting. A portion of the engine block that had torn through the firewall into the car's interior, was burning Tara's leg and she could do little to prevent it. Although barely touching her skin, it nevertheless caused her to call for help and cry from the intense pain. She called for her daddy, for Arlon. Out loud, and in her mind, she beseeched him to come and help her. Her desperate pleas caused the man beside her to chortle and choke on the phlegm and blood from his busted nose.

Tara watched with growing fear as the man managed to reach into his pocket to withdraw a mobile phone. As he was unable to talk clearly through busted lips, he texted someone. Tara was very worried about the use of the mobile phone so close to petrol and fumes. She had seen the warning signs all too often at the petrol stations, warning about the dangers of naked flames or mobile phones anywhere near the bowsers while the fuel was being pumped into the vehicles.

CHAPTER SEVENTEEN

Fire!

The single thought and the gruesome images flooded Arlon's brain with a manic urgency that filled him with dread. He stumbled awkwardly, landing sideways on his injured ankle on the steep and slippery slope. The pain tore through his leg like wildfire, making him cry out suddenly in the deathly silence. The fog had drifted in as they ascended slowly up the central gorge to the top of the ridge.

Betty swirled about at the sudden noise and disturbance behind her. She had felt his emotional pain and the associated images of fire only seconds before the sharp cry of agony escaped the strange man behind her. Hildy had implanted a connection with the man in her mind, and she was unable to rid herself of the troubling mental highway on which they both travelled. She saw flashes of a sweet face in the flames, crying out desperately for help. Betty correctly assumed that the face belonged to Arlon's daughter. She was about to communicate an important piece of knowledge with the man immediately before he slipped, inflaming his injuries further.

His sudden cry of pain in the middle of the silence also meant he may have given away their position, or, at the very least, alerted the enemy to the fact that someone had escaped the cottage. Betty prayed that the sound had not carried to the youths at the bottom of the property.

Her prayer went unanswered, for she could detect excited shouts coming from the direction of the chicken coop. Apparently, the young men had been cunning enough to send someone to guard that exit. That young man was now shouting out to the others that he had heard someone farther up the ravine. This elicited a swift response from the others, who were soon heard whooping and hollering their war cry as they raced around the clearing to the rear.

Betty worried that they had not managed to gain sufficient distance to outrun the pursuing party. However, Arlon was in no condition to continue immediately. She urged him to rest on a nearby log while she placed her hands either side of his head.

Arlon felt the familiar brush against his mind, sensing the machinations of the new force binding with his, enhancing and strengthening it until the combination managed the pain. He felt the physical debilitation receding as he pushed himself to concentrate on the task, accepting the assistance of the other mind in correlation with his. It still felt bloody weird to the man who relied so heavily on all things 'normal'. It was a surreal experience for Arlon as the gentle tendrils of foreign thought pulsed along his neural pathways as if they were his own.

The pain subsided until it barely existed. Arlon felt invigorated once more, sufficiently to continue with some urgency, for they were alerted to the sound of hoof beats, the sturdy and methodical thumps of the sure-footed Clydesdale owned by the Cabbage family, making its way up the ravine behind them. Unbeknownst to Arlon, the pursuing party was being hindered and distracted by any number of forest dwellers, including the more unlikely creatures such as snakes and spiders, falling upon the hapless youths.

In silence, Arlon and Betty resumed their upward journey to the top of the ridge, where they would almost double back on themselves along the crest, where the forest growth was sparsest. Arlon felt nothing of the debilitating pain or the weakness he experienced before. He could still sense Betty in his mind, despite all his efforts to dispel her. Fiercely independent, Arlon loathed needing to rely on others for anything. He knew he had to work on that aspect of his personality for the sake of his wife and child, but for the moment he yearned to fly solo once more.

"It isn't me wishing to stay in there, Mr Grey. It's Hildy pushing me. She is a very strong lady. At least her mind. I can't resist her and neither should you. We are only trying to help," explained Betty breathlessly, as the gradient became an almost vertical slope.

Though the steep slope taxed their energy, it had the benefit of being nearly impossible for the horse to negotiate. It would slow down their pursuers considerably, as they would have to dismount and follow on foot. Betty hoped the young men would give up rather than exert themselves. As the ridgeline would be descending to a degree, the going would be easier for Arlon and herself, allowing them to gain some valuable distance.

"So, she's okay, then?" asked Arlon after a long while.

"That remains to be seen. Her mind is strong, the rest...?"

The unfinished sentence hung ponderously in the swirling mists. Arlon did not wish harm to anyone, especially on his account. He couldn't feel bad about it and sometimes wished he could, just for a moment or two. He was always classified as such a cold bastard by pretty much everyone he encountered. It took too long to explain himself when meeting someone new and generally they didn't believe him, anyway. His condition was, if anything, mentally exhausting.

When they ascended the ridgeline, the fog remained below. Though still dark, the moonlight provided enough of a glow to navigate the larger obstacles. Ahead of them at ground level, Arlon witnessed the amber eyes intermittently peering back at them, guiding them on their journey. Arlon could not make out the shape of the creature belonging to the haunting eyes. It could have been a dingo, a domestic dog, a fox or something similar. He had no idea.

Despite himself, Arlon became intrigued with the identity of their unseen scout. He could not for the life of him decide on its origins, nor could he imagine why it would be considered a miracle. A miracle, perhaps, in the fact that a wild or semi-wild creature was aiding them in their quest? Though very odd, it was not particularly miraculous, in Arlon's opinion. Just as he was about to ask a question...

"Needn't bother asking. I don't know and I don't want to know until Hildy decides to tell me," said Betty brusquely.

"Why the secrecy? If she's going to show us anyway...?"

"Men! Never satisfied that someone is helping them or respecting the wishes of those kind folk. No, they always have to ask questions, even if it's not in their best interest. You'll know when it's time, Mr Grey, and you'll not be hearing anything from me to the contrary. Even if I knew, I wouldn't say. It isn't my place. We are all risking our lives for you and now your daughter as well. You had best come to terms with that and stop trying to fight us along the way, Mr Grey."

"Just asking," said Arlon after a moment.

"Well, stop asking. Stop talking. Our voices carry easily from up here. I don't suppose that lot back there is actually up to following us, but you never know. We have quite a way to go and we should save our energy for the task at hand and for monitoring your injuries, shoring up your resistance to the pain. So, allow Hildy and me in and stop trying to handle it yourself," Betty demanded.

Betty had changed from the woman he had first met. Arlon imagined it had much to do with what had occurred to her simultaneously with him while under the old woman's scrutiny. She was no longer the mousy little creature with the weight of the world upon her shoulders. Her back was straight, her eyes clear, and her thoughts exuded strength and confidence where previously they were an insecure, depressive mush. The forceful tones she adopted when she spoke lately belied her slight frame and his initial impression of her.

Arlon surmised that she would make a worthy successor for whatever secret the forest folk kept. He had felt the old woman's energy waning as she withdrew. His intimate bond had allowed him to feel the weakness in her ancient heart and other organs. She had lived well beyond her slated years, waiting until the prospect of a successor had made itself known to her. Arlon sensed the slow withdrawal of her urgency, of her diminishing attempts to remain strong in her duties.

Arlon felt certain that Betty was also aware of that fact and thought it was the reason for her brusque demeanour; projecting some of the blame for Hildy's deterioration onto Arlon.

Behind them, in the eerie mists covering the mountainside, Arlon heard the distinctive clip, clop of large horse hooves over the stony ground on the top of the ridge they passed earlier. Evidently, the sheer gradient did not thwart the advance of their pursuers as Betty had hoped. Not that she mentioned that out loud. It came to him through her thoughts, which he was able to read with reasonable clarity, though quite how that worked, he couldn't be sure. Once again he surmised it was the result of the two-way sharing he'd experienced with Hilda Haggerty.

Without so much as a word spoken, he and Betty increased their pace. Arlon was aware of the pair of soulful eyes peering at them periodically from the darkness ahead. It was frustrating for Arlon to place his faith in others around him, much less some mysterious animal guided by a witch-woman! It was all too absurd for him, despite all evidence to the contrary. His logic simply refused to accept the facts as they presented themselves. He clung to his logical, scientific truths as passionately as others held to the words of their faith.

"You are a very stubborn man, Mr Grey, to your detriment. Without that animal in front of us, I would not have been able to guide us through this quickly enough to avoid those youngsters behind us," said Betty breathlessly.

"I didn't say anything."

"You didn't have to."

Arlon felt a breath of wind whispering past his cheek as he walked. A resulting thud in the trunk of the tree beside him caused him to halt. Reaching out blindly toward the place where he had heard the sound, he was shocked to discover the shaft of a crossbow bolt still quivering from being launched from the weapon. Arlon thought their attackers were armed with rifles or pistols; he hadn't suspected a crossbow or archer's bow.

"Betty, they're shooting arrows at us."

"Down!" she commanded. "That's Elmo. He's an expert

marksman with that crossbow of his, same as his old man, Colin. They rely heavily on silence when dealing with strangers and the like around their land. I didn't think the horse would make it up here. I was wrong. Howl!" she commanded.

"What?"

"Howl, like a dog or a wolf might. Howl, Mr Grey."

"You can't be..."

But she was serious. She began to howl just like an old bloodhound or wolf. From the darkness around them came a chorus of other howls joining in, until the forest was alive with the sound. Ahead of them, the glowing eyes reared up and down as that creature also let out a hair-raising yowl. Other animal sounds joined the fray, confusing and alarming the horse behind them. They heard a yelp from a human, followed by a desperate whinny from the startled horse as it reared suddenly, dislodging its rider.

The thump of a heavy body hitting the earth alerted Betty and Arlon to the fact that Elmo had been thrown from the spooked horse, which was now galloping away blindly through the darkness. Unless some miracle intervened, the Clydesdale was doomed to perish on its mad dash down the mountainside. The disturbing commotion distracted the pursuers long enough to allow Arlon and Betty to make their escape.

They ran as fast as they could, jinking this way and that at the last possible moment to avoid tree trunks and other obstacles in their path. Here, a large boulder appeared suddenly through the mist. There, a large tree fern obscured the path and the eyes of their guide, always just ahead. Arlon's coat began to weigh heavily upon his slim frame as it became soaked from brushing against the wet leaves and fernery. The descent from the ridge became a precipitous procedure requiring all their skill and stamina. Betty instigated a treacherous pace that Arlon found difficult to match, with his injuries playing a part.

Behind them, they heard the blundering pursuit by the oafish youths, steamrolling their way through the foliage with foolish abandon. Someone was going to get hurt badly this night, and the fleeing pair hoped desperately that it would not be either of them. The nightmarish run took them to the bottom of the ridge, where it met with the forestry road soon after.

The youths were gaining ground. Arlon could hear the laboured breathing and heavy footfalls getting closer by the moment. His injured leg was slowing them down. While the pain threshold was being managed, the nature of the injury did not lend itself to running for any length of time. Arlon was amazed at Betty Payne's resilience and stamina. She kept up a pace that Arlon would have had difficulty maintaining when in the best of health and physical condition.

Once they hit the road the going became somewhat easier, though they knew Elmo and his friend would soon be on them if they didn't hurry. The pain in Arlon's injured foot returned with a vengeance. He collapsed on the roadside, clutching his bleeding ankle where the vicious steel jaws of the animal trap had pierced down to the bone. He could go no further and refused Betty's efforts to work with him in an attempt to stifle the pain once more.

Arlon had had enough of running, enough of hiding, enough of everything. He rose from the road unsteadily, biting down on the ferocious agony working its way through his system.

"What - are - you - going - to - do?" asked Betty through great heaving gasps.

"Stand my ground. This has gone on for long enough," replied Arlon, once his breath had steadied.

"They have weapons. What can you hope to do against those?"

"Live or die. Makes no difference. I can't run anymore. You'd better go before they get here."

Arlon faced the way they'd come without waiting to see what Betty would do. She would either leave or stay. He didn't care. It was time to end the race if he was to have any chance at all of saving his daughter. Running away was not part of his DNA, never had been. He'd been allowing others to dictate his movements for him, which had to cease immediately. His instincts had never been wrong in the past and he trusted them now, more than he trusted the argumentative voices in his head.

Enough of eyes in the dark, bloody running around through pitch-black forests, depending on goodness knows what to guide thcm. Enough of tunnels and goofy sessions with old ladies in run-down shacks. Enough of feeling helpless and foolish by allowing himself to believe the weird nonsense these forest folk dreamed up. There were some things he couldn't yet explain, but that didn't mean there was anything metaphysical about it. He would find the answers eventually.

Arlon forced everything and everyone out of his mind. He'd had that up to his eyeballs and wanted nothing more of the interference he felt up there. He banished the lot from his mind, concentrating on the matter at hand. That was something he knew about in great detail, something he'd been trained to deal with for most of his life. Physical conflict was something he felt confident about. At least he knew he stood some semblance of a chance if he faced a real opponent. If he relied on all the airy-fairy nonsense he'd been asked to swallow, he was as good as a dead man and would not be able to help his daughter.

He was oddly calm and accepting of whatever fate had in store for him. He concentrated all his energies on the forthcoming conflict against an unknown number of assailants. He hoped there were just the two, Elmo Cabbage and his mate. He knew they had at least one weapon that shot short arrows. He guessed it might be a crossbow, though he couldn't know for sure. They could have a gun as well, but that didn't matter to him. He was beyond caring about what might happen. It was time to end it one way or the other.

From the darkness came a thudding sound as a heavy person lumbered into view in the dim moonlight. The fog had dispersed a little, allowing the area to shimmer ethereally. Arlon recognised the dull boy as Elmo soon enough. He couldn't see any sign of anyone else.

"Ya shouldn't-a stopped, old man, ya dead meat now," sputtered

Elmo through the heavy panting, holding his loaded crossbow steadily aimed at Arlon.

"You shouldn't have left your friend behind. You might have stood a chance with two of you," said Arlon, in a voice devoid of emotion.

"He-he'll be here soon enough, mate. Won't need him, though."

"Oh? Why's that?"

"Coz I have a weapon, ya dumb bastard. Whadda ya, blind?"

"I see the crossbow, Elmo."

"See where it's aimed?"

"Naturally."

"Well?"

"Well, what? I've trained with crossbows."

"Didn't ask if ya knew how ta use one, ya dumb shit. I said I have a weapon and yiz don't. Game over right there."

"You think?"

"Jeez, ya got some balls, I'll give ya that. Matter of fact, that might be where me second shot'll go. Pay ya back for what ya done ta me dad and mum."

"You going to talk all night or shoot the weapon?"

"Ya coming back wif me and..."

"Not happening, Elmo. I'm not going anywhere with you or anyone else. I have to get to my daughter because your dumb-arse father pranged his car with my girl in it. Don't know how *he's* doing, but my daughter is in danger, maybe injured, maybe dealing with fire. I don't know exactly."

"Bullshit! Daddy gone ta get them two and he's on his way back wif em," stated Elmo uncertainly.

"You were expecting them back ages ago, Elmo. They didn't show up, did they? There's been a smash."

"How would ya know if there was a smash, anyway?"

"I'm not getting drawn into that right now. Make your move, Elmo, I'm getting impatient."

Elmo looked about him with concern. "Where's that woman

what was wif ya?"

"Told her to go back. Where's your mate?"

"He run outta breath way back. Don't matter. Like I said, I got a weapon and yiz don't."

"I don't need a weapon, shit-for-brains."

"I'm warnin' yiz..."

"Fire, damn you!" whispered Arlon, in the most contrived malevolence he was able to produce.

"I will..."

"Now! Fire the bloody weapon, you coward."

Elmo fired off a nervous shot directly at Arlon's head.

Utilising his untold hours of training, Arlon captured the quarrel between his hands, only centimetres to the side of his head. In the wink of an eye, Arlon whipped the projectile back at Elmo before the moron had the chance to insert another into the crossbow. The sharp tip embedded itself in Elmo's shoulder. The boy cried out in stunned alarm and pain, dropping the crossbow. Arlon stepped forward gingerly to pick it up. He tossed it casually into the thick fernery at the side of the road.

Elmo slunk to the ground, cradling his shoulder and whimpering pitifully. Arlon stepped over to him.

"H-h-how'd ya do that?" Elmo asked in wide-eyed awe.

"I told you, I've trained with crossbows."

"Thought ya meant ya fired 'em at targets and that."

"That's what I wanted you to believe. I've had arrows and quarrels fired at me for years as part of my training. Of course, they always had blunted ends in case I missed. Hurt like hell just the same, though. Nothing teaches you to learn faster than pain. Can't tell you the number of times I went home with some nasty bruises and even blood. How are they tipped?"

"Huh?"

"Your quarrels, do they have field points or broadheads?"

"I..." Elmo didn't get to finish as Arlon snatched the protruding end of the quarrel and withdrew it before Elmo knew what was happening.

"Here's what's going to happen now," said Arlon, once Elmo had stopped screaming. "I'm going to continue to my car and you're coming with me. After we get to my daughter and see to her needs, I am going to take you, my daughter, and possibly your father, to the hospital in Healesville. I need to explain something to you on the way. Betty will take care of your wound until we get there. Understand?"

"Bullshit..."

Arlon pressed his rubber-booted foot on the wound until Elmo gasped. "I'm not arguing with you or giving you a choice. Get up and walk ahead of me back to my car, or you'll wish I'd thrown that thing straight into your heart. Betty, can you come back now, please? We need to get a move on," cried Arlon to the forest.

The dense fog was wafting back in through the forest, cutting down the amount of light coming from the moon. Only when Arlon felt a hand touch his elbow did he realise that Betty had materialised at his side. Allowing her to guide them, Arlon and Elmo followed close behind as they travelled the distance to Arlon's vehicle. Arlon retrieved the spare key from its hiding place; he hoped that everything was in working order.

Betty ushered the large boy into the rear seat, where she attended to his wounds with a first-aid kit supplied by Arlon. The car started immediately and soon had the interior warming them, as Arlon reversed the car along the narrow side track where he'd left it a lifetime ago. So much had happened he'd lost track of the days.

CHAPTER EIGHTEEN

"Bullshit!" exclaimed Elmo. "No way that's true. Dad said..."

"Your dad didn't know. He was fooled by your grandfather. This feud has been of your own doing for all these years. Roman Cabbage removed his son's eyeball as payment for the trespassing accusations. Roman despised his disadvantaged son, Cory. His wife had to intervene on many occasions when it seemed he was going to follow through with his threats to end the lad's life. When Roman was presented with the perfect opportunity to finally do something about his retarded son, he wasted no time in doing so. Jason Haggerty was appalled by the event and played no part in the actual removal of the eye, despite casually mentioning an eye for an eye by way of recompense for the trespass."

"Nuh-uh. No way ya could know that. Ya wasn't there. None-o-yiz were."

"Well, that much is true. We weren't there. Jason Haggerty was there and he relayed what he knew to his daughter, Hilda. You know she has...special...qualities?"

"Bloody witch!"

"Her father carried the guilt of Roman's actions with him his entire life. He never recovered from the shame and disgust he felt, according to his daughter."

"Nah, ya wrong, mate. We been findin' bodies without eyes in the forest for a long time. That bloke...Jason been doing it ever since the run-in with me gramps," said Elmo, after taking a while to think about what was being said.

"The eyes...are taken posthumously," declared Arlon.

"Huh?"

"After they died in your traps."

"Why?"

"Hmm, not entirely clear on that point myself. It seems the eyeballs are fed to some..."

"STOP!" cried Betty.

Arlon hit the brake pedal hard, causing the Prado to veer treacherously close to the precipice off the dirt track. The skidding vehicle came to a halt with its passenger-side tyres halfway over the lip.

"What? What is it?" asked Arlon with eyes wide.

"You can't tell him," warned Betty, sitting beside Elmo in the rear seat.

Arlon turned in his seat to face the woman with a glare that could turn her into a pillar of salt.

"Are you insane?" he asked. "You risk all our lives by shouting 'stop' while we're travelling on a slippery dirt road in the mountains, and all you mean is that I should stop talking to protect your ridiculous secret?"

To Elmo, he said: "I can see now why you're keeping the feud going. I would be, too, with such insanity going on. You're all as bad as one another, you know that? I think you should have a fully-armed conflict to eliminate your kind once and for all. Now, I want you to listen very carefully, Mrs Payne. You are in my car and my rules apply. I will discuss anything I choose in here and you are free to step out any time you feel the urge."

Arlon waited until the nuisance of a woman made up her mind to stay or leave. Finding a contrite understanding in her eyes to remain in the car, Arlon turned back to concentrate on the road once more. The thickening fog made the going treacherous enough without having orders barked at him from the rear-seat driver. While he realised his attempt at ending the feud was feeble at best, he thought it deserved a chance if he could explain a few truths to the boy. Unfortunately, Arlon also understood that the boy could not influence the man who controlled the Cabbage household.

Arlon turned his mind back to the pressing problem of finding his daughter. If Colin Cabbage had done anything to harm Tara,

Arlon determined that the man would no longer be using up earth's good air once he caught up with him. Arlon had never before felt the urge to inflict harm on anyone, despite being capable of doing so and having done so on numerous occasions when he could do nothing to prevent it. What he felt towards Colin Cabbage was vastly different from the defence mechanisms employed in his past. He wanted to inflict all manner of hurts upon the man who harmed his child. He saw a grisly end to the man in his mind, brought about by Arlon's hand. He saw rage. He saw brutality and revenge. These were alien concepts in Arlon's history.

It seemed that whatever had changed Arlon during his last assignment had the capability of fuelling the darker side of human emotions as well as the more positive aspects. In the dimness of the car's interior, Arlon's cobalt-blue eyes began to emanate a sinister glow. The other occupants, each caught up in their particular thoughts, were unaware of the mysterious illuminations...until they both became aware of the increasing speed.

"Don't you think you should slow down a little, Mr Grey?"

Betty's question was greeted with total silence. She blinked with concern at the fern fronds whipping by as the Toyota Prado careened along the rough track at breakneck speed. The fishtailing rear end of the heavy vehicle threatened to push them over the edge, as the speed increased and the high-pitched revs screamed the engine's protest. Hairpin turns and switchbacks appeared out of the wall of thick fog, while the occupants of the car were pitched from side to side. The driver encountered and manoeuvred the vehicle around each bend with the precision of a well-trained rally driver, yet Elmo and Betty were screaming in panic.

No amount of pleading reached the maniacal driver as the vehicle plunged headlong through the wall of fog with no indication that the driver was aware of the road beyond the bonnet of the car. The glare from the headlights bouncing off the curtain of fog reflected onto the occupants of the vehicle, clearly illuminating the horror and panic on the faces in the rear seat. Just when they believed it could not get any worse...

The lights went out.

The ride through hell continued without any form of lighting. Without it, the bouncing, bashing, bruising ride seemed to escalate in severity. Betty and Elmo clung to each other for dear life, despite their animosity. Elmo's injury opened anew, and an outpouring of blood soaked his shirt.

Through the panic and the insane jostling, Betty somehow managed to connect with Hilda Haggerty. Together they tried to locate Arlon within their minds. Together they were appalled at what they found. Arlon was not himself. His mind was being overcome by a malevolence. From a starting point of no emotions, through an incident of overwhelming love, came the opposite. Arlon was unable to cope with the hatred, the sensations of rage and revenge boiling up inside him for his enemies: the enemies hurting his girl.

Arlon, what you saw was only one possibility, not an absolute. You pictured your girl dying, burning alive in that overturned vehicle, but it isn't a given. You have the sight of what may be as well as what is. You need to calm yourself and examine your mind to find the present. Find your girl, find Tara, in your mind in the here and now. You must determine her present condition before you accept a fate you have seen for her. More lives are at stake than hers alone. Please, Mr Grey, please...

Suddenly the car slowed, and Arlon broke from the single destructive thought consuming him long enough to take note of his surroundings. He turned the fog lamps on once more and slowed the vehicle to a suitable speed for such treacherous terrain. The eerie bluish glow emanating from his eyes faded.

"What the fuck ya doin', ya maniac?" screamed Elmo, when he finally found his voice.

"Are you two all right back there?" asked Arlon quietly.

"Lemme outa here," cried Elmo.

"You need that wound looked at by a professional," replied

Arlon, in an annoyingly calm tone as if nothing had transpired out of the normal.

"No point in turning up at the hospital dead, ya whacko!"

"Hmm, are you dead?"

"Are you all right, Mr Grey?" asked Betty, who appeared pale.

"Fine."

"What happened?"

"Not entirely sure. Thought you might be able to supply some sort of an explanation," said Arlon.

"Hildy and I managed to see some of it. Seems whatever you experienced on your last assignment has some lingering effects. You're experiencing emotions for which you're ill-equipped, especially the darker side. Most humans learn to deal with emotions throughout a lifetime, whereas you are dealing with them suddenly and unsuccessfully. You were allowing your rage to rule you. I picked up something else, though. Something seemed to be driving those raw emotions, fuelling and intensifying them. I must say that I wasn't able to stay there long. It was devastating, paralysing. If Hildy hadn't been in there with me I doubt I could have escaped the power of it."

"What the fuck are ya talkin' about? Ya both a pair-o-fruitcakes! Get me outta here."

"Elmo, shut up. I will not be responsible for the death of another member of your family," said Arlon, as he brought the vehicle to a halt. He turned in his seat. "Listen, although I can't show it, I feel a heavy burden for what I did to your mother. It's as close to feeling guilt as possible for me. What makes it worse is I knew I could inflict damage by doing what I did. I had other options at my disposal, other options that would not have caused such injury."

"Didn't you say you acted in self-defence?" asked Betty.

"Yes, but it wasn't an excuse. I'm fully trained in the martial arts and didn't need to resort to such measures. Elmo, whichever way this turns out, I'm sorry. It's small comfort when a boy has lost his mother and if I could change it, I would. Now, I've injured you and it seems the wound has opened. That's on me, too. Betty will do what she can to help you stop the bleeding. I, I don't know what came over me just then. I apologise to both of you. I have it under control now and Miss Haggerty is helping with that. As soon as I locate my daughter I will rush you to the hospital, I promise."

"Yiz all witches, then?"

"Enlightenment comes in many forms, Master Cabbage. My knowledge comes from years of reading books. Miss Haggerty has learned different lessons from losing one of her senses. It amounts to the same thing. Years and years of dedicated practice. She has honed her skills to a great degree. We've all felt the benefit of that. She not only had her father explain what happened all those years ago, when he visited your grandfather's farm and received the eyeball, but she also saw the truth of that moment when she looked into his mind many years later. Think about it logically for a moment. Is your father or grandfather the type of man to allow someone to gouge out the eyeball of a family member without a fight? It had to have happened the way she told me.

"Roman Cabbage detested his retarded son, possibly the result of inbreeding. Roman was the son of a related couple, as were his children, and Colin's, when he took his aunt for wife, bringing Irma into the picture. You are the result of a union between a father and his daughter. Your father is your grandfather and Roman is your great-grandfather."

"Nah, ya wrong, mate..."

"Think about it. Why did Irma call Colin, Daddy?" asked Arlon kindly.

"But..."

"You weren't to know. You've only ever known him as your father, and Irma as your mother. Irma is Colin's daughter from his wife, Roman's sister. I'm using the term wife when, in fact, there was probably never an official wedding."

"Does, does that mean I'm gonna be...ya know...retarded?"

"Well, you're not the sharpest pencil in the pack, but you won't be suddenly turning into a drooling imbecile or anything, at least not until you're much, much older."

"Can this wait?" asked Betty with some urgency, after seeing to Elmo's wound. "He's bleeding heavily."

"Hmm, I don't like the look of that. Damn!"

"I don't think we can delay getting him to the hospital," said Betty.

"I-I'm going to try something," said Arlon, vacating the driver's seat.

He walked around the car to the passenger-side rear door. Elmo flinched as it was opened by the strange man.

"Mrs Payne? I want you and Miss Haggerty to remain outside my head for the time being. No matter what you see, you mustn't interfere," explained Arlon, as he stood in the doorway of the vehicle.

"What is it you're going to do?" she asked.

"Yeah, whatcha gonna do?" echoed Elmo, fear etched on his features.

"I need you to be perfectly still, young man. Betty, you've seen what happened to me, yes? On my last assignment?"

"A little."

"Well, I don't want any of that to filter through to either you or Miss Haggerty by being in my head when I attempt to use that...energy. It plays havoc with people's emotions, and you sensitive folks are likely to crumble if you cop a dose of it."

"How are you going to...use it?"

"Not even sure if I *can* harness it yet. Only one way to find out. If I don't try something this boy will exsanguinate."

"Shit, what does that mean? That ex-sandwich-thing?"

"You'll bleed out," answered Arlon.

"Oh."

"Now keep still and shut up so I can concentrate. Whatever happens will be for the good. Understand?"

"No!"

"Good. Betty, take your hands away and remove that temporary dressing."

To his credit, Elmo did become stone-still, mostly through mortal fear. Betty, curious, pushed along the seat towards the other door. Arlon placed his left hand on the site of the bleeding wound and his right hand lightly on top of Elmo's head. Arlon asked Betty to turn off the interior light. He did not wish to drain the battery while the motor was off. He concentrated to reach a state of deep meditation, to gain access to his higher brain functions. Minutes ticked by on the dashboard clock in the darkness of the interior.

Moments turned to timelessness as warmth emanated from his left hand directly into the wound of the lad, whose eyes were as big as saucers from the fear that coursed through him. Inexplicably, at least to the others, Arlon's hand began to emit a soft glow. When he opened his eyes they shone with an eerie blue radiance.

Elmo squirmed slightly as the heat began to pour from the man's hand. The weird shine from the man's eyes, coupled with the searing heat produced by his hand, made Elmo ready to run, screaming, the first chance he got. The heat increased until Elmo felt his flesh was on fire. He muttered in pain, unable to prevent the sounds escaping his lips.

Arlon concentrated all his efforts into the hand above the boy's injury. He could feel the energy flowing from his brain, down his neck and chest, into his left arm and, finally, his hand. He believed he saw through his hand, through the boy's epidermis and musculature, right to the bone. He visualised the repairs that were required. He envisioned the closure of the wound, along with the repairs to the sinews and muscles therein. The harder he concentrated the more energy he released from wherever it resided.

Ghostly tendrils of steam spiralled up from the hand that glowed an angry red. Elmo writhed and whimpered as the heat became almost unbearable. Arlon pushed down hard to limit the amount of disturbance the boy could bring to bear. Elmo shrank back from the glow in Arlon's eyes. He screamed suddenly as the searing heat burned its way through the layers of flesh on his chest.

Betty watched in fascination and awe. She had seen some inexplicable events occurring around Hildy before tonight, but nothing came close to matching the spectacle she was witnessing. Exactly how the man achieved it left her confused. That he seemed to be succeeding was not in doubt, despite the boy's pitiful cries.

Betty did not think much good would come from Arlon's use of the mysterious blue energy. She'd had a taste of it while assisting him earlier. No doubt Hildy had experienced the backwash from being in his head as well. As far as Betty was concerned, it was evil. The horrific foreign ambience of it had her petrified when she encountered it. Betty did not believe Arlon, or anybody, would be able to contain and control the force. She had witnessed the almost demonic possession it had hold of him earlier. That was scary enough without it getting into her head.

Elmo began to relax as the fierce glow abated, the area cooled and the light withdrew from Arlon's eyes. When Arlon pulled his hand away there was no visible sign of the injury, though blood stained the area significantly. Elmo seemed to be in a daze, closing his eyes and drifting into a slumber.

Betty gave an involuntary yelp when she saw the result of Arlon's ministrations. She never would have imagined it possible. She gave him a look of suspicious awe as he unbent himself to step back from the vehicle. He stretched his back to straighten out the kinks. Without a word spoken, Betty watched as he made his way back to the driver's side of the car and drove off.

CHAPTER NINETEEN

"How did you do that?" asked Betty quietly.

"I don't know," answered Arlon.

"How did you *know* you could do it?"

"I didn't."

"Then...?"

"How's our patient?"

"Sleeping it off."

"Good."

"Did you have a hand in that as well?"

"In a roundabout way."

"What does that mean?"

"I think you can figure that out if you want to."

"Not natural...that."

"Oh? You saying faith healing is new and unnatural?"

"That wasn't faith healing."

"What was it then?"

"Evil. The devil's work."

"Now who's being unnatural? Evil? Healing someone's wound is evil? Better not tell doctors that. I don't think they'd appreciate it. As far as that bunkum about the devil, you can keep that for those cult movements you attend and believe in."

"I don't attend any cult meetings..."

"Oh, I thought you said you went to church?"

"That's blasphemous!"

"Only if you buy into the concept of religion. What I did was help a fellow human being with whatever skills I may have, be they learned or inherited. Nothing evil or malicious about it. Did you think we could have made it to the hospital in time to save him?"

"It wasn't you did that. It was..."

"Don't give me some balderdash about demonic possession now, please. There *is* a foreign aspect to me. I'll give you that. It isn't a demon and it isn't even intelligent. It's a form of energy. It diminishes a little every day. I experienced it on my last assignment and it hasn't left me yet. Instead of ignoring or shying from it, as if I should be scared of it, I choose to use it, if at all possible, when it is warranted. I deemed it warrantable a few moments ago to save the life of that boy."

"It took control of you. I saw it."

"True. Hang me by the neck, then, or burn me at the stake, is it? Burn the witch? Maybe drowning? If I drown, I wasn't a witch? Yes, it took control of me for a time. Do anger and rage not get a hold of ordinary people at times? Is there no forgiveness for my momentary lapse?"

"You're making fun of me."

"No. Just pointing out some of the hypocrisy in your beliefs."

"Nobody said it was perfect."

"Oh, but they do. Your priests would have you believe that religion is the only true path to perfection and life everlasting. Of course, you can only ratify or verify that claim by dying, and then it's too late if it isn't true. You'll have wasted all that time praying, kneeling, repenting and confessing. What I experienced, that energy? It comes as close to the spark of life as I think it is possible to get. As close to true creation as any human in history."

"If I hadn't seen what you did with my own eyes I never would have believed it was possible," admitted Betty reluctantly.

"Yet you believe that another person performed all those miracles without ever having witnessed it? Loaves and fishes, walking on water?"

"That's..."

"Not so different. You saw me heal someone, does that make me the son of God?"

"You shouldn't say such things."

"In for a good 'smoting', am I? I wasn't being serious. Even if I had the energy permanently, I still wouldn't be the creator of life as we know it. Researchers create life all the time during their careers. Creating microbes and genetic anomalies to heal and to augment crops, kill insects or malicious weeds. All sorts of creation happening every day. You play a hand in creating variations of chooks, don't you?"

"I only use what God has already created."

"If God created perfection, why are you changing that design? Isn't that blasphemous?"

Betty was about to say something, then hung her head in shame. Arlon did not come to her rescue nor feel the need to shame her further. They fell into mutual silence.

Arlon concentrated on negotiating the steep and treacherous terrain to leave the forest. The dense fog made that more difficult. Arlon was a good driver, a safe driver, he felt. He would not have described himself as being gifted or skilled where driving was concerned, yet he negotiated each turn and twist in the road with unerring precision. With only his fog lamps showing a dismal yellowish glow against the bank of thick fog obscuring the road beyond the bonnet of his vehicle, it was challenging to ascertain how he managed to drive so confidently and expertly.

CHAPTER TWENTY

Betty slowly became aware of the paradox, raising her level of alarm to borderline panic. There should be no way the driver could continue in the pea soup enshrouding the vehicle. The same eerie glow, though greatly subdued, was apparent in Arlon Grey's magnificent blue eyes. She was enthralled and appalled by the image she saw in the rear-view mirror. She had seen that same gleam in his eyes during his demonic lapse only moments ago, when the...thing took control of him. She admitted that this was different. She could feel the calmness as opposed to the manic display earlier. It worried her no less.

Betty peered at her fellow back seat passenger, oblivious to everything that transpired after being miraculously healed. The stench of him was overwhelming in the confines of the vehicle, with the heater cooking up the sweat and stink to a nauseating boil. She couldn't believe she had clutched him only moments ago. She wanted to escape. She wanted surcease from everything that had occurred from the moment her son went missing a year ago. She regretted ever having left the forest in the first place, falling for that...man! That pompous, arrogant, pious man who had managed to capture her heart despite all that she saw was wrong with him.

She wanted out of the forest back then. She was desperate to be away from that confinement. She was losing herself, her identity, her individuality, while she remained trapped in the bloody forest. She'd run across the Cabbages before. She'd been told they had something to do with the demise of her parents, but nothing was ever proven. She had only Hildy's word for that. Her 'special' ability gave her the knowledge of that incident, which she related to Dot. Dot eventually told Betty when she believed she was old enough to bear the truth. She wasn't. Betty told herself she would never be old enough to accept the truth of the incident stoically, unemotionally.

When she looked at the disgusting excuse for humanity that was sprawled over the seat beside her, snoring loudly, with the stench of rot and filth emanating towards her on each foul exhalation, Betty wished she could end his rotten existence and the feud once and for all. Too much blood had been shed over the years, there had been too much hatred and secrecy. If it all came to a head because of her interference, then it was probably past due. Her only regret would be that it seemed Hildy might not be with them much longer. Betty knew that Hildy had been hanging on for only as long as it took to find a suitable successor. Betty had agreed to the proposal with trepidation.

She *did* want to return to the forest; of that she was certain. She'd had quite enough of what the outside world had to offer. She missed the comforting reclusiveness of the forest life, the peace and contentment among the simple folk living there. It surprised her to feel that way after yearning desperately to leave it since the age of ten. Her Aunty Dot and Uncle Alex were wonderful human beings, yet the closeness of the cottage and cloying atmosphere of the forest back then had threatened to overwhelm the young girl, crying out for space and deliverance from banality.

Her one desire since spying a magazine in a doctor's office once had been to create beautiful dresses like the ones she saw therein. The magnificent gowns on the equally glamorous celebrities adorning the pages of that glossy magazine captivated the young, impressionable mind of the girl. With her foot-pedal sewing machine she had made an admirable job of creating her wardrobe for years. But her clothes were nothing like the examples she saw in those few pages, that bible of exquisiteness and sartorial splendour.

Those and many other dreams foundered after falling pregnant to a man who did not regard the creation of anything more than a practical and shapeless frock to be worth the time and effort to produce. Although she loved her bundle of joy when he came along, just like any other mother, she pined for the life she had lost and her unrequited ambitions. She cried for the world denied her artistic contributions to form, style and colour on the elite frames of the gorgeous and famous women who could afford her haute couture.

She had never admitted her deepest desires to anyone but herself. That ingrained and urgent requirement to create was squashed down deep when she married and had a child. She supposed her hobby of raising bantams was a way of creating? A far cry from the illustrious career and magnificent gowns she envisioned in her portfolio, but a pitiful attempt at salvaging that dream, nonetheless.

How she had once loathed all that living in the forest represented. Now, she had inherited and accepted the mantle of responsibility as far as 'the secret' was concerned. The secret was kept by them all, despite not understanding much or knowing the full details. It was a secret worth dying for, Hildy and the others had mentioned on many occasions. Betty wondered if any secret was worth dying for. It didn't make sense to keep perpetuating the infernal feud over a lousy secret.

She pondered what the strange and enigmatic man had told Elmo Cabbage about the origins of the feud. She supposed Hildy had implanted that vision, those memories of her father's, into his head. Could they be taken as the truth, the only truth? Or were there other versions, other variations on that truth, as there were with most things in life. Nothing was ever as cut and dried as people would like them to be. Lawyers and barristers had a field day with the truth in courtrooms across the globe every day, dissecting it, layering it, disguising it and ignoring it as suited their cause.

Betty was tired. She no longer grieved for her son, though she missed him terribly. She was exhausted because of the problematic circumstances surrounding life in the forest, a life she'd agreed to resume. She was weary of the never-ending war taking place there. She was fearful of the outcomes inevitably following this trip with Arlon Grey and Elmo Cabbage. It was bound to result in yet more bloodshed and rage. No one, least of all Elmo, would be able to disseminate the convoluted mess that had begun so long ago, to convince Colin Cabbage that it was all unfounded, that the Cabbages had no right to continue their promise of revenge against the Haggerty family and their friends.

Hatred was endemic of the Cabbage clan. Without it, Betty thought they could well lose all purpose in their miserable lives; such was the strength of their ingrained lust for vengeance. It had driven their existence for so long that any other way would be anathema to them.

The adversity of living in the forest, with that constant threat to their existence by the Cabbage clan, made a very special kind of person. Betty doubted she had the stamina and strength to withstand those conditions for as long as her aunt and uncle or Hilda Haggerty had. As if all that wasn't bad enough, along had come Arlon Grey, with his horrible non-personality and his demonic eyes, fuelling the volatile situation into an all-time lethal climax.

Betty didn't know what to make of him or whatever it was that invaded him. She couldn't bear to peer too closely while she was in his head. Nor could Hildy. It weakened her immensely.

Hildy! It always came back to her, centred on her, emanated from her, into them all. The secret! The eyes! All the stuff about eyes.

However, what Hildy had was acceptable to Betty, after a fashion, explainable, natural and often most helpful. Betty experienced and gained some of what Hildy manifested. It was nothing like that which possessed the man in front of her; Arlon Grey, private detective from the Bizarre and Mysterious Detective Agency. What she witnessed where he was concerned did not seem acceptable or natural in the least. It was frightening and intolerably alien and evil.

"It's not right," she mumbled, loud enough for Arlon to detect sound without the ability to accurately make out what was said.

"Hmm, sorry?"

"Using that...thing," she accused.

"What are you talking about?" asked Arlon, honestly perplexed.

Arlon peered at Betty in the rear-view mirror and saw the worry lines creasing her brow in the muted light within the vehicle. He quickly turned his attention back to the front.

"Using that...that evilness in any form is just...wrong!"

"I still have nothing, not a clue, not a sausage!"

"That power. You're using that thing to drive our way out of here, doing things a body shouldn't be able to do. No way can someone normal see through that out there. And your eyes are shining again, so I know."

"Oh, I see. Without that mystical, 'evil' power I should not be able to navigate through this fog? Is that what you're implying?"

"And the eyes..."

"Yes, shining, you said?"

"Not right."

"No, it wouldn't be in your mind, would it? Only, you aren't being either sensible or logical about it. You aren't questioning anything with an open enough mind to make an accurate assessment. You're judging circumstances based on your indoctrinated and narrow view. Had you the capability of employing your grey matter in methods of your own making, then you might have looked for other explanations to those anomalies. Like the eye shine, for instance. Couldn't possibly be because of the blue screen from the satellite navigation instrument I turned on recently, could it? And the fact that I can see through the fog would have nothing to do with that same instrument accurately producing images of the impending conditions before the car? You know, showing me exactly where the road twists and turns, enabling me to engage those turns with confidence? I can't see through the fog, but a satellite can."

Betty closed her mouth before she could utter a sound in further accusation. She leaned forward to examine the screen in the centre of the dashboard. It did have a soft blue emanation, and the screen showed the road ahead clearly, with the little arrow icon showing the car's position relative to the road. Betty watched silently as a sharp bend appeared on the screen, which Arlon negotiated confidently without the ability to see beyond the bonnet of the vehicle.

What Arlon did not tell Betty was that his use of the instrument did not give them any warning of oncoming traffic or hazards of fallen trees and such blocking the road. His other senses were assisting him in that regard. Not that he would mention it to the woman. Arlon supposed she had a right to be spooked after what she had witnessed earlier. It wouldn't do much good to try and explain anything to her in her present state of mind.

Besides, what he was utilising was not the remnants of the strange energy still lingering in his system. He was using the information bequeathed to him by Hilda Haggerty, who persisted within his mind despite his request for her to discontinue the practice. He sheltered her as best he could from exposure to the energy while she occupied his cerebral temple. He hoped it would not adversely affect her if he failed to maintain that shield.

He observed his passenger shifting in her seat uncomfortably after being put in her place so effectively by him. He'd embarrassed her, he guessed. He didn't care, couldn't care, even if he'd wished. It wasn't callousness. He had never cared about anyone or anything until Clarice and, later, Tara came into his life. Even then, he could feel a sense of caring only when an external force imposed itself on his persona, exposing him to the realms of emotions. It was an area of personal exploration he did not wish to repeat.

Regardless of that, he did feel an urgency, a nearly-panicked impulsion to get to Tara. His daughter needed him and he refused to accept that he was unable to reach her...in time. He saw the flames engulf her in his mind over and over. That, and the thought of Colin Cabbage harming her, drove him to that out-of-control state he had experienced earlier. The overwhelming sensation left him breathless with its intensity. He vowed never to allow it to occur again.

He dreaded what he might find at the end of his search, or how the present assignment would end. There had been an emptiness in the depths of his being before he'd encountered Clarice. That half-filled chalice overflowed when Tara entered his life. He had no desire to evacuate that vessel, no wish to return to that previous state of nothingness. He wasn't able to pluck from his depths the ability to express that information; not as a normal human could. His condition prevented even the presence of alien energy to permanently breach that well of indifference. What he gained was ephemeral and brief. It diminished daily. Soon, it would vanish entirely...he believed.

Tara Blaze-Grey and Clarice Grey had become his world: without them he would find it difficult to continue living. Tara, especially, showed fierce loyalty and dependence on him. An inexplicable love and an unbreakable bond had developed between them. His connection with her was so strong he ached. A physical malaise entered his body when he saw his daughter in the flames. He wasn't able to comprehend a life without her in it. He hoped that Clarice was not involved in any of the troubles he'd seen.

The Toyota Prado snapped out of the thick fog so suddenly that Arlon almost overshot the main highway to careen over the opposite edge. He threw the steering wheel into a tight turn, causing the car to travel for a short distance on two wheels before the remaining tyres thumped heavily to the asphalt. When Arlon managed to bring the vehicle back under control he drifted calmly to the side of the road.

"What now?" asked Betty.

"I have to figure out where to go."

"Could only be in that direction, towards Lake Eildon, surely?" said Betty, pointing in the direction the Prado was facing.

"That would be a logical assumption."

"So?"

"I need to get my bearings. I need to find Tara, up here," said Arlon, pointing to his head.

"Why?"

"There was an accident. That much we know, right?"

"According to Hildy, yes."

"Do you know where they ran off the road? It's night, cloudy, hiding the moon and stars. No way to see where they came off the road unless they left a clear trail, and I don't think we are going to be that lucky. I have to get a fix on her position in my head or we could be driving around aimlessly for the rest of the night."

"Could call the cops," she suggested.

"I lost all credibility with the cops when I brought them to Noel's car, which you and your family disposed of. Thanks for that, by the way."

"It was..."

"Skip it. I need to concentrate, so keep it quiet for a moment."

Arlon relaxed into his seat and closed his eyes. He had parked the vehicle in the small section of highway where there was a reasonable shoulder. He'd used that same section to perform the U-turn several times in his search for the forestry road that led off the highway. He turned off the engine and the lights. Only the screen of the navigation instrument continued to provide any form of illumination within the vehicle until it, too, faded to black.

Without the heater blowing warm air through to the back of the vehicle, the air soon turned cooler. To Betty, the drop in temperature had the benefit of reducing the stench wafting her way from the lad next to her. The absolute darkness was a blessed relief from the cloying atmosphere of the thick fog with the headlights reflected at them, yet she wasn't comfortable with it. She daren't intrude upon Arlon Grey's thoughts to determine the methods he employed in his attempt to locate the girl. She supposed he would not require anything other than what Hildy and she had...she hoped. Unable to resist, she peeked.

She screamed.

CHAPTER TWENTY-ONE

They were too late.

It didn't take very long to reach the exact location where the vehicle had left the road. Arlon saw the glow and smelled the smoke before they turned a bend to discover the path taken by the out-of-control vehicle. A very uncomfortable lump formed in Arlon's throat. It was painfully obvious that the flickering glow was not the beginning of a conflagration, but the aftermath.

Betty watched anxiously as the car approached the scene of the accident. She had seen the grisly images swirling around Arlon Grey's mind, coupled with the acrid taste of the unfamiliar energy within. The power of the emotions behind those thoughts caused her to scream. She was unable to cope with the sudden influx of heightened rawness in those feelings, in the mind of the man who professed to be devoid of such things. It scared her senseless.

Arlon parked the Prado as far to the left as he was able, given the limits of the narrow highway. He turned off the engine and the lights and sat for a moment in the dark, regulating his breathing, steeling himself for the task ahead. He knew he was too late to be of any assistance to the occupants. Unless one or both had been thrown clear during the accident, they would not have survived the inferno. The flames were dying, having consumed everything of a flammable nature within the car.

Instead of rushing headlong down the steep embankment as most grieving fathers would have done, Arlon was astute enough to realise it would only endanger himself and anyone else accompanying him. He didn't like that he could think calmly and logically at such a time. It only proved how callous he must appear to others. Not that he cared how he appeared to others. It bothered *him* that he was unable to express his grief. It bothered him more than he could adequately explain.

With a sigh of resignation, Arlon opened the door to step out into the frigid night air. He crossed the road to the opposite shoulder, peering downwards where the remnants of fire continued burning in the car, which remained relatively vertical, supported by the trunk of the tree into which it had crashed at treetop level. A small area surrounding the vehicle continued to smoulder, though the moistness of the grass and fernery had reduced the ability of the fire to spread.

Betty reached his side. She stared at the pitiful scene helplessly, unsure if she should say something. In the end, she decided that anything she said, no matter how well-meant, would not be appreciated. She did not want to accompany the man down to the crash site. She'd seen enough in his mind without wishing to have the real image burned into her retinas, where they would stay for a lifetime. Just as she set her mind to think it would be near impossible for them to descend, at any rate, the strange man suddenly walked off to the right, along the side of the highway. Before she could ask him what he intended to do, he left the road.

Using the miniature L.E.D. flashlight attached to his key chain, Arlon made his way, haltingly, down the near-vertical gradient. Gravity assisted his passage while he groped for one large tree fern after another to avoid careening out of control to the bottom of the mountain. His heart beat faster than he had ever experienced during the most gruelling of training and exercise regimes he tortured himself with. The leaden heaviness he felt inside made the journey an arduous one.

When Arlon made it to the level of the car wreck, still some twenty-odd metres from the forest floor, he did his best to avoid peering inside the car immediately. He searched the scorched area around the vehicle first, attempting to identify any signs that the passengers had been tossed free, or made it out under their own steam. He saw nothing to increase his confidence. There were no bodies outside the car, alive or otherwise.

Arlon closed his eyes as he reached the front passenger side of the car, where he knelt in readiness to view the interior. He slowly opened his eyes, after depressing the small button on the miniature light. He saw only himself. Edging a little closer, though the beam barely penetrated the car, Arlon was able to see beyond the reflection from the blackened side window.

Empty!

CHAPTER TWENTY-TWO

Arlon was exhausted when he finally regained the road at the top of the steep incline. His injuries were once more bothering him to the point where walking became a painful experience. He had taxed his foot and his arm severely during the struggle to ascend. The slipperiness of the rotting vegetation and the soft soil made progress seem nearly impossible, with Arlon gaining a few precious steps upward, followed by one or two back, until he reached the next solid trunk he could cling to.

"Gone," he said, bent over nearly double when he reached the asphalt, where Betty was waiting anxiously.

"Gone? Gone where?"

Arlon peered at her between laboured breaths as if he couldn't believe what she had asked.

"Sorry, that was probably a stupid question."

"You think?"

"What now?"

"Any ideas?" he asked, while remaining bent over.

"One."

"Surprise me."

"I'm thinking that Colin had someone pick them up. He has one of those satellite phones, I'm told; it doesn't rely on local cell towers. He could have made a call if he survived."

"Any clue as to where they may have been taken?" asked Arlon, as he slowly straightened and regained his even breathing.

"Thinking like a Cabbage and knowing he has your daughter with him..."

"His place?"

"I can't think of anywhere else he might go, unless either one of them is injured enough to warrant medical attention. Wouldn't take them to a hospital, though. Probably a private doctor they keep in their pay."

"Knowing his personality, if that were true, he would order the doctor to come to him at his residence, that filthy hovel in the middle of the bloody forest again. Makes my skin crawl, thinking of my daughter in that cesspool of bacteria. I can't fault your reasoning, though. It makes sense. You know where the turnoff is?"

"Not really, no. An idea of the general vicinity only," admitted Betty.

"In that case, our passenger will have to enlighten us."

"Don't like our chances of that happening. He's still out like a light and not likely to cooperate, anyway."

"I may have to...encourage him a little."

"I won't stand by to see you hurt that boy, Mr Grey. I don't like him very much but he's been through enough already."

"He chased us through the forest on horseback with a crossbow."

"Like I said, I don't like him much. What he is was done to him through that nasty piece of work, his father and grandfather before him. According to Hildy, it all started with that Roman Cabbage, you said? His nastiness has filtered down through the rest of them, but I can't stand by and watch someone, a young man, tortured, no matter who he is."

"Even though your son probably died as a direct result of getting caught in a trap put there by those people, possibly even Elmo Cabbage?"

"Even then," she asserted.

"Well, just as well I had no intention of using physical methods of persuasion, then, isn't it? I am not a person like that, Mrs Payne, like that lot. I didn't heal him only to injure him again at my leisure."

"I can't say that I like the idea of the alternative, if that's the case."

"Are we back to evil again?"

"Shouldn't be using that...whatever it is."

"Oh, I see. Back to hypocrisy again. You and Miss Haggerty are perfectly fine using this mind trick, but everyone else is damned?"

"Miss Hildy doesn't use it for..."

"Oh, spare me the sanctimonious garbage about using power or knowledge for the good of people or the betterment of their lives. Missionaries have been hiding behind that flawed rhetoric for centuries."

"You don't like religion much, do you?"

"Oh, the principle behind all the silliness is okay; be good to each other, don't kill or steal and such. It's all that other rubbish that leaves me shaking my head sometimes. Arcane ceremonies and blessings are given by ordinary men who feel divine guidance instructing them to convert the masses to their way of thinking. Better to give than receive would work if churches did some more giving instead of fleecing the poor of every last cent. Buildings and artworks cost millions of dollars, which could all be better spent by assisting their followers in a more realistic sense. No, I don't have a very high opinion of religion."

"You don't believe in God?" she asked.

"Most certainly not. If we were created, then we, this entire universe, is nothing more than specks of life on a petri dish, and whoever is in charge of that experiment is not going to waste their time by trying to communicate with it or help it, or explain the bloody meaning of life to it. Just as our scientists study bacteria under a microscope every day and have no thoughts about befriending the organisms, granting them wishes or giving them false hopes of an afterlife."

"That is a very sad outlook."

"No, it's a realistic outlook. We live, we die, and what we make of our existence should be made in the present. Now, I have a daughter to find. I didn't create her, but I have every intention of locating her by whatever means necessary. You may stay out here and freeze if you object to my methods. I don't care. I thank you for your assistance in getting me here, even though everything is your fault, to begin with."

"My fault?"

"Oh, not by engaging my agency, no," said Arlon, interpreting the look of consternation on her features. "By lying and then drugging me after I informed you that I had located your son's vehicle, which you then had your friends remove. Everything from that point onwards is directly attributable to you. By trying to maintain this ridiculous secret of yours you have endangered the lives of me and my family. If you try to interfere with me or obstruct me in any manner from here on, I shall leave you in the middle of the forest you love so much and I will inform the media about *everything*," said Arlon, with a look that brooked no argument, as he returned to the car.

Arlon sat in the front of the dark vehicle concentrating, as Betty slipped in behind him. After a moment or two of deathly silence, their other passenger began to stir and mumble. Elmo Cabbage tossed his head from side to side while Betty frowned with worry. Elmo then settled into a calmness, his head gradually nodding rather than shaking. Betty witnessed no signs that the boy was suffering or in any way stressed. It seemed to her that he was simply engaged in a dream.

When Arlon opened his eyes a few moments later, he was satisfied with whatever information he had gleaned from the boy. He started the car to bring the satellite navigation unit to life. He knew the Cabbages normally parked a kilometre or two from the actual house, travelling the last stretch by horse or on foot. He had seen the route taken by Elmo in the boy's mind, and it appeared as though he could accomplish the trek in his car if he engaged the four-wheel-drive option with the lowest gear selected.

"You said you wanted to know where the turnoff is. How are you going to find their house?" she asked.

"I left a transmitter there on my last 'visit'. I won't be able to pick that signal up until I get closer to the location."

Without pausing for a reaction from Betty, Arlon turned on the headlights and flicked on the indicators, ready to return to the highway. The heater took quite some time to warm the interior of the car again. Elmo slowly woke from his induced slumber.

"What? What did yiz do ta me?" he asked in a rising voice.

"Nothing bad. Calm down," ordered Arlon.

Surprisingly, Elmo did as he was told. Betty suspected she knew the reason.

"Where we goin'?"

"To your place."

"Hah! Not gonna find it in a month-o-Sundees."

"I already know where the house is and you just told me how to find the turnoff."

"Bullshit!" he said, with doubt creeping into his voice.

"You talk in your sleep, Master Cabbage."

"No way I tell no one where the road is, even in me sleep. 'Sides, ya can't get up ta the house in this. Ya knew that before."

"Maybe, maybe not. We'll soon find out. The entrance to your private road isn't too far away. I guess your father wasn't headed in that direction with my girl because he wanted to get to the Haggerty residence. After the crash, which he managed to survive somehow, he must have called for help and decided to return to his house, possibly to await medical treatment for himself or my daughter."

"Wouldn't waste no treatment on ya brat."

"He would if he felt he needed her in good health for an exchange. When I offer your life in exchange for my daughter we'll see exactly what he thinks of his son."

"You can't do that. It's not right," argued Betty.

"I thought I'd made it abundantly clear what I expected from you, Mrs Payne. Care to walk?"

Betty remained silent for a time.

"Ya didn't tell me what yiz did," said Elmo sulkily.

"Still bleeding, Master Cabbage? Still feeling pain?"

"It bloody hurt," he groused.

"I imagine so, yet I am also sure it was worth it to survive. You aren't dead, Master Cabbage. That is what I did. I saved your life, which is more than you, your mother or your father would ever do for another human being.

"You are the product of a bad seed, Master Cabbage. By all accounts, Roman Cabbage was just immoral, through and through. I won't say evil, because that has too many religious overtones. Rotten to the core and beyond does not do him justice. I've been inside Hilda Haggerty's head, and, in turn, her father's, who witnessed the atrocity perpetrated by Roman Cabbage. I've heard the screams coming from that room over the garage where Cory Cabbage lived once he was forced from the main residence.

"Possibly the result of an incestuous relationship, Cory was born with mental disabilities. That didn't sit too well with Roman's grandiose opinions of himself and his ideals of perfection. Nobody loved Roman Cabbage more than himself. His wife was nothing more than a breeding chamber for offspring who would carry on the perfection handed down to them by the best of the best, in his mind. Cory fell far short of those expectations. Were it not for the pathetic pleas and seductive enticements from his mother, the child would not have survived to adulthood."

"That's bullshit! No way yiz could know any of this shit," barked Elmo suddenly.

"From whom do you think Hilda Haggerty inherited her gift? It was her father. Jason had it without knowing it. He saw into Roman's mind that day, saw exactly what happened through Roman's eyes as the man ascended the stairs into Cory's room. He watched as Roman removed the pocket knife from its leather sheath on his belt while advancing on the scared and confused lad. He heard the pathetic pleas from the boy when he realised the danger he was in.

"It came slowly to Cory because his mental acuity was on the level of a five-year-old. What he was reacting to was the look in his father's eyes. His mother had warned him often enough not to speak in front of his father, not to be noticed or heard, for fear of a certain belting.

"Cory had even been dragged out into the forest once, when Roman was pissed to the gills and doped out of his mind with his product. The boy had never forgotten that episode. He remembered the bloodied axe in his father's massive hand as he was dragged deep into the towering mountain ash. His father had been killing a few chickens when the bloodlust came on him. Were it not for a well-placed root protruding from the forest floor, Roman would not have tripped so badly that Cory was able to escape his clutches and run to his mother.

"Cory saw the same murderous look in his father's eyes when he came at him with a pocket knife. Jason felt the excruciating pain as Roman sliced through the superior and inferior rectus muscles, popped the boy's eyeball out of its socket, and then severed the cord behind the eye.

"Jason Haggerty never forgave himself for causing so much grief and agony. He hadn't imagined that asking for the trespassers to be punished would result in such cruelty. He didn't think it possible that anyone would take him literally when he quoted the passage from the Bible. Jason was never the same man after that. He also managed to shut his mind to elements that allowed him to see into the mind of another without ever having a clue that it existed. But his daughter had the gift, which she explored and perfected over time. She saw it all and so did I. I wish I hadn't."

"Can't be true..." whispered Elmo.

"Did you ever meet your... Did you ever meet Roman?"

"Nuh. Heard about him when daddy got drunk sometimes. Cursin' him and hatin' him all the while."

"Father and son are two peas in a pod, I reckon. I can't see that same trait in you, Master Cabbage. I know you were following orders when I was being held captive by you lot, but I didn't sense the same amount of venom in you. I think you are possibly more of a victim than a willing participant. I see you being forced through fear to obey your father and follow his instructions."

"Ya dunno what ya talkin' about, mate. Shut ya hole."

"You know you're going to prison after all is said and done here, right?"

"Bullshit!"

"You grow dope and you assaulted me. That's enough to put you away for a while, let alone all the rest of it. Your father is going away for the rest of his life for everything he did. You can enjoy him as your cellmate while you're inside. I'm sure that'll be a barrel of laughs for you."

"Won't get ta that," said Elmo with a knowing smirk.

"I won't go to the local cops, Master Cabbage."

"Who then?"

"I doubt your old man's reach will stretch as far as the federal level. One way or the other everything ends tonight. Once I have my daughter safe I'm going to make sure this stops." Arlon stopped the car in the middle of the highway, then turned to face Betty. "And I'll tell them everything, Mrs Payne, everything."

Arlon swivelled back to face the front, stepped on the accelerator and moved off. The turnoff to the small road leading to the Cabbage property wasn't difficult to locate if you knew what to look for. The satnav had the road on its screen. It ended around three kilometres in. The fog thickened the farther in they proceeded. Elmo continued to grumble and complain in the back seat, while Betty remained mute.

Arlon could almost hear the cogs grinding away in Betty's head as she mulled over all her options for damage control. In her mind, there was simply no future in which she could envisage a happy ending if the truth came out, all of it. There was, however, a distinct advantage to the feud ending at long last. That was a given. What she couldn't abide was the secret being revealed to the world. She thought long and hard how she might bring about Arlon Grey's failure to accomplish that task.

Betty accepted that the man had every right to be upset, even though he wasn't upset in the ordinary sense. She had inadvertently placed lives in danger by bringing him and his family to the valley. He had already been injured, and who knew what had happened to his daughter and his wife? She had seen the man try unsuccessfully to phone his wife several times on his mobile. She assumed he had tried to contact his daughter as well. Cell phone reception in the forest was a hit-and-miss proposition at the best of times.

Betty watched as Arlon turned the car into a steep descent off the main highway onto another dirt track leading to the Cabbage property, though not directly to the house. Once again, the strange man was using the satnav to make his way through the pea soup of fog surrounding them. She heard Elmo mumbling incoherently beside her and wished he'd stop. She needed to concentrate on the problems she and the forest folk faced.

Hilda Haggerty had entrusted her with the responsibility of ensuring the safety of their secret, and she had no intention of betraying that trust. Had she thought judiciously, she might have discovered that it was that sort of narrow thinking that had caused so much hardship for Arlon in the first place. Removing her son's car from where he led the police was the first strike against him and his credibility, leading to his capture by the lump of a lad beside her, stinking to high heaven once more within the heated vehicle. Everything had descended downhill from there, underground, right down to the Haggerty property.

Only one single strategy came to her mind, short of killing the man. If she and Hildy combined forces to enter his mind and wipe out any memories he had of his misadventures in the Yarra Valley, it might provide the relief they sought. It would be a delicate plan to implement without his knowledge. Betty wasn't even sure it was feasible. Her knowledge of the practice, so recently acquired, was fragmented at best. Her thoughts were interrupted by the slowing of the vehicle.

Arlon drove up to a carport of sorts, well-hidden under dense foliage. The structure offered a hiding place for a vehicle and its occupant hoping to escape detection from the air. It was nothing more than four supporting poles holding up a corrugated iron roof, though little of the structure could be seen through the profusion of climbing ivy and ferns.

Arlon saw nothing more than a narrow trail leading from the area. His satnav would be of no help to him as far as navigating the terrain was concerned. The transmitter he'd placed in the cabin gave him the coordinates to input into the satnav, showing a destination off road somewhere but no clear indication how to get there. He was unable to see much beyond the beam of the dim fog lamps.

Arlon resigned himself to scouting the way ahead on foot before venturing farther in the vehicle. He would need to examine the condition of the soil and distance between tree trunks to ascertain the credibility of his plan. The moment he exited the car the bitter cold delivered a telling punch. Sitting inside the car with the heater turned up to maximum did not prepare him for the sudden assault. He closed the door quickly to preserve the heat inside the car.

"Told ya so," said Elmo smugly, when Arlon returned.

"When are you ever going to learn not to underestimate me, Master Cabbage? I don't give up. I am perhaps my own worst enemy in that regard, but I never quit, especially where my family is concerned. We either attempt to reach your house in the nice warm car or freeze our butts off by walking. Hmm? Care for a brisk hike through the woods? What about you, Mrs Payne? Or maybe you would both like me to leave you here while I proceed on my own?"

"In the car, with the heater goin'?" asked Elmo foolishly.

"You wish," answered Arlon flatly, as he turned to the front once more.

Arlon engaged the 4WD drive by pushing the button to lock the hubs, and selected low range and the lowest gear. His motor could easily handle the strain of extended distance in low gear. The hardest part would be the unforgiving terrain and the numerous obstacles. Without the luxury of the satnav or clear vision, because of the fog, he would have to resort to 'other' means.

"Mrs Payne?"

"Yes?"

"I have to utilise my inner demons, using your vernacular, to proceed. I understand your misgivings. I know you don't approve and that is your prerogative. What I can't have is you distracting me or attempting to prevent me from using it. If you feel strongly enough about it to wish to exit the vehicle, then now is the time to do so. Once I start I won't stop until I've achieved my purpose. Attempting to gain my attention while underway will only place us all in danger. Make up your mind, both of you, now," he ordered.

"What the fuck is ya talkin' about? What demons?" asked Elmo in a near panic.

"The same demons that healed you and took hold of me for a time. I'll control that aspect. You have to trust me on that score. I don't have time to discuss or debate the issue. Forgive me, you don't have a choice, only Mrs Payne."

"Why?"

"You're my hostage, my negotiating chip. Without you, I have nothing to bargain with. Not that I think I have a strong position, even with you. Mrs Payne?"

"I won't last long out there in that," she said.

"Do you agree to my conditions and accept that you will endanger our lives if you suddenly decide to interfere or object?"

"I suppose," she said uncertainly.

"No, not good enough. I need a firm response. Understand that I will use it on you if you give me no choice."

The sudden intake of breath by Betty told Arlon all he needed to know. She wanted nothing to do with what she deemed evil and demonic.

"Fasten your seat belts and I want absolute silence. No sudden sounds or movements outside the natural jostling within the car."

Arlon turned off the car lights and concentrated, falling into a semi-meditative state within moments. He kept his eyes closed to prevent his passengers being alarmed by the blue emanation from his eyes, should it reappear. He carefully tapped into the diminishing well of energy, allowing its essence to augment his mental processes. He felt the odd, though familiar, sensations of something kick-starting lazy areas of his brain, parts not associated with everyday use. He felt the insertion of energy into those neural pathways like a warm, welcoming, liquid infusion.

He began to hear the thoughts of the other occupants within the vehicle. Their breathing became cyclonic and their body odours increased to almost unbearable in the cloying atmosphere. He felt their angst, heard their thoughts, shared their visions and goals. He withdrew from their minds quickly, so as not to disturb them, especially Mrs Payne, who would know what he was doing. He didn't want the backwash effect to expose them to the energy.

Once loose of the extraneous distractions, Arlon attempted to capture the topography of the route to the Cabbage residence. In his head, he pictured the narrow trail taken by the son and father on horseback when exiting or entering the property leading to the carport. His transcendental journey lifted him far above the canopy of the forest, while allowing him to see through the thick vegetation.

The force played wickedly with his emotions, though not in an evil capacity, as Betty Payne would have ascribed to it. It sought, rather, to enhance or build emotions beyond the normal experience. To Arlon, it was an introduction to emotions. To anyone else, it would be an increase of intensity to a level of incapacitation. Arlon worked with it, not allowing it to control or exacerbate his system. It had the strength to overwhelm him: experience had taught him that. So he drip-fed the energy into his thought processes to avoid being consumed and debilitated by it.

Without opening his eyes he started the vehicle moving forward. He located a route through the impossible terrain with relative ease, considering the number of obstacles. He turned the steering wheel abruptly to the left, then right, around a massive tree trunk blocking their path, unseen by anyone in the vehicle. The steep climb caused the motor to rev higher and higher. The powerful torque of the diesel engine enabled the vehicle to continue upward.

The occupants were jinked and jostled this way and that as the car lurched left and right, up and down. The lap-sashes of the seat belts cut deeply and painfully into their abdomens as their bodies strained against the webbing. Sometimes the car was near vertical and at other times it leaned precariously sideways until everyone felt sure it would topple. Arlon kept his eyes glued shut as he commanded the Prado to tackle the harsh landscape with scant regard for its engine or paintwork.

It was a demented rollercoaster ride worthy of inclusion in Dante's *Inferno*. Without the ability to view anything within or without the car, except for the faint glow from the muted dash display, Arlon's passengers grew ever more fearful for their lives, involuntarily crying out whenever they were flung against their restraints. They wholly believed that the vehicle would overturn at any moment and their lives would come to an end.

Without realising it, Betty was sending Arlon brief glimpses of her panicking mind, of her terror. Arlon also picked up on Elmo's terrified thoughts as they cascaded around his empty head. He was able to deflect most of the distracting and unhelpful messages entering his mind. He was driving blind and required every ounce of his concentration to manoeuvre the car through the impossible landscape. On several occasions he felt the rear tyres spinning hopelessly in the soft earth, losing all traction until the front tyres found enough purchase to get them going again. He conceded that it was a hairy ride if you were not the one in control of the vehicle. He doubted his ability to be a passenger in the same situation.

When the sound came, it didn't register in anyone's mind and, when it did, no one knew exactly what had caused it. To Arlon, it sounded as though a stone had hit the windscreen. That wouldn't have been worrisome if he were heading down the highway; an everyday occurrence. Only, they weren't on a highway, and any gravel or stones scattered on the ground would have been buried under years and years of the forest's detritus.

Arlon halted the car and turned off the ignition. The interior dash lights went out, the silence returned.

"That's far enough, arsehole!" came the gruff voice from immediately in front of them.

"Daddy!" cried Elmo, scrambling to open the rear door.

Arlon wasn't concerned. He had engaged the child locking mechanism, which prevented the passengers in the rear from opening their doors. Arlon used his hands to explore the sheet of glass in front of him until he came across the tell-tale hole. When he heard a slight moan from behind him, he guessed correctly that Betty Payne had been injured by the slug that had entered through the windscreen. He made sure to turn off the ceiling light before opening his door to slink out of the car.

Arlon's eyes glowed with the same blue quality Elmo had witnessed previously, when he saw the odd man opening the rear door. It had the desired effect of shutting him up and scaring the crap out of him. Betty grew weaker as blood flowed freely from the gaping wound. Luckily, or unluckily, as only time would tell, the slug had spent much of its momentum as it passed through the windscreen. A through and through shot could have caused irreparable damage. However, a slug lodged in a precarious position was just as deadly. The ricocheting slug had entered her chest at an oblique angle, tearing through several layers of tissue and muscle before nicking the lung, by the feel and sound of it.

Arlon placed his hand over the entry wound, reaching into her body with his mind, searching for all the nuances of the injury. His hand glowed red, as though held over a torch beam. From the red glow came shards of blue and white light as the heat penetrated deep into the flesh, the muscles, tendons and sinews, finally reaching the damaged organ. Betty writhed weakly as the heat burned her. She screamed as she tasted the barest hint of the blue energy. Elmo yelped in sympathy, knowing what she was experiencing.

Betty collapsed into a heap when another shot interrupted Arlon's ministrations. She was breathing steadily, but not completely out of the woods, as Arlon came slowly back to the present. He had not completed the repair. Betty was still in danger. He hoped he had done enough to stave off the major threat until he could resume the intervention. The second shot went nowhere near the vehicle. Colin Cabbage was firing blind.

"Next one is for ya brat, arsehole. Turn ya lights on so I can see yiz," demanded Colin from the haloed glow Arlon could just make out through the misty darkness.

Arlon leaned back out of the vehicle.

"I have your boy here. You almost shot *him* with that first round," shouted Arlon.

"Bullshit!" came the reply.

"Fair enough, keep shooting then. I don't care if you kill him or not."

"Elmo? Ya there, boy?"

"He can't answer you from inside the car and I won't let him out."

"Whatcha proposin'?" came the query, after a long pause.

"Straight trade. Your boy for my girl. I go away after the exchange and say nothing to anyone."

"Fat fuckin' chance!"

"While my daughter is within earshot of you, I would appreciate it if you kept the language civil."

"Talk how I bloody want."

"Then there'll be consequences."

"Hah! Whatcha gonna do?"

Colin's sudden yelp, followed by a clatter as he dropped his weapon, could be heard clearly by Arlon.

A few moments later, he said: "What, what did ya do? What was...?"

"Just a little trick I picked up. Tell your people to back up, away from this car, and return to your hovel," Arlon demanded.

Colin yelped again as he leaned down to pick up the weapon, intending to let loose with several shots. His voice was somewhat subdued and a little groggy when he next spoke.

"What the fuck...ahhh!"

"I told you, keep the foul language down around my daughter. I won't warn you again," insisted Arlon, with his eyes blazing blue.

Elmo was squirming against the seat, attempting to release himself from the seat belt and move to the front of the vehicle while Arlon Grey's mind was distracted by his father. Unfortunately, something was preventing him from physically accomplishing the task. In his mind he knew what he wanted to do, but his body refused to respond to the orders it received.

"Do as he says, Jonesy and Boof. He's doin' a witch thing on me, like someone is piercin' me noggin," ordered Colin.

"We can take him, Col...ahh, shit!"

Jonesy and Boof were writhing in agony on the forest floor only twenty or so metres from Arlon's position. Once released from the mental torture, they gathered themselves quickly, crawling back to the house, cursing and moaning all the way.

"Well, seems we got us a Mexican stand-off, don't we?" suggested Colin. What ya don't know is what kinda mess ya girl's in, and what might happen if you don't stop what ya doin'. Might be I got it set up so she dies in case something happens ta me. Might be I need ta do something ta prevent it, like. Might be she's tied ta an electric device what will zap her bad if I don't reset the two-minute timer it's connected ta. Might be I'll remove the circuit breaker ta allow the full force ta juice her up. Get her all nice and crispy for ya."

"Miss Tara Blaze-Grey?"

"Daddy?"

"It's me. Is he telling the truth? Are you hooked up to some sort of electrical device?"

"Yep. I'm scared, Daddy."

"It's okay to be scared. What you need to know is that I'll get you out of this."

"Like last time?"

"Yes, like last time."

"Mummy? Mummy?"

"She isn't here. I'm here, though."

"I just reset the timer. Ya got two minutes ta surrender or the kid lights up like a Christmas tree," warned Colin, his voice dripping with hatred and venom.

"I have your son," declared Arlon.

"Do what ya want with him. Useless bloody retard! Need some new blood ta spawn me a better one. Might have me a new breeder already. One minute!"

"Go, go, go," came the command from nearby.

The forest ignited with movement and sound, accompanied by several moving flashes of greenish light. Several persons stormed the front of the cabin, with several more entering from the rear. Arlon was momentarily confused and stunned by the unfolding events. He heard many shouted orders and confirmations from the shadows amid the blazing flares lighting up the forest around them, turning night to day. Arlon thought he heard a female voice among the voices, sparking recognition of sorts.

"Mummy!"

CHAPTER TWENTY-THREE

Colin Cabbage was on the floor, his hands cable-tied behind his back, with his co-conspirators, Jonesy and Boof, when Arlon came through the front door of the house after the all-clear signal was announced. Five tall, fit men, dressed in black tactical police gear, stood around languidly, allowing the adrenaline in their systems to slowly dissipate.

Arlon recognised the night vision gear and the Kevlar vests of the Australian Federal Police. When he spied Clarice comforting their daughter, he became truly confused.

"Clarice?"

"Hi, Arlon."

"What's going on?"

"You remember my brothers?"

"I guess."

"What I couldn't tell you, when they attended our wedding last year, was that they are members of an elite force within the A.F.P., dealing mainly with drug trafficking and firearms. They're undercover, mostly, which is why I invented occupations for them or avoided the questions when you asked. At the time they were deep into a two-year operation. They only wrapped that one up a month ago, with arrests the public will never be aware of and a massive haul of narcotics that will be used to trap more players eventually."

"Truth is, Arlon, that while we've had our sights on this Cabbage clan for nearly a decade, we have never been able to catch them in the act. Local cops always tipped them off if we came sniffing. We never made it this far into the forest, either. What we find here when we do a thorough search should be very interesting. You nearly spoiled the whole operation by turning up here when you did. We were about a minute away from storming the house when we heard your car," said the eldest brother.

"Now, let's see if I remember you all. You're Brian, the oldest, then Ben, Barry, Bobby and Bart? And you're all with the A.F.P.?"

"Sorry, we couldn't admit that before, Arlon."

"How did you end up here?"

"That would be because of me," admitted Clarice.

"When the princess went missing and I saw where she went, I had to call in the big guns."

"Are you all right, Miss Grey? The accident? The fire?" asked Arlon, going down on one knee in front of Tara, who was sitting on Clarice's knee.

"I'm okay, Daddy. The fire didn't start until they got us out of the car. He hit me," said Tara, pointing at Colin Cabbage.

"She's fulla shit. I never..."

The blow came suddenly and stunningly. Arlon had whipped around in a flash to land the telling punch to Colin's face, which he had raised from the floor when commenting. Arlon's blow connected solidly with his jaw, sending the man's face hard into the floorboards.

"I told you to watch your language around my daughter," warned Arlon in a deathly whisper.

"I can understand your frustration and your anger, Arlon, but he's now officially in our custody and he can't be messed up when we bring him in, much as I'd like to wipe the smirk right off his lousy face," said Brian.

"I don't get angry. Gag him if you have to but keep him from mouthing off obscenities in front of my daughter."

When Arlon rose, he was deep in thought.

"Wait a minute. How could you have known where Miss Grey was? I only guessed myself a short time ago."

"I've known where you both were all along, at least, the vicinity," said Clarice. "Remember those new phones I purchased for you and Tara? They have an app installed which allows me to track you both with my phone. Unfortunately, I didn't have the car, so I wasn't able to do anything about it myself. I called in my brothers, who were only too happy to have a chance at finally nailing one of their top targets."

"The son is in the car, or maybe trying to make a run for it. I...I have a confession to make. You'll have to arrest me as well. I'm responsible for the death of the boy's mother. I admit that it was in self-defence, just...well, I used an excessive amount of force, which resulted in her death. Pretty sure there are a few charges that you can attribute to me."

"Yeah, ya better arrest the mong...him," spat Colin through a bloody mouth.

"One of the reasons Clarry was able to get us here so quickly, and the reason we associated the kidnapping with the Cabbages, was because we were already in the area. We had triggers out to alert us in case any of the Cabbage clan turned up at a hospital or doctor's surgery. The moment Irma was admitted to the hospital's database we were alerted, and made arrangements to have her spirited away to a federal institution, where she's being cared for. We concocted the story of her passing to prevent Colin from attempting to locate her. Sorry, sis. It was probably that ruse that made him kidnap Tara."

"Ya saying me girl's alive?" asked Colin in disbelief.

"That's right, Cabbage, and she's willing to testify against you. She's been giving us a mountain of information that brought us here and will see you in custody for the rest of your miserable life. You've been read your rights, want a lawyer?"

"Fuck ya!"

Brian leaned down and knocked Colin out cold. Arlon gave him a questioning look.

Brian shrugged. "He was resisting arrest. Bobby, go get Elmo from the car or chase him down if he did a runner. He'll be spending quite a bit of time with his father very shortly. Too old to go to juvie even if he does have the mentality of a minor. Doubt he'll be lucky enough to get the loony bin."

Bobby acknowledged the order given by a superior. Before he left the house to attend to the boy, Arlon spoke.

"There's an injured woman in the car as well. We need to get her seen to, unless..."

"Unless?" mused Clarice.

"Hmm, something you might want to see."

Arlon led Tara, Clarice and three of her brothers to the car, where he performed his minor miracle to an astonished audience.

"Okay, someone care to fill me in here?" asked Brian, who seemed somewhat spooked.

"We only told you a small part of what happened to us on that island, Bri," said Clarice. "I'm still not sure I want to try to explain what happened to Arlon, because it sounds so...impossible."

"That glowing in the eyes, that has something to do with it?" Brian asked Arlon.

Arlon nodded without saying a word.

"That woman was shot by Colin Cabbage, right? The first shot we heard?"

"Yes. Missed me by millimetres in the front seat. I have to hand it to Mr Cabbage for his accuracy, given the veil of fog we were in."

"You...healed her?"

"Yes."

"If you weren't my brother-in-law I would have *you* put up for a trip to the loony bin, you know?"

"Yes, I wouldn't blame you."

"Arlon? I don't understand. I thought you said it was decreasing, almost gone?"

"I thought so, too, only it becomes stronger with use. The more it intensifies, the more I can accomplish with it," stated Arlon with a hint of regret. I drove here using nothing but my mind, without car headlights, without the ability to physically see anything through the fog."

"What-what else can you do?" asked Clarice with concern.

"That is so cool, Daddyo," piped in Tara, still clutching tightly to Clarice's legs.

"You reckon, kiddo?"

"Uh-huh," she replied.

"That would be 'yes', young lady," admonished Clarice.

"If I hadn't seen it, I wouldn't have believed you, that's for sure," admitted Brian. Bobby, get Elmo out of that car and handcuff him before he messes up his underwear. He looks like he might faint with fright any second."

"I did the same for his wound and he was already disturbed by that. Do you *have* to arrest him? He's been brought up wrong and doesn't know any better."

"Courts will probably go easy on him with that in mind, but we do have to officially arrest him as an accomplice in the cultivation of cannabis and a lot of this other stuff. But it's always been the patriarch we've been after. He's the one we suspect of travelling to Melbourne to hand over his product, which is then distributed throughout the country, making it a federal matter.

"Listen, Arlon, we need to get the prisoners back to our base of operations, as far away from local authorities as we can get. Bloody cold out here and I don't want to hang around that filthy hovel for too long. We'll leave someone here to guard it while the rest of us get out. We hid our vehicle near a carport or something down near the bottom, then made our way in here on foot. Can you drive us all back?"

"Be a tight squeeze."

"Anyone who doesn't fit in will stay behind with Bobby to guard the house and begin searching the grounds at daybreak. We'll have a team transported in as soon as we get word to headquarters in Canberra."

Epilogue

Deep in the temperate rainforests of Victoria's rugged hinterland, on the eve of the winter's solstice, with crisp, white snowdrifts decorating the tips of the numerous mountains surrounding the area, in a ravine known to only a handful of locals, Hilda Haggerty led her small party down the length of her property.

With mere starlight penetrating the chilly darkness, Hilda Haggerty hummed softly as she held out her hand with a morsel to tempt the local fauna out of hiding. Almost everyone watching recoiled at the grisly sight of the human eyeball she held.

Her exhalations formed small clouds of vapour in the still night air. The temperature was below freezing, as expected for that time of year in the Victorian forest of towering mountain ash.

She was the last Haggerty. The secret would have perished upon her deathbed had Betty Payne not agreed to resume the ritual.

Not alone this time, in the dark, unafraid and highly attuned to her surroundings, Hilda waited patiently on her stump beside the permanent creek, listening to the gentle splash as the crystal-clear waters washed against the many stones and boulders in its downward path. Much had occurred in the clearing of late and Hilda held grave fears that her guest might not appear, might no longer be able to appear. She felt intensely sad about that possibility.

All that she did, everything she accomplished each year, was designed to follow through with the promise made to her father. She had continued the ritual he began in his youth, before she was born, before he met her mother. Her entire philosophy of life revolved around the anniversary of her birth, to continue the crucial act of reunification with nature.

Succumbing to lethargy and her ageing anatomy, Hilda blinked in an attempt to remain awake. Gradually her eyelids descended as gravity and age took their toll. Unable to remain awake for the first time since being introduced to the sacred tryst, Hilda nodded off, releasing the morsel she held in her hand to tempt the creature from its forest refuge.

Betty and Arlon stood behind Hilda Haggerty, supporting her ageing body. Tears came unbidden to Betty's eyes as she felt the last breath escape the old woman's lungs.

The morsel rolled from Hilda's wrinkled and liver-spotted hand onto the frosty grass at her feet. From there it continued for a metre down the slope before coming to rest against the base of another small tree stump.

Staring up blankly from its final resting place, the gelatinous globe remained there while the small troop vacated the clearing, believing the special event would not occur that year and, perhaps, never again. Alex and Arlon carried the lifeless form of Hilda Haggerty back up to the cottage, where they toasted her passing with mulled wine.

"Come with me, Mr Grey?" asked Betty.

"Where to?" he asked.

"Back out there," she explained.

"Why?"

"To witness the miracle, of course."

"Weren't we out there for that exact reason only moments ago?"

"No, we went out there with a wonderful woman to share her journey one last time. She always knew she wouldn't live long enough to see it happen again. She wanted me to take you all out there again so that I could sit on the stump in her place and reveal the miracle to you all. We are the caretakers of that magnificent privilege."

"It's getting very late for Tara to be up, Arlon. She can hardly keep her eyes open," said Clarice.

"What about it, kiddo? You up for it or not?"

"Arlon?" queried Clarice.

"Miss Grey is perfectly capable of knowing her mind. She'll soon tell us if she's too tired."

"I want to go, Mummy," said Tara firmly.

"Uncle Alex and Aunty Dot?"

"In for a penny, in for a pound, my dear. Lead the way if you think something will happen," said Dot with a warm smile.

Arlon faltered slightly as he passed through the doorway behind Clarice. He reached out automatically to brace himself when his hand found Clarice's shoulder.

"Arlon, are you okay?"

"Sure, just a momentary lapse. I need some sleep and a good holiday, I think. Just...away from this cold and the lake?"

"Too right, mate. You've earned it. We all have."

They walked together, following the others back down toward the stump near the creek. Although Arlon had reassured Clarice that he was feeling fine, she couldn't help but notice a glint of blue shining from his eyes that worried her.

"I'm surprised this experience hasn't affected Tara more. I would have had horrific nightmares if that had happened to me at her age," said Clarice, as Tara skipped ahead of them to join Dot and Alex, who had grown quite fond of the young girl.

"Good," stated Arlon, too quickly for Clarice's liking.

"Arlon Grey! Did you have something to do with that?"

"I couldn't let this experience scar her for life. She deserves some happiness in her life, don't you think?"

"Of course I do. It's just, well, we discussed you using this...gift. You said the more you use it the more intense it becomes. What if you can't control it?"

"It will have been worth it to prevent that girl having one more day of sadness or fear. Her external bruises are fading but the mental injuries would have stayed with her forever."

"Promise me you won't use it too much, Arlon, please?"

"Now, Clarice..."

Clarice turned on him with her hands planted firmly on her hips.

"Okay, okay, I give up. You know I can't compete with that Clarice who bossed her big brothers around."

They joined the others at the bottom of the clearing. Betty asked everyone to stay behind while she sat on the stump. She bade them remain perfectly silent. The torches were turned off, leaving only the stars to cast their ethereal glow upon the small clearing.

Teeth were beginning to chatter noisily before a movement could be seen from the ferns on the other side of the creek. Peering every which way to ensure the area was clear of danger, the shy creature slunk through the icy waters of the creek to a distance of two metres from Betty, who was smiling fit to burst.

The mouths of those behind Betty opened in awe as the exotic creature glanced up at her with purpose. Its movements were slow and deliberate, indicating age. Arlon nodded his head appreciatively when he saw the creature's face clearly for the first time, then the distinctive stripes on its rump when the animal turned toward the lower stump where the eyeball rested. Gingerly, it made its way to the waiting morsel, which it picked up gently in its mouth. With one last look at the assembled audience, it swallowed the globe and made its way back across the creek to disappear in the fernery.

"It's a Tasmanian tiger!" shouted Tara suddenly, startling them all.

"Clever girl, Miss Tara Blaze-Grey. Yes, a thylacine. A carnivorous marsupial believed to have been extirpated from the Australian mainland and New Guinea long before the last one was captured in Tasmania in 1930. Believed extinct, until now," explained Arlon in a voice that grew whisper-quiet.

Just then the forest shone with a renewed twilight ambience as if clouds obscuring the stars had drifted past. Only, when Clarice turned, she saw that it was Arlon who was shining. He was enveloped in a halo of shimmering blue and white. He was trying to speak, but no words came out, and he was reaching toward her, toward Tara.

When Tara ran to him and wrapped her arms about him, she passed right through. Clarice watched as Arlon smiled at her, a smile that was so uncommon on a man like Arlon Grey, a smile that was so welcome when it emerged on those rare occasions. He smiled knowingly, trustingly.

"Fight it, Daddy. Find a way to come back. I know you can," cried Tara pitifully.

The radiance grew brighter around Arlon, so bright it pained the eyes to look upon him. Tara screamed his name, crying out desperately for her daddy to come back, urging him to fight the forces at play. Clarice watched in horror, paralysed by the unfolding event. Gradually, Arlon Grey dematerialised and then became nothing more than a wraith-like, misty outline, before wafting away on the gentle breeze that suddenly blew into the clearing.

The End

PREVIEW BOOK 4 IN THE B.A.M. DETECTIVE SERIES.

THE GUARDIANS

WITH CLARICE GREY
BOOK 4

BY JOSEF PEETERS

CHAPTER ONE

"Happy birthday, pumpkin. Sweet sixteen and never been kissed...I hope?"

"Mum, that's so lame," scolded Tara playfully.

"What? Who kissed you then?" asked Clarice in a mild panic.

Tara unwrapped the present carefully, making sure not to tear the pretty wrapping paper. She would save it for decorating pages in her scrapbook. Inside the brightly printed paper, Tara found another layer, even more exotic and colourful than the previous one.

"I suppose this is going to be paper all the way through, is it?"

"No, I just thought you'd appreciate some more lovely paper for your scrapbook. I hunted all over to find a few designs I didn't think you had."

"They're gorgeous. I haven't seen this type at all. Where did you get them?"

"Sent for them online."

Tara unwrapped the last layer to find the back of a picture frame. Her breath caught in her throat when she turned the large frame around. It was an oil painting depicting her and Arlon together, taken from Tara's favourite photo of them both. It was a perfect rendition of the pair, in a sensitive pose capturing his magnificent blue eyes and her happy grin in the arms of her beloved father. She stared at the painting for a long while as Clarice observed.

Tara had never grieved for the man she adored beyond measure. The days, weeks and months following his disappearance were not the unhappy experience Clarice had expected them to be for her daughter. She'd accepted the tragic event with stoicism and maturity beyond her years, but Clarice suspected that Tara was holding back.

The subject had been raised periodically and Tara seemed almost flippant in her responses, which troubled Clarice. Subsequent conversations with analysts and therapists, and even hypnotherapy over the years, failed to produce any of the expected emotions.

Clarice couldn't help herself, allowing the tears to come, but Tara remained dry-eyed.

"Oh, I hope I haven't done the wrong thing, princess. I thought you might like a painting done to hang on your bedroom wall. I'll take it if you..."

"You'll do nothing of the kind. It's mine. It's the best present in all the world and I love it, Mum. Thank you," said Tara, rising to hug her mother.

Tara sat beside her mother on the austere lounge suite in the house they had inherited from Arlon Grey. She reverently touched the gilded frame and then placed her hand gently on his face in the painting.

"I miss him so much..." sobbed Clarice.

"I know, Mum."

Tara placed a comforting arm over Clarice's shoulder.

"Don't you?" asked Clarice, in a sterner tone than she would have liked.

"Of course I do, Mum. What sort of question is that?"

"You've never said anything, never cried, never spoken about him, nothing. Anyone would think you didn't give a fig," she blurted out, regretting her words the moment they left her mouth.

"I've never felt that he left us. I always feel that he's watching over us, me. Mum, I hear him sometimes," admitted Tara reluctantly.

"What? What do you mean?" cried Clarice in alarm.

"Oh, don't go having a cow. I don't mean I can hear voices. No, I mean I hear him sometimes, in my sleep, in my mind, as I could on the island. Of course, I miss that he isn't here in the flesh, but I just never felt his loss like you did. I've never felt he was truly gone."

"Really?"

"Absolutely. I was sad when it happened, but...I don't know, it's just that..."

 "What?" Clarice insisted.

"You know when you can be alone in the living room, for instance, and not feel lonely because there is someone in another room of the house, in a bedroom or bathroom. It's like that. Somehow I can't see him or touch him, but I know he's there. Whenever I've had a problem all I had to do was think of him and I would get an answer, or the problem would be solved somehow. When I was bullied at school that time?" Clarice nodded. "I spoke to Dad in my dreams and the next day those girls came up and apologised, just like that. Never had trouble with them again after that."

"You never told me that."

"I couldn't figure out what happened exactly, so I didn't want to start telling you something that made no sense. You think he's happy, Mum?"

"Oh, what a question. Is that like an existentialist question or something?"

"You know I'm not religious, Mum. We both know where he went."

"You believe he went into that..."

"Other dimension, Mum. Say it."

"Other dimension? Is that truly what you think happened?"

"Of course, don't you?"

"I never knew what to make of it."

"That's because you didn't want to handle it. If you think about it logically, it's the only explanation. His use of the energy caused the increase in its presence, or intensity, and drew him into the other dimension. Maybe he survived. Maybe he learned to use it more. Maybe he found a way to get closer to this dimension and can speak to me sometimes if the planets are aligned or some such thing. You know, a cosmic connection?"

"And maybe that's just a whole heap of wishful thinking, young lady."

"It's why I don't feel sad like you, Mum."

Clarice's mobile phone buzzed and vibrated on the kitchen marble benchtop.

"That's the business mobile. I'd better get it. Could mean work for me."

"Don't know why you won't take some of my inheritance money so you don't have to rely on that income anymore. I'd still have heaps left over."

Clarice rose from the sofa, ignoring Tara's generosity, to fetch the phone that was still vibrating so much it was likely to drop off the benchtop.

"B.A.M Detective Agency, how may I help you?" she said into the phone.

"Yes, this is Clarice Grey. Yes, that's how it's spelt, why...? I'm sorry? Look... No, you may not know my daughter's name. I am ending this call... It, what happened? When was this? Every night? My name? Can you send me some photos? Give me your number just in case it disappears from my phone. I'm technically challenged that way. I'll give you a call once I've studied the photos and discussed it with someone."

Clarice remained pensive after she disconnected the call. She stood in the kitchen shaking her head slowly from side to side.

"What was it, Mum?"

"Hmm? Oh, just a business call."

"Oh golly gee, that's so informative...NOT!"

"Tara Grey, you don't need to be told everything, you know?"

"No, I don't know. Whatever happened to 'sharing everything and not holding back'?"

"Well, *you* haven't, have you?"

"What?"

"You never said anything about what you just told me. About feeling Arlon with you, and that you think he went to that other place."

"I always thought you were intelligent enough to assume he went there and that I didn't need to explain."

"Nothing simple about it. No telling where he went."

"Oh, I get it now!" said Tara angrily.

"What? What is it you think you get, missy?" challenged Clarice.

"You're angry with him because you think he could have done something to prevent it."

"Nonsense..."

"Yes, you are. You think he allowed himself to go or even encouraged it."

"Well, he certainly had the power, didn't he?" Clarice admitted.

"When you open Pandora's Box, you don't necessarily have the skills to operate everything you find in there. Daddy would never have intentionally left us. He loved us with all his heart."

"Don't be so naïve, Tara. He couldn't love. Maybe he can express love wherever he ended up. Maybe he is a happy man at last. He wasn't one for this world, that's for sure."

The ping on her phone alerted Clarice to the incoming message. When she swiped the screen, she furrowed her brow as she concentrated on the small images.

"Mum? Is everything all right?"

"Damn! I don't want to ask, but you're so much better at this tech stuff than I am. How do I get these pictures from my mobile to my computer so I can enlarge them?"

"Mum, how can you run a professional agency and not know how to do that?"

"Don't help your mother then, if that's how you're going to be."

"Give it here," demanded Tara, with a sigh and a smile.

Clarice watched her daughter unfold herself from the sofa to stand to her full height in front of her. Clarice had to look up to view her daughter's features. At sixteen, Tara towered over her mother, with long legs and blossoming curves, accentuated by tight jeans and T-shirt. Her long hair shone with an anthracite brilliance, highlighting and framing the perfectly-proportioned face and enigmatic green eyes.

Tara accepted the proffered mobile, which she quickly attached to Clarice's laptop, after searching a kitchen drawer for the cable. She set them both up on the kitchen bench, where she began the process of transferring the pictures from the phone.

Tara's sharp intake of breath told Clarice that she had succeeded in the task and had opened the file to view the pictures. She didn't immediately say anything, wanting Tara's take on the photos without influencing her in any way.

"Mum? Why is my full name, Tara Blaze-Grey, emblazoned on this bloke's wall alongside yours?"

"He claims they reappear every morning, no matter how many times he removes them or repaints the wall."

"How long has it been happening and where is this?"

"Seven years."

"Jesus, that's..."

"Yes. That's exactly the length of time that Arlon has been missing," whispered Clarice sadly.

"Where?" asked Tara with growing concern.

"A little seaside town called Tannum Sands."

"Mum, that's where..."

"I know," said Clarice quickly.

"Is it the same house?"

"I don't know that yet."

"Do his parents still live there?"

"No, they moved to Brisbane with Arlon when he was still fairly young. I think they're in a retirement home now. I only ever spoke to them once after we were married. That was bloody awkward, I tell you. Horrible people. I'm glad we never had to do our duty by visiting them regularly. Not that we were together all that long," said Clarice with a sigh.

"So, if it is, how do our names mysteriously appear on the walls of Daddy's childhood home for seven years while he's been missing?" asked Tara quietly.

"We're being offered the brief to find out, according to the message on the phone. That fellow said he finally made the connection with the names when he came across our magazine ad, with my name as the contact on it, in a doctor's waiting room."

"I knew it," Tara said, almost to herself.

"Tara Grey, I will not have you going down that road. I forbid you to think like that."

"Like what?" asked Tara pointedly.

"You know what I'm talking about," replied Clarice, with her fists on her hips.

Tara laughed.

"What's so funny?"

"Daddy always said not to go up against you when you strike that pose. He was the only one who ever used to call me by my full name as well. It has to be him."

"Tara, I don't want you to get your hopes up," said Clarice, going to embrace her. "It will just end in heartache for us both. I'll tell him we don't want the case."

"I'll go there myself if you do that," warned Tara, in a voice so low that Clarice almost missed it.

ABOUT THE AUTHOR

Josef, born in Düsseldorf, Germany, immigrated to Australia with his parents in 1964. A near lifetime of creative pursuits has culminated in his desire to produce entertaining stories. Josef lives with his wife in the tiny outback town of Moulamein, NSW, Australia, where they own and manage a small caravan park, while they each indulge in their own artistic endeavours.

If you would like to follow the author and keep up with his latest books, please visit his website;
http://lakesidecaravanpark.wixsite.com/josef

If you enjoyed reading Josef's book please leave a review on either Amazon or Goodreads.

www.ingramcontent.com/pod-product-compliance
Lightning Source LLC
Chambersburg PA
CBHW070009120726

47909CB00003B/848